"I'm gonna ask you one more question, Mitchell, and you might live a little longer if you answer it: who was the squeaky-voiced little man in that barn with you and Lively?"

Mitchell spat in the dust, then spoke with a snarl: "Ain't got nothing to say to you," he said.

Jubal cocked the Colt. "Your choice, Mitchell. But since you're not gonna talk to me, I've decided you're not going to be talking to anybody." He pointed the gun at the man's chest. Kane was looking Mitchell straight in the eye when he pulled the trigger.

THE GUNS
OF
BILLY FREE

DOUG BOWMAN

A TOM DOHERTY ASSOCIATES BOOK
NEW YORK

This is a work of fiction. All the characters and events portrayed in this book are either products of the author's imagination or are used fictitiously.

THE GUNS OF BILLY FREE

Copyright © 1998 by Doug Bowman

A Forge Book
Published by Tom Doherty Associates, LLC
175 Fifth Avenue
New York, NY 10010

Forge® is a registered trademark of Tom Doherty Associates, LLC.

ISBN: 0-812-59028-7
Library of Congress Catalog Card Number: 98-8267

First edition: December 1998
First mass market edition: January 2000

Printed in the United States of America

0 9 8 7 6 5 4 3 2 1

In memory of Kirby and Estelle: Daddy and Momma

THE GUNS
OF
BILLY FREE

I

Sheriff Barlow stood beside the seldom-used path, staring at the body. "It's Deputy Morrison for sure," he said, pointing to the swollen face and empty eye sockets. "Look at that red hair. Look at them buckteeth. Buzzards have pecked his eyes out and something's chewed off one of his ears, but that's Sid, all right."

"Damn tootin' it is," agreed Will Kipling, the man who had discovered the body. "Prob'ly killed last Monday, the same day he disappeared. Been shot right through the forehead, and I'll betcha Amy Shelton's oldest boy is the one done it."

"The tall one?" the sheriff asked. "The one who had it out with the Evans bunch awhile back?"

"One and the same," Kipling said, drenching a flat rock with a mouthful of tobacco juice, some of which splattered onto the body. "The way I heard it, he beat them two oldest Evans boys up for no reason a-tall, then pulled a six-gun on the rest of the family. People say he can knock a squirrel's eye out with that damn gun, too." He sprayed the rock again, then wiped his mouth with his sleeve. "I tell you, Sheriff, that boy's bad news, and the quicker we get him outta this community, the better off we're all gonna be." He pointed to the corpse. "There ain't no doubt in my mind that he's guilty of that right there. Ain't nobody else around here that woulda done it."

Mainly due to the fact that no one else had shown any interest in the job, Lambert Barlow, a man believed by many to have never had an original thought in his life, was now serving his second term as sheriff of Greene County, Mississippi, and had hired the illiterate Morrison only six weeks ago.

The forty-year-old Barlow was a skinny, dark-haired man who stood about six feet tall and weighed no more than a hundred forty pounds. Continuing to stare at the body of the slain deputy, the sheriff scratched at his chin, which sprouted a four-day growth of salt-and-pepper beard. He spoke to Kipling: "That boy goes by a different name than the one claimed by his mammy, don't he?"

"He went to school under the name of Billy Free," Kipling said, "so I reckon that's his name. Hell, Amy Shelton's crazy, so I doubt that even she knows how many husbands she's had. Several years difference in the ages of them three boys, and I don't believe any two of 'em's got the same last name. There's a girl lives in that cabin, too, but I don't know how old she is. I ain't never seen her up close, but from a distance, it looks like she's beginnin' to take on a little shape."

The sheriff scratched his chin again, then looked at Kipling blankly. "What makes you so sure that this Billy Free done the killing, Will?"

"What makes me so sure?" Kipling asked indignantly. "What makes me so sure? Hell, I'm surprised that you'd question my judgment, Lam."

"Now, don't go getting mad, Will," the sheriff said meekly. "I ain't never doubted your judgment, and I ain't gonna start now. If you're convinced that Billy Free done it, then I reckon he did. You always was real smart."

"He done it, all right," Kipling said. "We ain't gonna find him this early in the day, though. We'll wait till about midnight, then kick in that cabin door."

The sheriff stood staring off into the woods for a long time, then turned to face Kipling again. "How come we need to kick in that Shelton woman's door, Will? Couldn't we just knock on it?"

Kipling grunted disgustedly. "Knock on the door? Knock, you say?" He spat the worn-out quid of chewing tobacco into his hand and flung it down the hill, then stood shaking his head. "Don't be expectin' no help from me if that's the way you're gonna do it, old buddy. You just go ahead and start knockin' and callin' out, then see if you ain't lookin' into a gun barrel when that door opens." He mounted his mule and turned the animal toward town, his new Winchester rifle lying across his saddle.

Sheriff Barlow, astride his swaybacked mare, followed close behind. "Wait up, Will!" he called loudly. "You ain't never told me wrong; we'll do it your way."

Kipling waited for the sheriff to come alongside him. Then the two rode into Leakesville side by side. They decided to inform the undertaker that his services were needed, then swear him to secrecy, lest word that the deputy's body had been discovered find its way to Billy Free. "We don't want that boy to have no warnin' that we're comin' after him," Kipling said. "He's done killed one man, and he won't hesitate to do it again."

"That's right, Will."

They sat their saddles in front of the sheriff's office for a few moments, as Kipling gave Barlow a few last-minute instructions. "Don't say a word to nobody but the undertaker, now, Lam. I'll get my two brothers and meet you right here at midnight. If Billy Free gives us a problem, we'll take care of him once and for all right on the spot."

"That's right, Will."

The sheriff stepped inside his office and closed the door while Will Kipling headed home to his farm.

Snaggletoothed, with a crooked potato nose, large, protruding ears, and a shock of thick, wiry brown hair, Will Kipling was not a handsome man. He was about forty years old, and although primarily a farmer, he also owned vast acreage of prime timberland between Leakesville and the Alabama line, all of it acquired by both hook and crook.

And though he had few real friends, Kipling's decisions and opinions were usually deferred to by Greene Countians, for most of the men, including Sheriff Barlow, were afraid of him. And with good reason: Kipling stood six-foot-six and weighed at least two hundred fifty pounds, and had been running roughshod over smaller men all of his adult life. Those he could not intimidate with his size, he would not hesitate to pound to the ground with his fists. His reputation was known throughout the county, and few men opposed his will.

Only three years ago a Leakesville jury, largely chosen by Kipling himself, had rendered a verdict in his favor against an Alabama paper company. The object of the squabble had been five thousand acres of timberland on the east bank of the Chickasawhay River. Though every man in the county knew that the company was the rightful owner, when the trial was over the property belonged to Will Kipling. And though the jury's decision was immediately appealed, a second jury handed down the same verdict a year later. Kipling later sold all of the pine timber off the property, most of it to the same paper company he had stolen it from.

The theft of the timberland was not the only hoax Kipling had pulled off in a Greene County courtroom. He had acquired most of his holdings by having handpicked juries rule that his forged deeds, surveys, and bills of sale, all prepared by a crooked lawyer in Jackson, were valid.

The Greene County courthouse had burned in 1874, and not a single document had survived. Since there were now no existing records of real estate titles and transfers in the county prior to 1875, and all of Kipling's claims were dated several years earlier, he had won each and every case, and his deeds were now duly registered and recognized by Greene County officials.

Two elderly women were on record as saying they had seen someone of a very large stature sneaking through the alley behind the courthouse shortly before it burned, but both were reluctant to name any particular individual. That Will Kipling himself had been the man in the alley had been suggested by a few brave souls, but there was simply no evidence, and no one was ever charged with the arson. At any rate, Kipling was the only man who had gained anything from the midnight fire.

Will Kipling took his time riding home, reliving events of the past three years and planning his next move. He was indeed the man who had torched the county courthouse, the final obstacle that stood between himself and the execution of a plan that had been more than five years in the making, a plan that he believed would eventually make him wealthy.

He had already profited handsomely from his strategically placed handful of dry pine kindling, and he was not done yet. He would soon be in a position to challenge Amy Shelton for ownership of the sixty-acre tract that joined his own property just south of Ward Creek. The phony papers he needed would be coming down from Jackson within the next few days; then he would begin the legal proceedings.

The only person in the county likely to argue Amy Shelton's side of the matter would be her oldest son. The boy had spunk and had already exhibited an unwillingness to be intimidated by Will Kipling's size. Last year, in front of the hardware store, he had sassed Kipling and bowed up ready to do battle, after the big man deliberately bumped into him to move him off the sidewalk. There was no question that Billy Free would put up a fight over his mother's property, but he was not going to be around. Tonight's midnight raid on that cabin would eliminate him once and for all.

Kipling did not plan to let Billy Free reach the jail. Once the sheriff had officially made the arrest and charged him with murder, the boy was going to attempt an escape, and good citizen Will Kipling was going to kill him. That would bring the case of the murdered deputy to a close. The big man smiled at the thought, then began to laugh aloud. He himself had killed Deputy Morrison, and he was going to get away with it. And of course, the fact that the deputy had not been killed where his body was found would never come into question.

Morrison had reneged on a debt, and it had cost him his life. He had bought a litter of pigs from Kipling a year ago last spring, and had agreed to pay fifteen dollars for them in the fall. The pigs had long since grown into hogs, and had either been sold or slaughtered and consumed by Morrison and his fat family. Each time he was dunned for payment, Morrison made a different excuse. Then, once he acquired a lawman's badge, he had brazenly begun to laugh the matter off each time Kipling mentioned it.

Last Monday, when the two men met on the main road and Kipling once again requested payment for the pigs, the deputy shrugged, laughed insolently, and asked Kipling what pigs he was talking about. The big man immediately put a bullet in the deputy's brain, then pointed the lawman's horse toward town and gave it a whack across the rump. Then he carried the body for a short ride on his own mule and deposited it beside the old Indian trail, where he had "accidentally" discovered it seven days later.

Kipling and his two brothers, both of whom were younger and considerably smaller than Will, met the sheriff in front of his office at midnight. All three of the Kiplings rode black horses, and all were armed with Winchester repeating rifles. Sheriff Barlow wore his usual sidearm, a .36-caliber Navy Colt that had been in his family since shortly after it was manufactured, in 1851.

The four men stood beside the sheriff's office for several minutes, holding on to the reins of their horses and speaking in low tones. Will Kipling finally raised his voice. "We've got a job to do," he said, throwing a leg over his saddle. "Let's get on with it." He turned his horse toward Amy Shelton's cabin, and the others followed. None of the four spoke again during the three-mile ride.

The small posse was still more than two hundred yards from the cabin when the resident hounds began to announce the fact that company was coming. "Damn!" Will Kipling said, jerking on his horse's reins and signaling the others to stop. "Ain't no way in hell we're gonna sneak up on 'em now. I didn't expect to run into no goddamn dogs."

The element of surprise had been lost completely, for even as the four men watched, someone inside the cabin lighted a lamp. The fact that more than one person was moving around inside could easily be determined by the number of silhouettes on the window shades. "Whole bunch of people in there, Will," the sheriff said after a few minutes. "This could get kinda nasty. You got any ideas?"

Kipling spat a mouthful of tobacco juice. "I'll think of somethin', Lam, just gimme a little time."

"Well, I don't want no shooting directly into that cabin, 'cause we know for sure that there's a woman and a girl in there. And then there's that youngest boy; hell, he ain't old enough to be no threat to us."

Both surprised and annoyed at Sheriff Barlow's sudden tone of authority, Kipling spoke to his brothers: "Did you hear that, boys? Did you hear that? The sheriff's gone soft in the head. Don't want nobody shootin' at that cabin, he says, and he thinks that youngest boy's too little to fight." He turned to the lawman, his voice reeking with sarcasm. "You got any more bright ideas, sir?"

"I certainly do," Barlow answered gruffly, offering proof that he could actually think for himself in a pinch. "I'm gonna walk up a little closer and try to talk to the boy, see if I can get him to come out on his own." He dismounted and handed his horse's reins to the youngest of the Kiplings, then began to walk down the road toward the cabin. With their rifles at the ready, the two older Kiplings reluctantly followed, leaving their younger brother to hold the horses. As the men drew closer, the hounds, being hunters, not guard dogs, ceased their barking and hid underneath the house.

"Billy Free!" the sheriff called loudly when he was forty feet from the cabin door. "This is Sheriff Barlow, and I want to talk to you! Come on out now, Billy!"

The response from inside the cabin was immediate. "What do you want to talk about?" a deep, youthful voice inquired.

"Well," Barlow began, "I just want to talk about some of the things that have been happening around here. I just want to—"

"He wants to talk about you killin' Deputy Sid Morrison and hidin' his body in the woods!" Will Kipling interrupted, yelling at the top of his lungs. "We all know you done it, so get your ass on out here before we come in after you!"

Another question came from the cabin: "Who's that with you, Sheriff? Who's that accusing me of killing the deputy?"

"That was Will Kipling talking, Billy; him and one of his brothers are standing here with me and they've both got Winchesters. Now, come on out and let's get this thing settled before it gets out of hand."

"I've never killed anybody in my life, Sheriff," the voice continued, "and I haven't even seen Sid Morrison since he became a deputy. Will Kipling probably killed the man himself. Half the people in the county know that Morrison owed Kipling money and refused to pay it."

Will Kipling exploded. "You hear that, Sheriff?" he yelled. "You hear that? That bastard just accused me of killin' one of my best friends, and I ain't gonna stand for it!" Then in a softer tone, he added, "Hell, Lam, you know I wouldna done nothin' like that. You know how thick me and Sid always was, don'tcha?"

When the sheriff did not answer, Kipling yelled to the cabin again: "Billy Free, this is Will Kipling speakin', and I done told you to get your ass out here. The sheriff's got a warrant chargin' you with murder, and you might as well face it like a man. Now, you know my reputation well enough to know that I don't run no bluffs. If you ain't out here in one minute, I'm gonna kick that cabin door in."

After a long pause, the voice in the cabin spoke again, louder this time, and with a definite tone of defiance: "The cabin door is not locked, Kipling!"

All was quiet now, and there were no silhouettes on the window shades to indicate any kind of movement inside the cabin.

Will Kipling stood in the darkness counting the seconds. He had noticed that Sheriff Barlow's manner had grown quieter after Billy Free suggested that Kipling himself had probably murdered the deputy. Was the sheriff at this very moment considering and maybe giving some weight to the young man's accusation? That could very well be the case, Kipling decided quickly.

The big man knew that putting a bullet in Billy Free was the only insurance policy he had against facing a murder charge himself if somebody decided to do a little digging. He had no choice in the matter now. He must get the young man out of that cabin, and he must kill him in the process. And the one-minute warning he had given Free had already expired.

The big man nodded to his brother, then to the sheriff. "Y'all keep your eyes on that door," he said. "I'm goin' in after him." He covered the forty feet quickly, then stepped up on the narrow porch. The door opened at his touch and he had just framed himself in the doorway when a heavy-caliber gun blast knocked him back into the yard. He was dead before he hit the ground.

Billy Free was on the porch for only an instant, then leaped into the yard and took up a position behind the corner of the cabin. Will Kipling's brother was firing now. Free took two quick shots at the muzzle flash, the second of which drilled the man dead center. He coughed once, then dropped his Winchester and fell to the ground. He would never move again.

The shooting was over in less than ten seconds. Sheriff Barlow, who had never even drawn his gun, was now lying on his stomach behind a log, afraid to even speak, lest he give away his position. The youngest of the Kiplings, the only one still alive, stayed in the background holding the horses, showing no desire to join in the fracas.

Free stood behind the corner of the cabin quietly for several moments. He had no doubt that the gun he had just silenced was a Winchester, for he knew the sound of that particular weapon well. Which meant that the shooter had been Will Kipling's brother, for Sheriff Barlow would not have fired into the cabin and had never been known to pack a rifle.

Finally, satisfied that the fight was over, Billy called out to the hidden lawman: "I know you're out there, Sheriff, so you'd better listen to me and listen good. I won't ever be in this cabin again, but my family will keep right on living here. If you ever shoot into it or allow anybody else to, I'll hear about it and I'll find you. That's a promise, Sheriff, and you damn well better remember it!"

Then, moving as quietly as a ghost, Billy Free disappeared into the night.

2

★

Sheriff Barlow and several men he had deputized combed the woods and riverbanks for the next three days, but no one discovered so much as a single footprint left by the fleeing Billy Free. Just before noon on the fourth day, the posse members held their final conference a hundred yards below Amy Shelton's cabin. There it was decided to give up the hunt. "I tell you, it's jist like 'at boy disappeared into thin air," hardware store owner Bill Colley said. "It's a damn shame, too. I'll bet old Jack McInnis'd turn over in his grave, if he knowed how his great-grandson turned out."

On his mother's side of the family, Billy Free was indeed a great-grandson of the founder of the town. About 1812, J. J. McInnis, familiarly known as Jack, along with his wife and children, built their home in a little clearing in the boundless forest, only a short distance from where the county court building would eventually stand. McInnis had come from Scotland and had first settled seven miles to the east. For many years he was the sole white man in the vicinity, although there were numerous nomadic Choctaw and other aborigines who paid him a visit from time to time.

Mobile was the nearest town of importance, and it was necessary to go there for such supplies as were not to be obtained from the soil, the forest, or the abundant game animals. Roads, there were none; a lonely, crooked Indian trail served as a horse-path over which frequent trips were made to the little town at the head of Mobile Bay, and a similar trail led to Jackson and other beginnings of civilization to the north. The Chickasawhay River likewise served as a highway during part of the year, and down it were floated such few products as the settlers had to sell. Flour, sugar, and other indispensables were brought back on the return trip.

With the organization of the district into the county of Greene, in 1811, the seat of government was established and given the name of Leakesville, in honor of Governor Leake, who was chief executive of Mississippi Territory at the time. A log building was erected to serve as the courthouse and county headquarters, but was burned soon afterward, as was its successor, in 1874.

Jack McInnis was not only recognized as the founder of Leakesville. He was considered by all to be the leader of the community, and either headed or was at least a member of every committee of importance in the area. And mostly because of his own relentless efforts, Leakesville acquired its own post office in 1840. McInnis himself became the town's first postmaster, and mail was delivered on horseback once a week.

Jack McInnis was also a businessman who eventually came to be financially well off. Though reluctant to invest his hard-earned money in the development of Leakesville itself, for he was not totally convinced that the town would last, he had nonetheless acquired extensive tracts of timberland on both sides of the river, as well as several hundred acres of cultivated farmland. When he died, at the age of eighty, his holdings were divided among his nine children and twenty-five grandchildren. Amy, the youngest of his granddaughters, received one hundred eighty acres of land and a sturdy log cabin, the same cabin in which she and her four offspring, the oldest of which was Billy Free, lived to this day.

Now, gazing up the hill to the cabin where Amy Shelton and three of her children sat on the porch returning the stares of the disappointed posse, Sheriff Barlow weighed Colley's comments for a long time, then finally spoke: "I don't know so much about that, Bill," he said. "I don't know that his great-granddaddy'd be all that surprised at the way the boy just up and shot the Kipling brothers. From what I hear, old Jack McInnis himself wasn't exactly cut from no holy cloth."

A man named Sinclair cursed loudly and kicked at a rotten log disgustedly. "I believe we'd have caught that boy three days ago if we'd sent somebody after Jack Lyndle," he said. "Jack's got some manhunting hounds."

Sheriff Barlow stood shaking his head. "Them dogs ain't worth a shit, Joe. Jack's got a pack of Walkers that he claims'll track a man, but he's the only one who thinks so. He brought 'em up here two years ago when Sam Arden broke jail, but they turned out to be worthless. Laid around licking their dicks for most of the morning, then when we did get 'em in the woods they took out after a deer and chased it all the way into Alabama. According to what I heard, three of 'em never did come back."

Sinclair stood quietly for a while, then began to chuckle. "Sorry I mentioned the dogs," he said, mounting his horse. Moments later, after the sheriff had officially dismissed the posse, the riders climbed the hill and took the road to Leakesville. Most of them turned their faces in the opposite direction as they rode past the cabin and the contemptuous stares of Amy Shelton and her children.

Although the ten members of the sheriff's posse had to a man declared Billy Free to be several counties away and long gone by now, that was not the case. In fact, at this very moment he was less than three miles from his mother's cabin.

When Billy was twelve years old, he and another boy of the same age had used a pick and shovel to dig themselves a hideout in the tall bank of the Chickasawhay, ten feet above the river's normal water level. The excess dirt fell into the water and washed away in the fast-moving current, leaving no sign that the conformation of the twenty-foot bank had ever been disturbed. A tall, leafy willow completely hid the cave's opening, and floods and high water over the years had only served to make the cavity deeper and wider. The young friend who had helped Billy Free dig the secret hideaway had died two years later of blood poisoning. Nowadays, only Billy and his younger brother, Toby, knew of the cave, and each had sworn never to reveal its existence to another party.

It was to the cave that Billy had run immediately after shooting the Kiplings, and he was still there. Since he and his brother had taken blankets and a lantern and spent the night in the cave on many occasions, he felt sure that Toby would know exactly where to look for him once the hunt by the sheriff's posse proved fruitless. Now Billy was beginning to wonder, for today was the fourth day.

His stomach had growled and fluttered for the first two days, but starting yesterday morning, he had begun to suffer physical pain from the lack of food. Though he had at times been forced to postpone a few meals over the years, he had never before been as hungry as he was at this moment. He knew that if his brother did not come soon, he would have no choice except to leave the cave and shoot something, for he must have food. A mallard duck had presented an easy target early this morning, but Billy had passed up the chance, fearing that the sound of the shot would bring unwanted company.

He had no water in the cave, and suffered unrelenting thirst during the heat of the day. But regardless of how uncomfortable he became, he refused to leave the hole during the daylight hours. He did crawl down to the river at least twice a night, however, drinking as much water as he could hold each time. Then, after brushing away any telltale signs of his passing, he would return to the cave, where he would soon doze off and dream of food.

Billy had known from the first day that the woods were full of men who were searching for him. During the first two days he had heard the sound of running horses and men yelling back and forth on an hourly basis. And more than once some of the riders had halted their horses beneath the canopy of the giant oak that grew directly above the cave. There they sat their saddles discussing strategy or sometimes telling jokes, while the object of their search lay in a hole no more than twenty feet below them, a cocked six-shooter in his hand.

Each time the searchers had talked for a while, then ridden away, never knowing how close they had come. If one of the riders had simply dismounted, walked to the riverbank, and looked straight down, he would have very quickly discovered the hiding place of his quarry. A discovery that would have no doubt cost him his life, for Billy Free had no intention of going to jail for a murder he had not committed.

Nor did he feel that he owed the state of Mississippi a single day of his life for shooting the Kipling brothers. He had no way of knowing for sure, but judging from the fact that they had not returned his fire, he supposed that they were dead. He had shot them both in self-defense, and Sheriff Barlow himself knew that to be a fact. Of course, in a court of law, the sheriff was highly unlikely to offer testimony beneficial to Billy Free, and the fact that the shooting had been witnessed by Free's entire family would mean little. A court prosecutor would probably find a law on the books that forbade the family's testimony, but even if it was allowed, nobody would believe it. Least of all a jury comprised of Will Kipling's cronies.

Billy sat holding the big six-gun that he had traded for last year. Its cylinder was full up and ready to go, and he had half a pocketful of extra shells. The weapon was known alternately as the New Model Army or the Artillery Model. Manufactured by the Colt company in 1873, the single-action revolver had met with immediate acceptance by both the military and civilians. Firing .45-caliber ammunition, it had tremendous knockdown power, and many handgun fanciers had early on begun to call it the Peacemaker.

Most of the men who kept track of such things claimed that the Peacemaker was the best revolver ever manufactured by anyone; and even though its recoil was considerable, the weapon was so well balanced that a quick follow-up shot, in the unlikely event that one was necessary, presented no problem. Its long barrel, which was a full seven and a half inches, made for more accurate shooting, and the black rubber grip with the design of an eagle on it that was common to most commercial models, as opposed to the one-piece walnut grip on those sold to the Army, was a comfortable fit for almost any hand.

Billy had bartered away an excellent saddle horse for his own Peacemaker, and had never regretted the trade. He had practiced with the gun until he became thoroughly proficient, and it now seemed like an extension of his right arm. At close range he could hit anything he could see, and had even brought down small game a few times just to see if he could. He discontinued this practice very quickly, however, for the heavy caliber destroyed so much meat that there was little left for his mother's pot.

He sat in the cave's small opening at sunset, waiting for darkness so he could crawl down to the water and quench his thirst. He had heard no men or horses all day long, and was wondering if the posse had given up the hunt. If so, he thought he would see his brother before daybreak, for it was difficult to believe that Toby did not know his older brother's whereabouts. The two of them had sat in this very spot at least a dozen times in the past, talking about how impossible it would be for someone to find them if they did not want to be found. Billy nodded at his thoughts and almost smiled. Toby knew, all right, and Toby would be here just as soon as he thought it was safe to come.

Billy slaked his thirst as soon as darkness fell, then again a few hours later. He had just gone to sleep and begun to dream about a bowl of his mother's potato salad when he was suddenly awakened by an indefinable sound. He tightened his grip on the Peacemaker, and lay still. A short while later he heard a sound that he recognized immediately. "Billy?" the familiar voice called from directly above the cave. "Billy, are you down there?"

"Yes, Toby," Billy answered excitedly. "Yes, I'm here."

"I figured you would be. I couldn't get here no sooner, 'cause they've been watching us too close. They finally gave up the hunt this morning in plain sight of the cabin. All of 'em's gone home now."

Toby scrambled down the bank quickly, halting his slide by grabbing one of the willow limbs. Then he crawled into the cave and put his arms around his brother's shoulders, hugging him tightly for a long time. "It's gonna be all right, Billy. You'll see."

"I'm so hungry, Toby. Hungrier than I've ever been in my life."

"I brought you some things. Momma says to remind you not to eat too much too fast; says it'll make you sicker'n a dog." They sat on the ground with their legs crossed while Toby opened a cloth sack and spread its contents on the ground. "She sent you some ham and biscuits," he said. "I baked you a few sweet potatoes myself. You go slow, now."

Billy wolfed down a biscuit so fast he almost choked, then began to peel one of the potatoes. "Is . . . are the Kiplings dead?"

"Both of 'em. They buried 'em two days ago."

Billy was quiet for a while, then spoke around a mouthful of food: "They brought it on themselves when they came on us in the dead of night, Toby. I don't know of any other choice that I had."

"You didn't have no choice, Billy. You did what you had to do, and Momma said the same thing. She knows you ain't killed no deputy. She believes the same thing you told Sheriff Barlow: that Will Kipling himself shot Deputy Morrison, then set out to blame the killing on you. She says Kipling never intended to let the case come to court, that he was gonna kill you before you even got to the jailhouse. I kinda believe that myself, Billy. Otherwise, why would he have wanted you out of the cabin so bad that he decided to drag you out himself? It wasn't none of his business, he wasn't no lawman."

Knowing that Toby was wise beyond his fifteen years, Billy had listened to him carefully. "It could be that the sheriff had deputized both of the Kiplings, Toby. If that's the case, I'm gonna be wanted for killing three men, all of them sheriff's deputies." He continued to eat slowly for a while, then added, "If I'm caught, I'm dead."

"That's what Momma thinks, but she says that the Greene County law ain't smart enough to catch you. She says that Sheriff Barlow ain't got enough sense to pour piss out of a boot, and that nobody else ain't gonna be hunting you unless a big reward gets posted. She believes that the reward business is gonna be coming before long, though."

Billy swallowed a chunk of half-chewed ham. "There'll be a reward, Toby."

"Sure there will, but it ain't gonna help 'em none, 'cause you ain't gonna be here." He began to crawl toward the cave's entrance. "I've got to get moving now, Billy, it's probably about eleven o'clock already. I'll be back in less than three hours, and I'll be bringing a whole bunch of stuff. I've been putting a pack together for you all afternoon, and Momma's added a lot of things herself. She wants you out of this country, and she wants you out quick. We're all gonna do everything we can to make sure you don't hurt for nothing while you're traveling. You stay in the cave while I'm gone, now. I'll whistle like a whippoorwill when I get back, then you can just climb on up the bank."

The wait for Toby's return was the longest three hours Billy had ever spent. Sleep was out of the question, for he was much too excited. He stuffed himself with food, then crawled to the river for water. Afterward, he lay in the cave thinking of home, and what his leaving was going to do to his family. He knew that he could count on Toby to look out for his mother, twelve-year-old Sarah, and five-year-old Tom. Toby was a tough young man even now, and Billy knew that he would get tougher if the situation did.

Sarah would probably miss him much less than would the others, for the relationship between Billy and his little sister had not always been smooth sailing. Sometimes it seemed that the two actually made an all-out effort to misunderstand each other.

Little Tom would cry often, however, despite the fact that he was usually in a world of his own, for Billy was the only father figure the boy had ever known. In his young eyes his older brother was the leader of the pack, a rank that must now be passed on to Toby.

Though his confidence in his brother Toby was almost unlimited, Billy was nonetheless a little concerned about his mother. Not nearly as much as he used to be, however, for she had not had one of her spells in a long time now. About a year ago, Dr. Ivy had changed her medication and started her on something that just might have finally done the trick, for she seemed to feel good all the time now, and was almost always in a good mood.

Many unknowing people in Leakesville had spread the rumor that Amy Shelton was crazy. The truth, however, was that she was a healthy, rational, and intelligent lady who had made more right decisions over the years than had most of the others in the community. Then, about ten years ago, she began to occasionally have one of the mysterious spells. At those times she would wander through the town and beyond, talking out of her head and failing to even recognize people that she knew well.

Billy had tracked her down and brought her home on countless occasions. Her pattern never varied: she would first wander up and down the streets of Leakesville for two hours, mumbling unintelligibly to one person after another, then walk down the west bank of the Chickasawhay for a mile, where she always took a seat beneath the canopy of the same blackjack oak. And there she would sit until one of her sons came to take her home.

Within a day or two she would be back to her old self, a condition that might last for several weeks or even a few months. Each time she had a relapse, Dr. Ivy would experiment with a different medication. Then, more than a year ago, he had finally hit on something that worked, and a few months ago Billy had made a special trip to town in order to tell him so. Nowadays, Amy Shelton took a spoonful of medicine in the morning and another at bedtime, and she was just fine every day of the week. She also laughed a lot.

Now that he had sat thinking on the matter for a while, most of Billy's concern for his mother's well-being had subsided. She was going to be all right, he had decided, and if problems arose, Toby would be there to handle them.

When he finally heard his brother's questionable imitation of a whippoorwill, Billy scrambled out of the cave and up the bank quickly, the sack containing the remainder of the food clutched tightly under his arm. The moon, which was in its first quarter, had just risen, and the brothers met in the shadow of the big oak. Toby stood holding the bridle reins of a gray mule. The animal was harnessed with a packsaddle to which were tied several individual packs, and the load appeared to be balanced very well.

"You overdid it, Toby," Billy said, pointing to the mule. "You're gonna need old Bob for the plowing, and to pull the wagon." He walked completely around the animal, then stood shaking his head. "You just take the mule on back home. I can carry everything I need on my back."

"Can you carry everything on your back that Bob's got on his?"

"Of course not, but I don't need that much."

"Momma says you do, so I ain't taking none of it back home. Ain't gonna take old Bob back either. Momma says we'll get another mule in a few days, and I've done seen for myself that she's got the money to pay for one."

"Momma? Momma's got money?"

"She sure does," Toby said, rushing his words. "I don't know how much, but she's got a lot more'n I ever saw before. She just walked over to the fireplace and pulled a loose rock out of the hearth, then pulled out the money. Looked to me like that old sock was half full of eagles, most of 'em doubles."

Billy began to shake his head again. "Momma with a sockful of money," he said softly, as if talking to himself. "I wouldn't have thought it in a million years."

"Me either," Toby said, "but I've seen it with my own eyes now. She said that she'd had most of it since before you were born, and that she'd even managed to add a little to it each year before things got so bad. Said she hadn't been able to save anything since the War, though."

Billy stood quietly for several moments, then asked, "Are you saying that Momma insists on me taking old Bob with me, along with all this stuff you've got tied on his back?"

"That's what I'm saying, big brother, and that ain't all." He laid ten double eagles in Billy's hand. "She says to put this two hundred dollars in your pocket and head west, and you're not to even tell me where you're going. When you get on out of this area, where nobody'll recognize him, she wants you to sell old Bob or trade him for a different pack animal, then buy yourself a good horse and saddle.

"Seems to me like you might be needing a rifle, too." He pointed to the packsaddle. "I put your other pair of pants and your old shoes in that pack. That blue shirt of mine is in there, too. It's way too loose on me, but it'll fit you just about right.

I never would fill it out like you will, 'cause I'm not ever gonna be as big as you. Everybody says that your daddy was a whole lot bigger man than mine, so I guess that's the reason." He laid the mule's reins in Billy's hand. "Momma was hoping that you'd be out of the county before daybreak, so you'd better get moving. Some time tomorrow you can look through the packs and see what all you've got, but I don't think we forgot anything." He put both arms around his brother and hugged him tightly. "Don't worry about us no more'n you have to, Billy. And don't you worry about Momma at all. Me'n Sarah'll both be looking out for her." He squeezed Billy's arm one last time, then turned and walked away.

Billy stood underneath the oak holding the reins for a few moments, watching his brother's retreat in the soft moonglow. He could see Toby very well for the first forty or fifty yards; then the image was lost to the night. "So long, little brother," Billy whispered softly, vainly trying to swallow the lump that had suddenly appeared in his throat. A moment later, he gave the reins a slight yank. "Come on, Bob," he said, then headed north. The date was April 28, 1877.

3

Billy traveled in a northeasterly direction for the next week, making an all-out effort to encounter as few people as possible, and avoiding conversation when he did. Two hours before sunset on the eighth day, he camped at a spring one mile east of Vicksburg. He built a campfire and put a pot of beans and bacon on to boil, then watered old Bob and staked him out on good grass.

While waiting for his supper to cook, he leaned back on his elbows and lay listening to the sounds of boat traffic on the Mississippi River. Occasionally he would cast his eyes toward the town. Even from this distance, he could see that Vicksburg had taken a beating during the Civil War, for the signs of devastation were everywhere.

Billy had decided several days ago that he would follow his mother's instructions when he reached Vicksburg. Tomorrow he would go into town and either sell old Bob or trade him for a different pack animal, then buy himself a horse and a cheap, used saddle.

He was not nearly as skittish about going into a significant town like Vicksburg as he might have been in the not-too-distant past. Only a short time ago he might very well have been detained by Yankee soldiers demanding to know his identity and where he came from, as well as where he was going and why. The Reconstruction period in the South was over now, however, and the Union soldiers had finally pulled out. And while many Southerners cursed the Yankees at every turn, others believed that the Republican government they had forcibly installed was working, and that the South was well on its way to a long period of record prosperity.

Actually, very few people had been touched one way or another by military rule, and some who lived in remote communities and did not stray far from home probably never encountered a Union soldier during the entire period. Billy Free was among the group who had never even seen a Bluecoat, and had one day found himself wondering if they even knew that Leakesville existed. Then, after thinking on the matter for a while, and considering the fact that the maps possessed by the Yankees were obviously good enough to win a war with, he decided that they knew, all right, but they also knew that the backwoods community was no threat to them and had nothing worth taking. Though Billy Free would never know it, his assessment of those particular facts was totally correct.

Now he stoked the fire, stirred the contents of his pot, and added a little water. Then he spread his bedroll and lay down. Resting his head on one of his packs as he watched the sun disappear into the earth a few miles to the west, he began to lay out his plans for tomorrow. After completing his horse trading, he would look around for a holster for his Colt. Then if he could find a used saddle scabbard at the right price, he might buy himself a rifle.

And he was going to need at least one more change of clothing, a matter that could be handled very quickly. He knew all of his sizes well, so there would be no reason to try on the garments before buying. He had long ago become convinced that he was not going to grow any taller, for he had been the same height at the age of sixteen that he was right now, one week short of his twenty-first birthday.

Standing as straight as a fence post, Billy Free measured six-foot-two in his socks, and though his broad-shouldered, one-hundred-seventy-pound frame still had some filling out to do, he was nonetheless muscular. His complexion was dark, his eyes metallic blue, and his dark hair, badly in need of a trim, curled below his ears. He had already decided to visit a barbershop next day.

He extinguished his campfire with several handfuls of sand just before dark, and while he was waiting for his supper to cool, he moved old Bob to new grass. Then he sat on his bedroll eating the beans and bacon straight from the pot. He drank the soup, then walked to the spring and washed the pot.

Then he called it a night. He lay on his bedroll for a long time thinking of the town he would visit tomorrow, a town that had been besieged and pounded with heavy artillery for weeks on end during the War. Even from his campsite a mile away, the scars that marred and disfigured the terrain had been plainly visible before nightfall.

Most likely because his own father had died at Shiloh, Billy became a rapt student of the Civil War. Any published material that he could find was studied closely, and the facts, figures, and details were indelibly imprinted on his mind. After sifting through the mountain of information that was easily available to anyone who could read, he had reached his own conclusion that the brutal facts of arithmetic had doomed the Southern cause right from the start: The North had 75 percent of the total wealth of the entire nation, 67 percent of the farms, 81 percent of the factories, and 66 percent of the railroad miles.

The Union Navy grew to 670 ships and 51,000 men, while the Confederate Navy counted scarcely 130 ships and 4,000 men. Indeed, the fact that the South had held out for four years and had inflicted more casualties on the Union Army than they themselves had suffered could be attributed directly to the South's generals and military planners, whose tactics most historians agreed were far superior to those of their Northern counterparts.

Billy's father, Carl Free, had died on April 6, 1862, when a Confederate army of 40,000 men under General Albert S. Johnston surprised and attacked a Union army of 45,000 men under Ulysses S. Grant. The two-day conflict became alternately known as the Battle of Shiloh and the Battle of Pittsburg Landing. Pittsburg Landing was located on the Tennessee River nine miles north of Savannah, Tennessee, and the name Shiloh was taken from that of a meetinghouse three miles from the landing.

During the battle, which lasted from dawn to dusk on the first day and was one of the most desperate of the War, the Union troops were steadily driven back, but General Johnston was killed, and his successor, General Pierre T. Beauregard, ordered operations suspended a few hours later. The following day General Grant, with 25,000 reinforcements commanded by General Don Carlos Buell, attacked the Confederates and forced them to withdraw to Corinth, Mississippi. Thus, Grant gained all of the ground he had lost the day before, and although the opposing armies had each suffered more than 10,000 casualties, the battle ended without a conclusive victory for either side.

Billy had not only learned all of these things, he also knew that, with medicine and medical facilities sadly lacking, more than 50 percent of the men wounded during the war died of their wounds, disease, or other causes. And he knew that one out of every four men involved in the Civil War had died on the battlefield, another sad statistic that he had just recently learned.

He did not remember much about his father, for he had not yet reached his fifth birthday when Carl Free went off to war. He did remember that his dad was much taller than most men, however, and he could easily recall times when they had played together like two children. Carl Free would sometimes walk through the woods for miles with his young son riding on his shoulders, pointing out and putting names to different species of trees, grasses, and wildlife. To this day, Billy remembered some of those piggyback rides, but try as he might, he could never recall any specific thing that his father had taught him.

He had known his mother's successive husbands much better, and both had been good men. Only a few months after learning that Carl Free had fallen at Shiloh, Amy had married Bud Patterson, and after less than a year of marriage, gave birth to Toby. A year later, after Patterson drowned in the Chickasawhay River, she married Tom Shelton, who consequently fathered both Sarah and Little Tom. Tom Shelton had died in a hunting accident a few months before Little Tom was born, and Amy Shelton had not been the same since.

The first inkling anyone had that her mind might be slipping was one day when young Sarah ran to the field where her older brother was plowing. She told Billy that their mother had been sitting in a rocking chair singing and nursing Little Tom when she suddenly jumped to her feet, threw the baby on the bed, then ran off into the woods screaming.

Billy did no more plowing that day. He pastured the mule and found his brother Toby, and the two spent the remainder of the day searching for their mother. When they finally found her she seemed perfectly normal, and was sitting under the same blackjack tree that would continue to be her ultimate destination each time she had a relapse. She hugged both of her sons and led them back to the cabin at a brisk pace. Once inside, she headed straight for the bed and picked up Little Tom. "Momma's little man must be starving," she murmered, unbuttoning the top of her dress and offering the baby a nipple. "That's Momma's pretty baby," she cooed. "Take your supper now." Little Tom began to nurse hungrily. Billy, who had been standing close enough to see and hear, stood shaking his head for a moment, then walked into the yard.

Now, only a short distance from the muddy Mississippi, with his destination much farther west, the thought crossed Billy's mind that he might never see his mother again. It was a dreadful thought, but he believed that he should not waste his time worrying about it. There was nothing he could do to change it. Nor was there anything he could do to change the circumstances that had brought on his being a so-called fugitive from justice. As the oldest male member of the family, he had been charged with the duty of protecting his mother and his siblings. And he had done no more than what he had to do to protect himself against Will Kipling and his unfounded accusations.

Billy had no doubt that Will Kipling had murdered the deputy. And he also had no doubt that if apprehended, he himself would die for Kipling's crime. Amy Shelton, whose eyes were more than a little difficult to pull the wool over, had thought the same thing, and had sent both money and supplies along with her instructions for him to leave the country. He knew that his mother was a very intelligent woman, and he intended to follow those instructions exactly.

About the same time his eyelids began to grow heavy, he resolved not to worry about his mother again. Her doctor seemed to have her problem under control, and Toby and Sarah were there to take care of her. Amy Shelton was going to be all right. He turned over on his bedroll for what seemed like the hundredth time, then went to sleep.

When he awoke at sunup, he walked to the woods to relieve himself, then built a small breakfast fire between two smooth rocks. He filled his coffeepot with water from the spring, tossed in a handful of grounds, and set the pot on the rocks. As he waited for the coffee to come to a boil, he walked north for a few paces to look at the grassy meadow in which he had staked old Bob the night before. The mule was nowhere to be seen.

Fearing that the animal had been stolen, he ran toward the meadow as fast as he could. As soon as he passed the treeline, however, he stopped suddenly. There, cropping grass a quarter mile away, was old Bob. Billy stood watching for a while. He was reluctant to cross the open meadow, for he was convinced that someone had deliberately turned the animal loose. There was only one way to get a picket pin out of the ground, and that was to pull it straight up: an impossibility for a mule on a forty-foot rope.

Keeping a sharp lookout in every direction, Billy walked backward for several steps and took a seat on the ground, his back leaning against the trunk of a large oak. He watched the meadow for half an hour, but the only movements he saw were those made by the mule: switching his tail at flies or walking a few steps to better grass.

When he finally decided to take the risk, Billy walked into the clearing cautiously. Then, seeing a large circle where the grass had been cropped close to the ground, he walked to the spot where the mule had been picketed the night before. He stood looking at the scarred earth for a moment, then began to chuckle softly. He could read the situation with one eye: in the darkness the mule had blindly stumbled into the picket pin with enough force to tear it out of the ground, then had dragged it behind him as he grazed farther down the meadow.

Deciding to leave the animal to its grazing for the time being, Billy returned to his campfire, where he took a seat on his pack and drank two cups of strong coffee. Then he went about preparing large portions of bacon and sweet potatoes. He would eat a hearty breakfast this morning, for he had a busy day ahead. And he intended to take care of his business as quickly and as inconspicuously as possible. Then he would travel northwest till he reached the solid earth of southern Arkansas, dodging the Louisiana marshes that he knew were at best difficult and in some places impossible to cross on horseback.

And he certainly intended to be riding a horse when he left Vicksburg. Walking at least twenty-five and more often thirty miles a day had already begun to take its toll on his body, not to mention the fact that he had been walking on sore feet since the very first day. One of his feet had blistered and bled within the first few hours. When he changed into his older pair of shoes on the second day, he got some relief for a while. Then the old shoes began to create new blisters in new places, and the going had been rough ever since.

By now, Billy had made a firm decision to go no farther on sore feet. As he sat beside the gray coals eating his breakfast and draining the last of the coffee from the blackened pot, he mentally added several pairs of socks and some comfortable footwear to his shopping list.

Two hours later, he was at the livery stable in Vicksburg, where he bought a horse and a used saddle for a total of forty dollars. Although at least a dozen horses of different colors and sizes were running loose in the hostler's corral, Billy had chosen a big, blaze-faced ten-year-old black with three stockings, and was confident that he had bargained for the best animal in the lot. Next he traded old Bob for a gray mule of comparable size, hoping that he might not even have to readjust the packsaddle. The liveryman explained that he liked old Bob better than any mule he had seen lately, but that it was totally against his principle to make any kind of trade without at least acquiring a handling fee. Billy offered two dollars boot, and the man accepted. They exchanged bills of sale, then Billy saddled the black and transferred the packsaddle to the new mule.

When Free mentioned the fact that he might be in the market for a cheap saddle scabbard for the rifle that he intended to buy, the hostler assured him that he had come to the right place; that he himself had one in the office that he was willing to sacrifice for the paltry sum of five dollars. Three minutes later, Billy bought the scabbard for two dollars, then attached it to his saddle with rawhide. He bought a small sack of shelled corn and added it to the pack mule's burden, then bade the aging liveryman good-bye.

He rode down the street and tied his animals at a hitching rail in the center of town, where he could conduct all of his remaining business within a one-block area. After getting a haircut, he headed for the dry goods store, where he bought a change of clothing and, after trying on several types of footwear, settled on a pair of calfskin boots. Though the soles of the boots were rigid and tough, the uppers were almost as soft as kidskin gloves, offering immediate relief to his sore feet. He walked out of the store wearing the new boots, carrying his shoes in a paper sack that the saleslady had offered.

At the grocery store, he bought a wide assortment of tinned goods, along with crackers, cheese, and a roll of Bologna sausage. He bought Irish potatoes, onions, salt, sugar, and more coffee. When he decided that he had enough supplies to last for at least a month, he returned to the hitching rail and added his purchases to his pack. Now, he would try to find a decent rifle at a good price.

Once the period of military reconstruction was over, the Union Army had headed north, leaving the Southern states to their own devices. Gun dealers, who during Reconstruction had been called "bootleggers," were suddenly legitimate, and their signs soliciting business were plentiful along the streets of almost any Southern town. Even from where Billy was now standing, he could see two gun shops. He chose the closest of the two, which, according to the sign out front, was a combination gun shop and hardware store. A tall, middle-aged man stood behind the counter. "Good morning," he said as Billy walked into the building. "Can I help you with something?"

Billy did not answer right away. He stood looking up and down the aisles and along the walls, clearly impressed with the large inventory. From where he stood he could see several racks of rifles, and dozens of handguns were visible beneath a glass counter. "I've got my mind on a used Winchester," he said finally. "That is, if I can find a good one at a reasonable price."

The man smiled broadly. "I believe you've found just what you're looking for, young fellow, 'cause I've got two used '73 models on hand. One of 'em's priced at twenty-eight dollars, and the other'n at thirty-five."

"If they're the same models, why so much difference in the prices?"

The man blew air into a book of cigarette papers to separate them, selected one, and poured it full of tobacco. "Actually, I suppose the action's just as good on one of 'em as it is on the other," he said. "But they don't look exactly the same, and that's the reason they've got different prices. You see, one of 'em is showing a little use, and the other'n is . . . well, kinda shiny."

Billy nodded, satisfied with the man's explanation. "I'll have a look at the cheaper one," he said. Moments later, he stood sighting down the barrel of the weapon, then jacked its lever action back and forth several times. He handed it back to the man quickly. "Whoever had that rifle sure didn't like it well enough to take care of it. The front sight's bent, and the action's dirty. You can even hear the grit in the mechanism when you jack the lever."

The man blew a cloud of smoke toward the ceiling. "Well, I don't really know anything about this gun, I just took it in trade a few days ago." He replaced it in the rack, and returned with the second Winchester he had spoken of. "Now, this one I do know something about. My brother-in-law bought it new, and he's a man to take care of things." He handed the rifle across the counter.

Billy knew immediately that the rifle was in excellent condition. He could actually see the oil glistening on its moving parts, and the action was smooth and almost noiseless. He sighted down the barrel one time, then announced: "I'll take it. I'll be needing a box of shells, too."

A few minutes later, he shoved the rifle in the saddle scabbard, mounted the black, and led the gray mule down the street in a westerly direction. He would not be looking around for a holster for his Peacemaker today, for he had just within the past hour decided to keep the weapon in his saddlebag, close to hand, yet out of sight.

As he rode along he could easily see that not everybody in the town was on hard times, for he had already been passed by two teams of blooded animals drawing expensive buggies, and several fine saddle horses were tied at the hitching rails.

As he neared the river, however, he saw more signs of poverty. Most of the people he saw were shabbily dressed and lived in dilapidated houses, and their animals, if they possessed any, appeared to be skipping meals on a regular basis. The fact that the town had suffered forty-nine straight days of continuous bombardment during the War was obvious to this day, and even more apparent down near the river, where a large portion of the heavy shelling had taken place. Billy took a good look at the devastation, then rode on without speaking to anyone.

An hour later, he paid to ride the ferry across the river, the fare for both man and animals being fifty cents. At first he had considered trying to save the money by seeking out a ford, but finally decided that a man might search for a lifetime and still not find one. This was the Mississippi. It was wide and deep, and when he thought of all the boat traffic traveling in both directions, with many of the vessels big enough and heavy enough to draw several feet of water, he decided that the big river might well be unfordable for its entire length. He finally coughed up the money and led his animals on board, thankful that the ferry was available. When he scrambled up the steep slope on the opposite bank a few minutes later, he was in Louisiana.

4

When Billy told the ferry operator that he was coming from Florida and was on his way to Arkansas, the man had advised him to head directly north. Otherwise, he said, crossing the many swamps and bayous to the west and northwest would surely present a problem for him and his animals. Then, laughingly, he added that, while the fifteen-foot alligators that inhabited those places would usually make no attempt to hurt a man, it was altogether possible that they might make a man hurt himself. He had still been chuckling at his own wit when Billy thanked him for the information and stepped off the ferry. Though Billy had not particularly liked the fellow, he decided to take his advice. After all, the man appeared to be at least fifty years old and probably knew what he was talking about.

Free rode at a walking pace till he was several miles west of the winding river. Then he turned due north, all the while keeping a sharp lookout for a spring or any drinkable water source for his animals. When no spring materialized, he made a dry camp half an hour before sunset. He himself would not be without water, for both of his canteens were full. His animals would not actually suffer, either. Both had drunk their fill back at the river and would be all right until tomorrow. He would make an all-out effort to find water for them in the morning, however, for it was beneath his principle to work a thirsty animal.

He dropped his saddle and his packsaddle under a tall pine, then picketed the mule and the horse a hundred feet apart. He gathered dead pine needles, twigs, and limbs and kindled a small fire, then dug out his coffeepot and filled it with water from a canteen. He added grounds and set the pot on the fire, then spread his bedroll while he waited.

By the time darkness had settled in he was busy eating cheese, crackers, and tinned fish, washing it all down with the best-tasting coffee he'd ever had. Tonight he was drinking Washburn's, a brand he had never heard of until he bought it in Vicksburg this morning. He licked his lips and refilled his cup, making a mental note to ask for the same brand the next time he bought coffee.

A short time later, after smothering his fire with dirt, he moved his bedroll away from the tree, dragging it between two small oaks whose tops were too close to the ground for birds to consider them as roosting places. He gave both of the bushes a hard shake just to be sure, for he wanted no bird droppings on himself or his bedding. Then he lay down and pulled one of his blankets over his head, for the mosquitoes had already gone to work on his face and neck.

Though the night was not cold, and the covering was uncomfortable, he would make every effort to stay underneath the blanket, for mosquito bites often created knots on his body the size of acorns, knots that would sometimes still be with him weeks later. Besides, he had heard that the pests might even be deadly, that at least some of the medical people suspected them of transmitting all kinds of contagious diseases. With that thought in mind and knowing that he would

probably cast his too-warm covering aside as soon as he was
asleep, he added another fold to the saddle blanket that he
was using for a pillow, then turned over and dozed off quickly.

Next morning, after building a fire and bringing his coffeepot to a boil, he cut several slices from the roll of Bologna
sausage and dropped them in the skillet with his eggs. A few
minutes later, he was eating a tasty breakfast. When he had
finished his meal he cleaned the skillet as best he could with a
stick and some leaves, then stored it in his pack. He would
scrub it with sand as soon as he came upon clean water.

He did not have to search for the water, for once he had
mounted the black, the big horse walked straight to a clear-
running spring a few miles to the north. Never once had the
saddler varied his course, but traveled the entire distance in a
literal beeline. And Billy had never had to tug on the lead
rope, for the pack mule had trotted alongside him most of the
time, not waiting to be led.

Some folks claimed that the reason animals could find
water so easily was because they could smell it for long dis-
tances, while others said that it was all a matter of instinct,
that clean water was completely odorless. Billy had never ar-
gued the point one way or another, but the fact that both his
horse and his mule had known the exact location of this particular spring had been obvious, and they had known it from
a distance of more than three miles. He had no way of knowing for sure, but he believed that the animals had indeed followed their noses.

He was in Arkansas two days later, and spent part of the
afternoon searching for a shallow place to cross Crooked
Bayou. He rode both north and south along its edge for quite
some time, but the water was so discolored that he could not
even make a guess as to its depth. He finally took his Colt
from his saddlebag to defend himself and his animals against
a possible alligator attack, then plunged in at the narrowest
point he could find.

Surprised that both the horse and the mule had taken to

the chore willingly, he was pleased to find that at no time during the crossing was the water more than belly-deep. The black even stopped halfway across and attempted to drink, but received a hard whack across the rump from its rider, who was anxious to cross the bayou as quickly as possible. Being from Southern Mississippi, Billy was no stranger to alligators and knew that their behavior was highly unpredictable. He believed that the stories he had heard about them attacking humans were greatly exaggerated, but he knew for sure that they had been known to kill horses, cattle, sheep, and hogs and that they considered smaller animals a delicacy, especially cats and dogs.

On dry land once again, he continued west. After traveling for little more than a mile, he came upon on a narrow trail that led northwest toward a higher elevation and what appeared to be an endless stand of hardwood timber. Though he knew that the trail had probably originated with the Indians, he could see that it was still being used to this day. No grass grew in its middle, and the tracks of many horses were visible, some of them only a few days old. And the majority of the tracks were deep, indicating that they were made by pack animals carrying heavy burdens. Deciding that the trail would eventually lead to a place bearing some semblance to civilization, Billy turned his horse onto it and kicked the animal to a trot. Maybe before sunset he would at least come upon a good campsite with drinkable water.

Two hours later, continuing to gain altitude as he rode deeper into the forest, he came upon a few acres of relatively level ground, where somebody had boxed up a spring and stacked large rocks around it. The ashes from dozens of campfires were plainly visible, and some thoughtful soul had even left a tin cup hanging on a limb that grew over the water. Billy knew that he would travel no farther this day. He used the cup to slake his thirst, then rehung it on the broken limb.

He unburdened his animals and watered them from the spring's runoff, then staked them close by and tied on their nose bags. He gave each of them a hefty portion of grain, because forage was almost nonexistent beneath the interlocking canopies of the leafy hardwoods, which included buckeye, hackberry, hawthorn, hickory, maple, ash, and oak. The shady hillside supported little small vegetation of any kind, and Billy suspected that in a few places the sun never touched the ground except during late fall and winter, after the trees had shed their foliage.

Once he had cared for his animals, Billy set about looking after his own needs. Deadwood was plentiful, and he was soon sipping hot coffee. His supper would not be ready for quite some time, however, for he had just now set a pot of red beans and bacon on the fire. He also planned to bake some sweet potatoes, but would wait a while before burying them in the hot coals.

He chose a bedding place twenty feet from the fire and swept it clean with a leafy limb. Then he spread his bedroll and took a seat on it, leaning back on his elbows as he waited for the boiling pot to do its work. Beside him, covered with a blanket, both his Colt and his Winchester were close to hand.

He heard the sound of horseshoes striking stones long before he saw the rider. As he sat staring down his back trail waiting for the man to round the curve and come into view, he slid his hand under the blanket and closed his fist around the grip of his Colt. Though he knew very well that most traveling people were simply trying to get from one place to another and posed no threat to anyone, he was taking no chances. He had only recently gained some firsthand knowledge of just how low some men could stoop.

The rider was a red-haired man of medium height and weight, who appeared to be about forty years old. His brogans, overalls, and flannel shirt suggested that he might be a farmer, and though he had a crumpled hat pulled low over his eyes, Billy could see that he wore wire-rimmed eyeglasses. Riding a broad-backed sorrel mare, he had a scrimpy bedroll behind his saddle and what appeared to be a small-caliber rifle in the boot. No short gun was visible.

The man neither spoke nor nodded a greeting as he rode past Free and on to the spring's runoff to water his animal. Then, as the mare drank, he pushed his hat to the back of his head and pointed to the hump under Free's blanket. "You're not gonna be needing that thing you've got in your hand there," he said in a deep voice. "I guess you could say that I'm just about as harmless as they come."

Billy nodded and smiled, but kept his hand under the blanket.

The man stripped his saddle, then tied the mare to a sapling a hundred feet away. After he had chosen a sleeping place, he walked to the spring, filled the community cup with water, and carried it back to his bedroll. Then he began to eat some kind of food from his saddlebag, washing it down with cold water.

Billy had removed his hand from under the blanket. He caught the stranger's eye, then pointed to the fire. "I've got more hot coffee in that pot than I'm gonna drink!" he said loudly, for the man was sitting at least fifty feet away. "You're welcome to it, 'cause I'll just pour it on the fire when I get sleepy!"

The man nodded, then dashed his water to the ground and walked to Billy's fire. He filled his cup from the coffeepot and took a sip. "My name's Red Lamb," he said, "and I appreciate your kindness." He pursed his lips and blew cool air into the cup, then sipped again. "This is the first cup of coffee I've had in nearly a week. Coffee's one of the many good things in life that I can't afford nowadays."

Billy smiled and pointed to the pot. "Drink it all," he said. "I've already had as much as I want, and I prefer plain old water with my supper, anyway." He added a couple of sticks of wood to the fire, then added, "I know what you mean about not being able to afford it. The stores were already charging more than it was worth a year ago, and the price has nearly doubled since then." He motioned toward his pack. "The coffee grounds I've got right there might be the last that I'll ever buy unless the price comes down. As much as I enjoy a few cups in the morning to get the day started, I can still take it or leave it."

Lamb chuckled. "I reckon I can take it or leave it, too," he said. "Of course, I'll keep on taking it as long as I can get it, but I sure don't think leaving it'll kill me. Like I said, I ain't had none for nearly a week, and I ain't dead yet." He lifted the coffeepot off the fire and held it at arm's length. "Once again, I appreciate your kindness." Then, with the blackened pot in one hand and the tin cup in the other, he returned to his own bedroll and continued to eat his supper.

Though Lamb had introduced himself right away, he had apparently been unconcerned that Free had failed to mention his own name. In fact, of the several people Billy had talked with since leaving home, none had asked his name. Nor had he volunteered it. He had no intention of changing it, but he had long since decided to make it known only when identifying himself by name seemed truly necessary. He knew that most people cared little about a man's name or where he came from, and that a lot of men considered it downright rude to ask. He also knew that the farther he traveled from Mississippi, the less cause he would have for concern.

Billy had no more than become comfortable with his thoughts when Lamb returned the empty coffeepot and set it on the ground beside the fire, where several sweet potatoes were now baking beneath a pile of hot coals and ashes. "You never did mention your name," he said, "so I thought I'd just up and ask."

Free answered quickly: "Most folks call me Slim."

Lamb smiled. "Well, most folks are sure gonna have to start calling you something else within the next year or two, 'cause you're gonna be a helluva lot bigger by then." He headed for his bedroll, adding over his shoulder, "Yessir, Slim, you're gonna be way too big to wear that name."

Billy ate his supper as darkness closed in, then kicked dirt over the fire. A few minutes later, he was sleeping soundly, his head resting on one of his packs and his weapons close to hand.

He was awakened half an hour after daybreak by the sound of a walking horse, and knew before he opened his eyes that Red Lamb was leaving the area. He got to his feet quickly and called out to the man, who had already guided his mare onto the trail: "No use in you rushing off, Red! I'll have some breakfast here in a few minutes, and you're welcome to eat with me!"

Lamb acknowledged the invitation by turning in the saddle and shaking his head, then waved good-bye and kicked his mare in the ribs. A few minutes later, he disappeared over the hill.

After washing his face at the spring, Billy led the black and the mule to the ditch and watered them. Then he tied on their nose bags and fed them the last of his grain. He would buy some more when and if he came to a livery stable or a feed store. He would always buy oats when he could find them, for they were the best feed that could be had for horses and mules. And it seemed that the animals knew what was good for them, for they preferred eating oats over any other type of grain.

Although most of the open terrain supported plenty of good grass at this time of the year, the small amount that grew in the hardwood forests was always cropped short, gobbled up by deer and other wild animals who were forever scrounging around for every last tidbit they could come by without exposing themselves. Though Billy would be careful not to overburden the pack mule, he would try to keep a small sack of oats or shelled corn on hand, for he had no reason to believe that he would be getting out of hardwood country anytime soon.

Half an hour later, he sat by the fire sipping hot coffee while the first of the several johnnycakes he would have for breakfast baked in an iron skillet. Several days ago he had eaten half of the jar of jelly that his mother had included in his pack, and this morning he would finish it off. As she had done every summer since Billy could first remember, Amy Shelton had made it from scuppernongs, a variety of muscadine grape cultivated throughout the South and named for the Scuppernong River in North Carolina. Of all the jellies Billy had tasted in his lifetime, he had found none better.

The sun was more than an hour high when he stepped into the saddle, took up the slack in the mule's lead rope, then guided the black onto the rocky trail. He had already decided that, if the trail was still heading in a northerly direction when the day's traveling was done, he would leave it. Then tomorrow he would turn west, for he had no desire whatsoever to see the north country.

The West was where a young man ought to be, according to most of the things he had read. One magazine had described Texas as the land of opportunity, a place where a man could find immediate employment with no questions asked. The writer claimed that nobody there was likely to even ask a man where he came from, for it was an unspoken fact that a goodly portion of the men living there were themselves wanted by authorities in other places.

Texans were largely unconcerned about anything anybody might have done in the past, the article had stated, and they would most likely gauge a man only by what type of life he was living at the moment. The writer, who claimed to have been to Texas several times, wrote that even Texas lawmen were exceedingly tolerant and slow to question any man who was minding his own business. Billy Free certainly knew how to mind his own business, and he was headed for Texas. Everything he had heard and read about the place suggested that he would be safer there.

He traveled north all morning and ate his dinner at a small

spring. About midafternoon, when the trail made a sharp turn to the northeast, he decided that he had followed it far enough. He turned the black off the trail, and, taking up the slack in the rope till he had his pack mule on a very short lead, began to pick his way west through the densest hardwood forest that he had encountered so far.

An hour later, he spotted a stand of small cottonwoods and a patch of tall green grass that signaled another spring. As he rode into view, a doe and her fawn trotted away from the runoff ditch where they had been drinking. They ran for only a short distance, then stopped to look him over. As he began to unsheath his rifle, however, the doe seemed to sense exactly what was about to happen. She quickly led her offspring into the nearby brush.

He unburdened and watered his animals, and picketed them on the first good graze he had come upon in several days. Moving about as slowly and as quietly as possible, he gathered an armload of deadwood. Then he leaned his back against a cottonwood to rest. He would not build a fire just yet. He would remain still and quiet for the next hour and do nothing to betray his presence, for he fully expected to have venison for supper.

When he finally decided that it was time, he jacked a shell into the chamber of his Winchester so quietly that he himself did not even hear it. Then he eased off into the brush in the opposite direction from that which the deer had taken. Billy was an accomplished hunter. He knew that deer usually live out their lives in a very small area, and will rarely stray from it unless frightened. The doe he had seen earlier had not been frightened. She had seemed to know that he was just passing through, and she had bolted into the brush only after he moved his hands in a way that she could not understand.

He hurried away in the direction from which he had come till he was out of sight, then circled to the south. He knew that he must get downwind of the doe, who was probably bedded down no more than a few hundred yards west of his campsite, no doubt planning to return to the spring and finish slaking her thirst as soon as the two-legged creature was gone.

After walking south for a few hundred yards he turned back west. He was not exactly downwind, but had a cross-wind that he thought was good enough. It was not a matter of whether or not the doe smelled him, for she had been smelling him ever since he rode over the hill. If her nose ever told her that he was getting closer, however, the hunt would be over, for she would lead her fawn out of the area at a hard run.

He continued to walk west till he was directly south of what he thought would be the doe's hiding place, then stood scanning the area to the north for a long time. Finally settling on an uprooted pine that rested in a patch of last year's tall brown sedge, he began a slow, noiseless stalk, taking one step, then waiting two. It took him twenty minutes to cover two hundred yards. Nonetheless, he had come far enough, for he could now see the doe lying in her bed with her attention focused on the spring, the place where she had last seen the two-legged creature. The flick of an ear had caught Billy's eye and given away the animal's location.

He squatted on his haunches as he continued to scan the field of sedge and the surrounding brush. The doe would keep, he had decided, for she suspected nothing out of the ordinary. Besides, he intended to take her only as a last resort. The fawn was his quarry.

When he was unable to spot the small animal during the first few minutes, he seated himself on the ground. Then, one clump at a time, he began to pick the tall sedge apart with his eyes, looking for anything that did not fit the terrain. After only a few moments he located not one, but two fawns lying about fifty feet apart and at least a hundred feet from their mother.

He waited no longer. When his rifle barked, the fawn nearest to him twitched once and lay still while the doe sprang to her feet instantly and left the country in a hurry, her remaining fawn close on her tail. He stood staring after the running doe long after she had disappeared. "One for you and one for me," he said softly, then walked forward to retrieve his supper.

He was still roasting venison two hours later. Though darkness had long since settled in and he had already eaten as much as he could, he had decided to cook up a few more pounds. Otherwise the meat would spoil quickly. When he was sure that he had prepared as much as he could eat within the next two days, he carried the remainder of the carcass a good distance from his campfire and deposited it where it would easily be found by a coyote or some other carnivore.

When he returned to his campfire he wrapped the cooked venison in an old newspaper and placed it in the fork of a willow, at least eight feet above the ground. He kicked dirt over his fire, then dragged his bedroll behind a clump of bushes. A few moments later he called it a night and did not open his eyes again until morning.

5

★

Billy spent his last night in Arkansas camped on the west bank of the Red River, and was in Texas an hour before noon the next day. He continued to travel west, and at midafternoon, riding parallel to the Texas and Pacific Railroad tracks, came upon a small settlement that, according to a weathered sign at the eastern edge of town, was properly called Atlanta. He sat his saddle for a few moments looking the place over. One glance was enough to tell him that the livery stable was at the west end of the town's only street. He could also see a small eating establishment next door to what appeared to be a one-story hotel or rooming house. He decided very quickly that he would travel no farther this day, and kneed his horse toward the stable.

A white-haired man who appeared to be at least sixty years old met him at the wide doorway. Wearing dirty, striped trousers and a thick flannel shirt that surely must be uncomfortably hot at this time of year, he offered a toothy grin, gave his wide suspenders an audible pop with his thumbs, then reached for the black's reins. "Shore 'preciate ya stoppin' by, young feller, so I'll be returnin' th' favor by takin' care o' yer animals jist like they wuz my own. Do it reasonable, too." He led the horse and the mule inside the building and went to work.

Billy followed, and began to ask questions concerning the community. The old man was a talker: "Yep, th' first ones of us 'at got here named th' place Atlanter," he said, stripping the saddle from the black. "Named it after Atlanter, Georgie, 'cause 'at's whur most uv us early settlers come frum." He placed the saddle on a wooden rack built for that purpose, then turned his attention to the mule's packsaddle. "Now, there ain't much money ta be made hereabouts," he continued, "but I b'lieve most folks git along mighty good without it.

"People livin' aroun' this town don't spend their time thankin' about gittin' a-holt o' no whole bunch o' money, 'cause ever'body's already got about all it takes ta git by. They grow ever'thang they eat and build whatever else they need." He stowed Billy's packsaddle inside the office, then continued to talk as he curried the mule. "I knowed all I needed ta know about this place th' first time I ever laid eyes on it. Th' Texas and Pacific Railroad weren't eeb'm done layin' them tracks out there when I told my two brothers 'at this wuz th' place fer us ta do our settlin' at. They both knowed it, too. We all three knowed this good soil'd grow jist about anythang a feller wanted ta plant, so this is whur we lit. My brothers, God rest their souls, have both passed on now, but I been here ever since."

When the old man finally led the animals down the hall toward the stables, Billy followed and stood watching till each of them had been given a good feed of oats and hay. Then, with his saddlebags across his shoulder and his Winchester cradled in the crook of his arm, he turned toward the front door. "I'll stay in town at least overnight," he said over his shoulder. "Might even hang around for a few days." Then he walked through the doorway.

"Jist suitcha self!" the old man called after him loudly.

A few moments later, Billy stepped up on to the board-walk on the north side of the street, then headed for a small building whose overhead sign identified it as the Cattlemen's Steakhouse. When he opened the door, he was looking into the eyes of a middle-aged gray-haired woman who sat on a tall stool behind the counter. "Come right in, young man," she said, smiling broadly and pointing to a nearby table.

When he had seated himself, she handed him the bill of fare, chuckling softly. "I suppose you can see that you're the first one in line this afternoon," she said, obviously referring to the fact that he was the only customer in the building.

"I guess it had crossed my mind," he said, offering a big smile of his own. He pointed to the bill of fare. "I already see what I want right there at the top of the page."

"The beef stew?" she asked. "Warmed-over beef stew?"

"Yes, ma'am, it always seemed to me like it tasted better the second time around."

"I've heard that before," she said, and turned toward the kitchen.

As he sat waiting for his meal, he could hear a conversation between the woman and a man with an exceptionally deep voice. Though he could make out none of their words, he assumed that the man was not only the restaurant's cook but most probably the woman's husband. His assumption proved to be correct a few minutes later, when the lady delivered an oversized bowl of stew to his table. "My husband used a bigger bowl than usual because he wants to empty the pot," she said. "He doesn't like to sell leftovers and told me to only charge you half price."

Free nodded, then dug in. After only a few bites he silently proclaimed the stew the best he had ever tasted. Not only had the cook not skimped on the beef, but the concoction had an overall flavor that was totally different from anything Billy could remember. Even after the stew was swallowed, it had an aftertaste that made him think about burying his face in the bowl. He wolfed it all down in short order, then called the lady back to his table. "Tell your husband that I'll be more than happy to empty that pot for him," he said, handing her the bowl for a refill. "And tell him that I insist on paying full price."

After finishing his meal, he sat at the table for another half hour drinking coffee and trying to decide where he was going. Since leaving Mississippi he had been traveling blind for the most part, seldom having any reliable information as to his exact whereabouts. For the past two weeks he had simply been pointing the black's nose west every morning, then holding the same course all day.

He knew that he wanted to go farther west and that he wanted to remain in Texas, but the crude map that he carried was old, probably made before much of the western portion of the state was even charted. He decided that he must at least make an effort to acquire one that was newer, for he wanted to avoid as many densely populated areas as possible. In fact, he would try to come by an up-to-date map before he left this town.

When he was finally ready to leave the restaurant, the lady met him at the counter. "Your dinner will be ten cents," she said.

"A dime?" he asked, shaking his head in disbelief. "Lady, I must have eaten close to half a gallon of beef stew, and I drank three cups of coffee."

She maintained a serious facial expression and continued to hold out her hand. "My husband says ten cents."

Still shaking his head, Billy dropped a dime in her hand and laid another one on the counter, then headed for the front door.

Back on the boardwalk, he leaned against the front of the restaurant for a few moments looking the small town over, then headed for a saloon he had spotted halfway down the street. Three saddled horses were tied at the hitching rail, and their riders, all three of them seated at the bar, gave Billy the once-over as he entered the building. He ignored their glances and pulled out a stool at the end of the bar. "I'll have a beer," he said to the middle-aged, bald-headed bartender.

The man drew the beer and began to walk in Billy's direction, sliding the mug of foamy brew along the bar before him. "I guess this one'll be on the house," he said, wiping his hands on his apron and refusing to accept Free's nickel. "You're the first man to order a beer today," he added. "Ninety-nine percent of the men in this town are whiskey drinkers."

Billy lifted the mug. "Thank you," he said, then took a sip of the brew.

"Maybe the boy can't afford nothing but beer, Horace," a loud voice called from midway down the bar. "Give him a drink of the good stuff on me."

When the bartender looked at Free with raised eyebrows, Billy shook his head firmly, then spoke to the man down the bar: "I appreciate the offer, but no thanks. It's not that I can't pay for my own drinks; I'm drinking beer because I don't like the taste of whiskey."

The middle-aged man, who wore a faded blue shirt and a high-crowned Stetson and sported a thick brown mustache, chuckled loudly. "Well, I guess by god that oughtta set me straight," he said, then chuckled again. "Yessir, I reckon that's enough to set me to minding my own business." He upended his whiskey glass, then slid off his stool and headed for the front door, his two drinking companions following close behind.

Now that he was down to one customer, the bartender pulled up a stool on the opposite side of the bar. He refilled the mug and accepted Billy's nickel, then seated himself and began to talk. "That man wasn't trying to be smart-alecky about what you were drinking," he said, "and he was sincere about wanting to pay for it. His name is Bill Durden, and he's just about the nicest sort of fellow you could ever hope to meet."

Billy smiled, and nodded. "That's good to hear," he said. "I wasn't offended by what he said anyway. I just thought I needed to explain to him why I didn't want a drink of whiskey."

The barkeep chuckled. "Well, you made it plain enough, and I could tell that Bill got a kick out of your straightforward answer." He sat quietly for a while, then asked, "You gonna be in town long, or are you just passing through?"

Billy was on his feet now, draining his mug. "Just passing through. In fact, I expect to be on my way again tomorrow." He set the thick mug on the bar and waved away the man's attempt to refill it. "I was hoping that I might find a better Texas map than the one I've got. Do you suppose there's any place in this town that would have one for sale?"

"I don't think anybody around here sells 'em," the bartender said, shaking his head, "but there sure ain't no shortage of maps. The Texas and Pacific Railroad made sure of that, not to mention the land speculators who come around several times a year passing out maps and trying to talk everybody into moving to West Texas." He pointed over his shoulder toward the office. "Hell, I've probably got two or three of 'em in there in a desk drawer."

Billy smiled. "I'd be glad to pay you for one."

"Pay, you say? Hell, there ain't nothing to pay for. Nobody couldn't get away with charging people money for them things, 'cause everybody that wants one has already got it. Them shysters ride all over the country just begging people to take a map or two, hoping they can eventually sell the poor devils a chunk of worthless property a thousand miles from nowhere." He slid off the stool and headed for the office, adding over his shoulder, "Even though I know that most of what the speculators are selling is bullshit, I'd say that the maps are probably correct, 'cause they sure wouldn't want nobody to get lost while they're delivering all their hard-earned money to 'em." He disappeared inside the office, and Billy pulled out the stool and seated himself again.

When the bartender reappeared, he laid the map in Billy's hand. "A good friend of mine who's traveled all over the West told me that this was the most accurate Texas map ever printed," he said. "It was put together by the Bekins Company of San Antonio, and their work is highly regarded by most of the people I know."

Billy spread the map on the bar and swept it with his eyes. "I'm sure it'll show me where I am and how to get wherever else I decide to go," he said. He refolded it and shoved it into his vest pocket. "Once again, I'd be happy to pay you for it."

"Dammit!" the man said loudly, appearing to be truly upset. "How long have you been in Texas, young fellow?"

"Just a few hours."

"Well, let me just tell you a thing or two, mister. At least twice you heard me say that I didn't want no damn money for that map; it ain't worth no damn money. Hell, I already knew you weren't no Texan, but if you're intending to be one, you might as well get to know the way things are out here. You see, us Texans don't charge people money just for treating 'em like human beings. You can travel anywhere you want to in Texas, and you'll see that I'm telling you right. No matter where you go or what you run up against, somebody's gonna reach out a hand to you.

"I'm talking about ordinary Texans, now, just plain old everyday people, 'cause I'd never say nothing half that good about some of the so-called authorities, the men who are supposed to be running the state. Nothing good to say about Texas lawmen, either, 'cause I'm convinced that more'n half of 'em are as crooked as a dog's hind leg."

"That might very well be the case anywhere a man goes," Billy said. He was on his feet again, offering a parting hand-shake. "I appreciate the map, Horace, and thank you for all the information."

The bartender grasped the extended hand. "I enjoyed talking with you," he said. "You already know that my name's Horace. You got a name?"

"Sure do," Billy said, laying his saddlebags across his shoulder and turning toward the door. "The name is Slim."

"Slim, huh?" the bartender called after him, chuckling. "Guess that name's as good as any other."

Back on the boardwalk, Billy made a beeline for the hotel, located at the end of the block on the opposite side of the street. Built of rough lumber, the single-story establishment appeared to be the newest thing in town, and even at this late hour of the day, with the sun very near the western horizon, a man stood on a high scaffold at the west side of the building, applying white paint to the uneven, mismatching boards. Billy nodded and waved to the painter as he walked by, and his greeting was returned.

He paid fifty cents for a room at the hotel and was not even asked to sign a register. The attendant, a tall boy not yet out of his teens, simply took Billy's money and handed him a key, saying, "Room six, right down the hall."

Billy entered the room and locked the door, then undressed and stretched out on the bed. He lay studying his map till there was no longer enough light to read it, then dropped it to the floor. He would not put a match to the wick of the coal-oil lamp, because he had no need for a light. He was tired and knew that he could very easily sleep till broad daylight. He made a firm decision to be on his way west again come morning, then turned his face to the wall and slept the night away.

6

Two weeks later, he camped at a spring two miles east of Stephenville. In his continuing effort to avoid densely populated areas, he had deliberately ridden south of both Dallas and Fort Worth several days ago. And today he had decided to bring his traveling to a halt at midafternoon. Both he and his animals were tired, and the spring offered an excellent campsite with good grass and lots of shade. Besides, he was hungry for a pot of red beans, and he would have plenty of time to cook them before nightfall.

He had staked out his horse and his mule immediately after his arrival, and had already moved their picket pins once. The hungry animals had begun to tear at the green grass as if there would be no tomorrow, and he expected to move them again before dark. But for now, even though he knew that supper was at least an hour away, he sat on his bedroll beside the small campfire hungrily watching the beans roll around in the pot of boiling water.

Earlier, he had sat studying his map for a while, trying to

decide just where he wanted to go. When he finally refolded it and returned it to his saddlebag, he almost spoke his decision aloud. He would simply wander along with wide-open eyes until some kind of opportunity presented itself. He believed that he had already traveled as far from Mississippi as he needed to, and that the name Slim was now completely unnecessary. His name was Billy Free, and from this day forward, when anyone asked, he would tell them so.

His chance came much sooner than he expected, for when he looked up from his daydreaming, he could see a rider approaching the spring from the south. As he had done on several other occasions when he spotted company coming, Billy removed his short gun from his saddlebag and laid it on his bedroll, covering it with the edge of his blanket. His loaded Winchester lay leaning against his saddle.

The rider stopped forty yards away and watered his bay gelding from the spring's runoff, then pushed his low-crowned Stetson to the back of his head and rode to Billy's campfire. Appearing to be about thirty years old, he was a six-footer who probably weighed about one-eighty. He had coal-black hair and a complexion the color of old leather, and with his red flannel shirt, faded jeans, and high-heeled boots had the look of a man who spent the major portion of his life outdoors. A dark leather gunbelt encircled his narrow waist, the holster of which contained a Colt revolver exactly like the one Billy was hiding under his blanket. The man looked Billy over for a few moments, then seemingly spoke without opening his mouth: "How long have you been here?"

Billy let him wait a while, then answered with a question of his own. "Is there some special reason why that should concern you?" he asked in the firmest voice he could muster.

The man's face remained expressionless as he answered through tight lips. "Special enough," he said. "That's my wood you're burning"—he waved his arm toward the meadow—"and that's my grass your horse and mule are eating."

Instantly taking on a milder disposition, Billy got to his

feet. "I just rode up about two hours ago," he said, his tone of voice softening considerably. "I've been working my animals mighty hard, and this spring just looked like a good place to stop for the night."

"It is," the man said. He threw his leg over the saddle and stepped to the ground, adding, "I've spent a few nights here myself when I was too tired to ride on home." He dropped his horse's reins to the ground and walked closer to the fire. "This is the southwest section of the Triple R Ranch, owned by Rachel, Robert, and Raymond Haskell." He offered a handshake, and for the first time cracked a smile. "I'm the one named Raymond."

Free grasped the hand quickly. "My name is Billy Free," he said, working up a feeble smile of his own. "I came from back east, and I haven't figured out exactly where I'm going. For the past several years I've been reading books advising young men to head west, so I finally saddled up and lit out."

Haskell nodded and was quiet for a few moments. Then he pointed toward Billy's campfire. "I've got a cup in my saddlebag," he said. "You got any coffee in that pot to spare?"

Free nodded. "Help yourself," he said. "If that runs out, I'll make some more. I've got plenty of grounds."

Haskell was soon squatting on his haunches sipping from his tin cup. A few seconds later, he sat down on the ground and stretched out his long legs. Finally he leaned back on one elbow and spoke again: "You don't have any idea where you want to go, huh?"

Billy shook his head. "I don't know where I should go, because I don't know what kind of choices I have. All I know about Texas is what I've read in books and magazines, and judging from what I've seen so far, I'd say they stretch the truth every chance they get."

Haskell chuckled. "We don't call it stretching the truth out here," he said. "We call it what it is: a pack of damn lies. I've read several of those books, and if I didn't know better, I'd swear that they were written about people in some other country. The writers of Western novels are not the ones who get my dander up. Even though most of them have never been anywhere near Texas, they tell you right up front that their work is fiction, so a fellow can live with that.

"It's the men with a financial stake in Texas who put out most of the bullshit, especially the railroads. You see, they own several million acres of land that used to belong to you and me. It was a handout from the federal government, didn't cost the railroad builders a damn dime. They're trying to unload it all on a bunch of unsuspecting people at fancy prices now, and they've hired an army of conscienceless bastards with good writing skills to do the job for them.

"And they'll write any kind of shit they think a dumb Easterner with a few dollars in the bank might swallow. Like I said before, they're heartless bastards with no conscience whatsoever." He emptied his cup and dashed the coffee grounds over his shoulder. "I have to assume that most of those writers attended a school of higher learning somewhere, but I know for sure that the schools didn't teach them to write that way.

"I sat through a few journalism classes myself while I was in college, and the first thing they tell you is to know what the hell you're writing about, then stick to the damn facts." He refilled his cup, draining the pot. "I've yet to read a truthful advertisement put out by the railroad," he continued. "I get mad as hell every time I see one of those posters they tack up in drugstores and hotel lobbies, and some of the ads they run in the newspapers are a little bit comical to a man who knows the country."

"I've seen 'em," Billy said, "and I probably believed most of 'em." He walked to the spring and refilled the coffeepot. When he returned, he changed the subject: "That spring puts out some of the best water I've ever tasted," he said as he dumped a handful of coffee grounds into the pot and set it back on the fire.

Haskell nodded. "It's probably been bubbling just like it

does now for thousands of years," he said. He waved his hand around in a circular motion. "This used to be a favorite campground for several different tribes of Indians. I've heard that some of the old ones still talk about the tornado that wiped out a whole village right here at the spring. They say it hit just before daybreak one morning and scattered bodies, tepees, and buffalo robes for miles. Their claim is that it killed more than fifty people, most of them children."

Billy sat quietly for a few moments. "I can certainly understand how that could have happened," he said finally. "Especially with them camped right out in the open like this. Seems to me that it wouldn't take much more than a strong breeze to sail a tepee away like a kite."

Haskell shook his head. "I don't believe their tepees were all that easy to move," he said. "I think the women knew how to anchor them down mighty tight, and they did it when they intended to spend more than a night or two in the same place. Of course it wouldn't matter how well they were tied down if the storm was a strong one, and I don't know of any other place that's entirely safe when the weather decides to turn nasty.

"I remember seeing a log church one time that had been hit by a tornado, and I had trouble believing my eyes. I mean, the church was a sturdy building that had been put up by men who knew what they were doing, but that wind just tossed it around like a toy and blew it to hell and gone. I don't think they ever did find all of the logs, and some of the ones they did find were broken like matchsticks." He was quiet for a moment, then added as an afterthought, "Now, I'm talking about thick, heavy logs, Billy."

"I know," Free said, nodding. "I've never been caught in a tornado or even known anybody who has, but I've been told all my life about how destructive they can be." He poured fresh coffee for himself and attempted to refill Haskell's cup.

"No more," the rancher said, getting to his feet. He stepped to the spring and washed his cup, then returned it to his saddlebag. "I've got to be heading home, and that's a good five miles north of here." He glanced at the pink horizon. "Looks like it'll be dark long before I get there." His bay gelding, which had stood in the same tracks ever since its reins were dropped to the ground, nickered as it sensed that its master was about ready to head for home.

Haskell mounted and kneed the animal forward a few steps, then stopped beside the campfire and rolled a smoke. "You're welcome to camp here till you and your animals rest up," he said. "Nobody's going to complain." He touched the end of his cigarette with a burning match, then blew a cloud of smoke to the breeze. "I guess maybe you're looking for work, but I don't have anything to offer you. Spring roundup's already over for us, and we just laid off three men last week. You got a trade of some kind?"

Billy shook his head. "I don't suppose you could say that. Farming and logging are the only jobs I've ever had; I've never done anything that every other man couldn't do." He smiled and waved his arm in a sweeping motion toward the barren terrain. "I don't see any logs around here, though, and I haven't passed a farm in more'n a week. Anyway, I don't want to farm or cut logs anymore; what I'm hoping I can do is get a job on a cattle ranch."

"Well, during the early spring and fall that's pretty easy to do, and the work is certainly not very complicated. I'm not denying that a ranch hand puts in long hours, but most of his work doesn't require a whole lot of heavy thinking. A man who knows how to ride well can usually learn the rest of what he needs to know mighty quick when he has to. Of course, if he expects to become exceptionally good with a rope, that's a different matter. Every outstanding roper I know has been fooling around with a lariat almost as long as he's been alive, and I think all of the good ones keep right on practicing till they die."

Billy nodded. "I believe you're right about that. I remember one of my neighbors back home who was mighty good with a rope. He was more than fifty years old, but I think he practiced just about every day. I learned how to use a lariat well enough to get by from him, but I don't think anybody would ever call me an outstanding roper."

"You don't have to be all that good with a rope to hold a job on a ranch," Haskell said. "There's always somebody else around to take care of that chore." He dropped his cigarette butt in the fire, then turned his horse's head northward. "Like I said before, I've got to be getting on home." Pointing across the grassy plain to his left, he added, "If you just keep traveling west, you'll run into one ranch right after another.

"Some of the bigger outfits employ a dozen men or more, and I believe they keep at least half of them year-round. You should just stop and talk to people every chance you get. If you ask enough ranchers for work, I'll guarantee you that somebody's going to put you in the collar." He kneed his bay and spoke over his shoulder. "Good luck to you, Billy." He headed north at a canter, and moments later, disappeared over the rise.

Even as Free walked to the meadow to move his saddle horse and his mule to new grass, he was still thinking of Raymond Haskell. He had taken a liking to the man and was wishing that the Triple R Ranch had been in need of a hand. If that had been the case, Billy might well have gone on the ranch's payroll tomorrow, he was thinking. Haskell had seemed mighty down-to-earth for a college-educated man, and Billy regretted the fact that he would probably never see him again.

When Free returned to the spring, he took his pot off the fire and set it on a nearby rock to cool. Then, as darkness settled in, he sat eating his beans straight from the pot, washing them down with yet another cup of coffee. A few minutes later, he kicked dirt over his fire and stretched out on his bedroll.

He lay awake for a long time wondering where he would be living and what he would be doing at this same time next year. Then he began to think once again of the rancher he had met today. Though the man could have been anywhere between the ages of thirty and forty, he had been a picture of health. Muscularly built and at the same time as slim and trim as a black snake, there had been no fat whatsoever around his narrow waist, and his gunbelt had appeared to hang on his hip naturally.

Billy knew that his own waist and hips were just as narrow, and even as he lay on his bedroll listening to the chirping crickets, he decided to keep his eyes open for a place that sold leather goods. He wanted a gunbelt and holster like Raymond Haskell wore.

The sound of the insects finally made him drowsy, and he slept till long after daybreak.

7

★

He rode at a leisurely pace for the next week, sometimes traveling as little as fifteen miles a day. He had bought a gunbelt at a small trading post in the new settlement of Eastland, and was now trying to get used to the feel of the heavy Peacemaker on his hip.

All of his life he had been told that a man could get used to anything, and he wholeheartedly believed that. Many men wore sidearms for most and sometimes all of their waking hours, and he would be no exception. He would buckle the belt around his middle when he put on his pants every morning and leave it there all day. The time might even come when he would feel uncomfortable without it.

He had made a dry camp last night, and spent the morning hunting a place for his animals to drink. The few inches of water that he found two hours later consisted of nothing more than a pothole in a deep gully, and was well on its way to drying up. He sat his saddle feeling sorry for his animals as they sucked up the muddy liquid noisily.

Billy knew that he was in cattle country. Their droppings were everywhere, and although he had seen none up close, he had seen at least a hundred head at a distance. He had long since begun to wonder where they did their drinking, however, for he had not passed a spring or crossed a single stream during the past two days. Of course, there was obviously good water around somewhere, he was thinking; he had just not known where to look.

Free had wanted to come to Texas since he was a small boy, but now he suspected that maybe he was a little farther west than he really wanted to be. For the past several days he had been riding deeper and deeper into what appeared to be nothingness, and grass and water were getting harder to come by with every mile. According to his map, New Mexico Territory was no more than a few days farther to the west, and he had no desire to go there.

By the time his animals had drunk their fill of the dirty water, Billy had decided to change course. He would head south immediately. He continued to ride west for the moment, however, for he was in a deep gully that ran in the same direction and had steep banks at least ten feet high. When he climbed out on the south bank a few minutes later, he suddenly yanked his horse to a halt and froze in his saddle, for it appeared that a lynch mob was at work a short distance away.

The largest pecan tree Billy had ever seen stood no more than twenty yards from the gully. Seven men on horseback sat underneath the tree, and two ropes with running knots fashioned into hangman's nooses dangled from one of its highest limbs. In the center of the crowd, two men, a Mexican and a Negro, were seated on bareback horses. Each man's hands were tied behind him.

Though Billy had been making no effort to approach quietly and every one of the men was aware of his presence, all gave him a quick glance, then ignored him. A giant of a man, who appeared to be about fifty years old and whose weight Billy estimated to be in excess of three hundred pounds, was no doubt in charge of the proceedings, for he was the only one talking. "Get it over with!" he commanded gruffly. "Move them horses up!"

One man led the horses forward a few steps, while another dropped a noose over the head of each of the condemned men. "Either one of y'all got any last words?" the big man asked. "Either one of you gonna admit that you're guilty?"

Neither of the men spoke. Then, at a nod from the giant, someone flogged the rumps of the horses. Billy had often heard of men kicking out their lives at the end of a rope, but had just now learned that such was not always the case. Neither the Mexican nor the Negro had moved a muscle when the slack suddenly came out of the rope. Maybe the drop had broken their necks and quickly rendered them unconscious, he was thinking.

Billy sat in his saddle feeling a bit sick to his stomach. Though he had no idea what he had run into and was somewhat concerned about his own safety, he had already made up his mind to take a few people with him if somebody made a move against him. He transferred the mule's lead rope to his left hand and continued to sit quietly, his now empty right hand very near his holster.

Then, as if suddenly becoming aware of the fact that they had a witness, the big man, followed by the smaller man who had spooked the horses, walked alongside Billy's mount. "Just taking care of a little business here," the oversized hangman said, pointing toward the dangling corpses. "Them two bastards shouldna never been on my payroll, and they wouldna been if it had been left up to me. My foreman hired 'em while I was in Dallas on business."

He rolled and lit a cigarette, then blew out a cloud of smoke. "Somebody's been stealing my calves right and left, and I got it on good authority that the problem all along has been that damned Mexican hanging there. He's been on my payroll for more'n a year, stealing me blind at the same time.

Of course he denied it, refused to own up to it right up to the time that rope snapped tight."

He pointed to the tree again. "There's another lying son of a bitch hanging right up there beside him. I caught that nigger staring at my youngest daughter." He took another puff from his cigarette and blew smoke through the wide cracks between his teeth. "Yes, sir, I saw it with my own eyes. Now, there ain't no question a-tall about what was going on in his mind. No, sir, none a-tall."

Billy nodded, hoping to give the impression that he understood.

The big man turned to face the tree, shouting to his underlings. "Cut 'em down and put 'em in the ground!" he said. "It's all over!" He stood quietly for a few moments, then spoke to Billy again: "You'd be wise to forget everything you saw here."

Billy nodded.

The big man made a few steps toward the others, then suddenly stopped. He turned slowly, then walked back to Billy's stirrup. "By the way," he said, seeming to be serious, "I'm gonna be needing a coupla new hands. You looking for work?"

"No, no," Billy said instantly, "I'm not looking for a job. I'm just passing through on the way to my mother's house in El Paso."

The big man scratched his chin for a moment. "El Paso, huh? What's the lady's name?"

"Edith Wisdom," Free answered quickly.

"Wisdom." The big man repeated, then scratched his chin on the opposite side. "I used to know a fellow from down that way named Frank Wisdom. Would you by any chance be related to him?"

"I don't think so," Billy said. "At least I've never heard any of my family or relatives mention his name."

The big man stood quietly for a few moments, then nodded curtly. "Well, I guess you're anxious to be on your way," he said, pointing over his shoulder with his thumb. "Like I said before, you'll be better off to forget what you saw here."

Billy offered a nod of his own. He headed south and did not look back even when he heard the bodies hit the ground after the ropes were cut. Moments later, he kicked the big black to a ground-eating trot. He knew that he would be in plain view of the hangmen for at least half an hour, for with the exception of the big pecan, the area was treeless for several miles in every direction.

He wondered if the Mexican had actually been guilty of cattle rustling. From listening to the big man talk, Billy felt his evidence had been scant; the man had executed a man on nothing more than what somebody else had told him. And what if the Negro had looked at the man's daughter in a lustful manner? Was that a capital offense?

The big man had professed to know exactly what was going on in the Negro's mind. Was that possible? No. The simple truth was probably that the oversized, overbearing rancher had been running roughshod over less fortunate men for so long that it had become a way of life with him, till he was completely without conscience. And it had seemed to Free that the man was a little bit weak in the head. The fact that he had just executed two of his own employees right before Billy's eyes, then offered him a job, would have been comical had it not been for the seriousness of the matter. Free began to shake his head at the thought. He wanted no part of the man. He was headed south—a long way south.

Later in the morning, after the shock of what he had witnessed had worn off, Billy began to think about the tree that had been used for the executions. Knowing that all trees are seeded by others of their kind, he was wondering how the big pecan had come to be standing completely alone in the middle of nowhere. That the wind had blown one of the nuts to that particular location was highly unlikely, he was thinking, and pecans were simply too large and too heavy for birds to transport. A turkey, maybe? Or a deer? Either was possible, he supposed, but he thought it more likely that the tree had been brought from somewhere else and transplanted. He believed that it was close to a hundred years old, and who had been living here a hundred years ago? The Indians, of course, and they had certainly known all about transplanting trees.

Satisfied that he had solved the mystery, Billy nodded at his thoughts. There was no longer any doubt in his mind: the Indians had transplanted the tree. Because he knew that some of the tribes had depended to a great extent on nuts and berries for food, he sympathized with those who had been forced to look to the fruit of such trees as the big pecan for sustenance.

Wild pecan trees grew all over Texas, and on several occasions Billy had attempted to eat some of the nuts. He found that they were very small, with an exceptionally hard shell, and the meager amount of meat inside was extremely difficult to dig out. And their bitter aftertaste was more than he could abide. Indeed, the wild pecans were a far cry from the meaty, soft-shelled, sweet-tasting commercial variety, which men had been grafting and regrafting for generations.

Once out of sight of the hangmen, Billy slowed his animals to a walking gait and traveled steadily till midafternoon. The sun was still three hours high when he reached the Colorado River. He crossed at a shallow ford, then camped on the south bank. Since graze for his animals was nonexistent, he poured the last of the grain in their nose bags. He would look for a place to buy more oats tomorrow.

He would also have to buy some supplies for himself, for even as he went through his pack hunting something for supper, he could see that he was either out of or very low on everything that a traveling man needed. He would eat potato and onion soup tonight, for he had nothing else to cook.

Deadwood was plentiful, and he gathered an armload quickly. He kindled a fire with several handfuls of dead leaves, then added wood. While he waited for the sticks to burn down, he chopped up his potatoes and onions and dropped them into half a pot of water that he had scooped up from the river. When he finally decided that the fire was just right, he set the pot on the coals and added a few pinches of salt and pepper, then sat back to wait.

Sitting in the shade, with his back against a tall willow, he began to study his map again. Earlier in the day he had begun to wonder if maybe he had already come too far west. Raymond Haskell had advised him to ask every rancher he saw for work, but he had seen no ranchers. In fact, he had not seen a single human being since early this morning. Nor had he seen a cow. On most days during the past week he had at least seen a few head at a distance, but not today.

According to his map, the Colorado River ran for hundreds of miles across Texas, adding the waters of many smaller tributaries to its volume as it traveled along its meandering, southeastern course. With a series of crooked lines, the map plainly showed where one small river after another emptied into the big Colorado. Which meant water, Billy was thinking, a whole lot of water.

And where there was an abundance of water, green grass was almost always plentiful. He thumped the map, then refolded it and shoved it back into his pocket. Wherever he found good grass and water, he had decided, he would also find cattle, and hopefully a rancher who was willing to take a chance on a greenhorn. He would begin to travel in a southeasterly direction in the morning, always staying within close proximity to the river. He would follow the Colorado because he believed it would eventually lead him to some of the big ranches; his map showed no more rivers to the west, anyway.

He finished his supper an hour before sunset and was at the river washing his utensils when he began to hear the sounds of rattling chains and wagon wheels crunching the dry earth. Then the big Concord came into view. He continued to sit on his haunches scrubbing the blackened pot with sand as he watched the canvas-covered vehicle, drawn by a team of exceptionally large horses, ford the river and come to a halt only a few yards from his campfire. A sandy-haired man who appeared to be about thirty years old stepped down and chocked a rear wheel.

Only after helping his passengers, a woman about his own age and a young girl about seven or eight, to the ground did the man acknowledge Billy's presence at the water's edge. He removed his hat and wiped his brow with his shirtsleeve, then waved. "Howdy!" he called loudly.

Billy returned the greeting, then walked back up the slope. He pointed to what was left of his campfire. "I guess you'll be wanting a fire," he said, "and all this one needs is stoking up a little. I've already eaten my own supper, and I have no further use for it." He motioned toward the pile of fuel he had gathered earlier. "Plenty of wood there, too. Just help yourself."

"We'll certainly do that if you're sure you're not gonna be needing it." The man walked to meet Billy with his right hand extended. "My name is Westfield," he said as the two men shook hands. "Of course, I've got a given name, but not many people ever bother to use it. Everybody except my family just calls me Sandy." He motioned toward the woman and the child. "That's my wife, Cora, and the little one's our daughter Mindy." The lady was a pretty brunette who stood almost as tall as her husband, and the loose-fitting, high-necked dress she wore failed to offer even the slightest suggestion as to the contours of her body. Both she and her daughter nodded and smiled after being introduced.

Billy returned the man's firm grip and introduced himself, then added, "You folks can just camp right here at the fire if you want. I was already planning to move my bedroll to a different location, anyway."

Westfield nodded. "Well, if it ain't gonna be putting you out none, I reckon we'll do that, Billy. Of course we'd consider it a pleasure if you'd come back in a little while and have a cup of coffee with us."

"Just whistle when it's ready," Billy said, then set about

moving his saddle and the rest of his belongings to a level place farther downriver. He relocated everything he owned in less than five minutes, finally placing his bedroll between two willow bushes fifty yards from the campfire. Then, trying his best to think of absolutely nothing, he stretched out to rest for a while.

After what seemed like only a few seconds, he heard Westfield calling his name. Realizing instantly that he had dozed off, he opened his eyes to see that darkness had already settled in. He answered the man's call, then got to his feet and walked toward the light. Westfield had lighted a lantern, and the family sat in its glow eating their supper. The lady pointed to a wooden tray that lay on top of a smooth rock. "Eat that," she commanded.

In addition to the coffee that had been mentioned earlier, the tray contained a johnnycake and a steaming bowl of stew. From his standing position, Billy could see that the pot on the fire was still half full, so the people had plenty. Without a word, he seated himself on the ground, picked up the tray and the oversized spoon, and began to follow the lady's orders. The food was delicious, and he ate it all without speaking.

Afterward, he dashed his coffee grounds aside and returned the cup and the empty bowl to the tray. Then he spoke to the lady: "Thank you, ma'am, that was mighty good." He chuckled softly, then added, "Considerably better than the first supper I ate tonight."

"You're quite welcome," she said, "and I'm glad you liked it. There's plenty more in the pot, there."

He shook his head. "No more food for me this day," he said. "I appreciate the offer, but I've already had more than I needed."

Westfield rose and dumped his eating utensils, along with those that had been used by Billy, into a wooden box beside the wagon. Then he reseated himself on the ground, well outside the lantern's glow. "We've been heading south for more'n a week," he said, "and I guess we've got about three days to go. My wife's brother owns a trading post a few miles west of San Angelo, and he's invited us to throw in with him. We took him up on the offer right off, 'cause I don't see how it could be any worse than working for the railroad; never knowing whether you've still got a job from one week to the next."

When it became obvious that Billy had nothing to say on the matter, Westfield spoke again: "I don't normally ask a man a bunch of questions," he said, "but I've just been wondering where you came from, and where you're going."

"I came from back east," Billy said, "a long way back east. As for where I'm going, I don't have the slightest idea." He chuckled. "I'm gonna have to find some work before too much longer, or figure out some way to get along without eating." He pointed downriver. "I've decided to just follow the water and see what I run into."

Westfield nodded. "You'll find a job," he said. "Work is usually found where the water is, and I'd say that the Colorado waters as many farms and ranches as any other river in Texas."

"That's what I was counting on," Billy said, getting to his feet. He stretched his long arms above his head, fighting the urge to yawn. "I guess I'll be getting on back to my bedroll. Thanks again for the supper." He walked a few steps, then stopped and turned halfway around. "I'll be leaving at daybreak, but I'll do it as quietly as I can, so I won't wake you folks up."

Westfield laughed aloud. "You won't be waking us up, 'cause we'll already be awake." He continued to smile. "Besides, you're gonna be hurting our feelings if you ride off without having breakfast with us."

Free, knowing that he had nothing in his own pack to cook, thought on the invitation for only a moment. "Well, I certainly wouldn't deliberately hurt anybody's feelings," he said, "so I guess you can count on me being around. Thank you again, and good night." He headed for his bedroll and did not look back.

He saddled the black and buckled the packsaddle on the mule at dawn next morning. Shortly thereafter, Cora Westfield called him to the best breakfast he had eaten in weeks: scrambled eggs, smoked ham, and molasses to pour over his hot flapjacks. He ate as much as he could, thanked her profusely, then went to help her husband harness and hitch up the team.

Then, as the two men stood beside the wagon saying their good-byes, the lady appeared again, handing Billy something wrapped in a newspaper. "I fixed you a few flapjacks and some more of that ham to eat later on," she said. "Just put this in your saddlebag, it'll keep till you're ready for it."

Billy accepted the bundle, thanked Cora Westfield once again, then headed for his horse. A few minutes later, he pointed the black's nose southeastward. Just before he disappeared downriver, he turned in the saddle, intending to wave one final good-bye. The Westfields had already climbed aboard the wagon and headed south, however, and were paying all of their attention to the terrain before them. Billy waved in the wagon's direction anyway and kicked his saddle horse to a trot.

8

A few days later, Billy was sitting beside his morning campfire on the east bank of the North Concho River. Contrary to his usual habit, he had slept until an hour after sunrise, for he had been very tired when he went to bed. Now, while several slices of smoked ham were heating in his skillet, he poured himself a cup of coffee and began to take stock of his surroundings.

He had arrived at this particular location on the advice of a complete stranger, and he now believed that the man had pointed him in the right direction. The fact that he had finally arrived in ranching country was obvious. From where he was sitting, he could see at least a dozen longhorns grazing on the eastern slope. The river was not on his map, and Billy realized that he had found it purely out of blind luck.

Two days ago, while following the Colorado, he had met a man who advised him to turn back west, saying that he believed Billy's search for employment would be much more fruitful along the North Concho. "One ranch right after another in that country," the man had said. "Seems to me that the only thing you'd have to do is let people up and down that river know you're hunting work."

Dressed fit to kill, the man drove an expensive buggy drawn by a matched team of Morgans, so it stood to reason that he must know something. Billy had pointed his mount westward, and after two days of steady riding had arrived at the North Concho just before dark last evening.

After a breakfast of smoked ham and grape jelly, he was down at the river washing his utensils when he realized he had company. With the lush, green grass muffling the sound of his horse's footfalls, the rider was no more than twenty yards away when Billy noticed him. The man dismounted and tied his animal to a low-hanging tree limb.

Billy finished his chore. "That coffee's still hot," he said.

The man appeared to be about forty years old. And though he stood no more than five-nine, he probably weighed at least two hundred pounds. He had brown eyes, dark hair that was graying at the temples, and a weathered complexion that had obviously seen its share of strong wind and hot sun.

Without a word, he turned to his saddlebag and extracted a tin cup, then stepped forward and filled it from the coffeepot. Standing beside the fire and blowing into the hot coffee, he took several sips before he decided to speak. "I saw your smoke more'n an hour ago," he said finally, "but I had a cow I had to see about. I figured you'd be gone by the time I took care of her, but I see you ain't."

Billy slung the remaining water off the skillet and laid it on his pack. "On most any other day I would have been gone before sunup," he said, turning to face the man. "But I've just been traveling so much lately that there ain't a whole lot of go left in me." He smiled broadly and pointed toward the grassy meadow, adding, "Not much left in my animals, either."

The man nodded. "I can certainly understand that, 'cause I've been known to wear out a horse or two myself." He took another sip from his cup. "How long you been on the move?"

"More than a month," Billy answered as he went about putting his cooking and eating utensils back in his pack. "I've been in the saddle almost every day since I crossed the Mississippi River."

The man stood quietly for several seconds. "Long ride," he said finally, "and ain't nobody out here gonna hold the fact that you're an Easterner against you. Every white man in Texas with any age on him came from somewhere back east. You looking for work?"

"Are you offering me a job?"

"I guess you could say so," the man said. He pulled a sack of tobacco from his vest pocket, then began to blow on a book of cigarette papers to separate them. "Of course you'd have to meet my boss. He'd want to talk with you." He was quiet until he had finished rolling his cigarette, fired it, and taken a deep drag. Then, with a stream of smoke pouring from each nostril, he spoke again: "My name is Casey Springer," he said, "and I'm foreman of the Flying W Ranch. Noah Winter is the owner, and we're standing on his property at the moment." He offered a handshake.

Billy gripped the hand firmly. "My name is Billy Free," he said, "and that job you mentioned would certainly be a big help to me. I guess I should tell you right up front, though, that working on a ranch would be brand-new to me."

Springer blew another cloud of smoke. "I figured that out already, but you won't have any problem handling the job I'll be turning over to you. My line rider up on the north boundary quit two days ago. I think he was in love and had to get back home to his sweetheart." He ground out his cigarette butt with his boot heel, then chuckled softly as he asked the next question: "Are you in love, Billy Free?"

"Nope."

"Then I suppose you'd probably make a good line rider. There sure ain't nothing complicated about it. If you can ride a horse and tell one brand from another, you'll do just fine. One part of the job that takes a lot of getting used to is living up there in that shack by yourself for weeks at a time. It can get mighty lonesome in the summertime, and downright unbearable during the long nights of winter. Of course we usually try to relieve a man just before he starts talking to himself." He began to chuckle. "I reckon the biggest drawback is that you have to eat your own cooking."

"I've done that for most of my life."

The foreman nodded. "You think you want to sign on, then?"

"I know I do."

"All right," Springer said. He pointed to Free's grazing animals. "I'll wait for you while you pack up and saddle up, then we'll go to the house and have a talk with the boss."

Billy put his pack and his bedroll together in record time, then brought his animals from the meadow. A few minutes later, he mounted the black and took the slack out of the mule's lead rope, saying, "Lead the way, Mr. Springer. I'll be right behind you."

9

★

Riding in a northeasterly direction, neither man spoke for the next two hours. When Billy's curiosity finally got the best of him, he kneed the black alongside the foreman's mount. "How big is the Flying W, Mr. Springer?"

The answer came quickly: "The ranch covers a little more than fifty-one sections, and everybody living on it calls me Casey. That's what I want you to do."

"All right, Casey." Billy grew quiet and allowed his horse to fall slightly behind again as he weighed the foreman's answer. He knew that a section of land actually amounted to a square mile, and he was having a hard time imagining one man owning so much. Fifty-one square miles! Hell, it would take a fast-stepping horse all day just to walk across it.

"From the southeastern border to the northwest corner is a good two-day ride," Springer said, "and it's all what I think most folks would call expensive property. More'n thirty-two thousand acres of the best grazing land in Texas, with plenty of water in every direction. Makes no difference where a cow happens to be standing, she ain't never very far from a drink. So many creeks and springs on this ranch that nobody's ever bothered to count 'em, and the river runs along the entire western boundary." He chuckled, then added, "Don't guess the Colorado's been dry since the beginning of time."

Billy nodded. "How many cattle are on the ranch?" he asked.

"A little more than a thousand head, I reckon; a man never knows the exact number. In the past, we've run anywhere from a thousand to two thousand head, but two thousand's way too many. The ratio that I like to see is about twenty head of fully grown stuff to each section of land. I sent a herd to Kansas two months ago, so we're down to about the right number now."

A few minutes later, Springer brought his horse to a halt at the top of a rise. "There she is," he said, motioning across the slope toward the large cluster of buildings. "A big artesian well up there on the hill waters the whole layout."

Billy sat looking the place over as the foreman began to put a name to each of the tin-roofed buildings. Springer pointed first to a big log house with a wide hall running through its middle. "That's where the Winter family lives. The boss built it himself more'n twenty-five years ago, back when he was able to put in a day's work.

"That smaller building farther down the hill is the bunkhouse, and the one off to the left of it is the cook shack, where we all eat. The cook sleeps in it, too. Of course you can see the barn and the corrals, and that big shed behind the barn is the blacksmith shop. The rest of them sheds and buildings are just places where we store a lot of things that we'll probably never need." He exhaled loudly. "Are you ready to ride over and meet the old man?"

Billy nodded. "As ready as I'll ever be."

They rode past the barn and the bunkhouse to the spacious yard, where they dismounted and tied their animals at one of the three hitching rails. Moments later, they stood in the hall, where Springer began to knock on a hardwood door as he called his boss's name.

A deep voice invited them in, and Billy suddenly found himself standing before a white-haired man who had no doubt once stood several inches taller than Free himself, for even though he was now stoop-shouldered and leaning on a cane, his snowy head was nonetheless at least six feet above the floor. He was standing directly in the middle of the room, leading Billy to believe that maybe he had gotten up from his desk intending to answer Springer's knock personally, but had had difficulty walking to the door.

"I'm sorry to bother you, Mr. Winter," the foreman said, "but I know you always like to meet a man before he goes on the payroll. I reckon I've found somebody to take Joe Perry's place up on the north boundary." He pointed to Billy. "This young man goes by the name of Billy Free."

Billy stepped forward with his right hand extended, but the old man ignored it. "Ain't shook nobody's hand in forty years," he said, moving back to his desk falteringly. He seated himself, then continued. "Now, it ain't that I don't like you, understand, 'cause you look like a nice young fellow to me. But I just figured out a long time ago that all that handshaking stuff is a buncha shit." He shuffled some papers on his desk, and added, "No, sir, a handshake don't mean a damn thing." He reshuffled the same stack of papers back to their original position, then spoke to his foreman. "Like I said, Casey, the young fellow looks like a good one to me. Put him to work if you've got a mind to."

"Thank you, sir," Springer said, "I'll do that." He turned to Billy and jerked his head toward the hall.

Billy was just about to step through the doorway when he heard the old man call his name. He stopped in his tracks and turned to face the aging rancher. Winter sat quietly for a few moments, then pointed to the gun on Billy's hip. "Do you always wear that thing around your middle?" he asked.

"No, sir," Billy said, "only when I'm traveling. I've been in the saddle for more than a month."

Seeming satisfied with Billy's answer, Winter nodded. "Very well," he said.

As Billy followed the foreman across the yard, Springer continued to talk. "That packsaddle you've got is big enough to carry everything you'll be needing for at least a month, so you can just buckle it on one of the saddle horses you'll be taking up to the line shack. We'll load the pack from the storeroom later this afternoon, so you can get an early start in the morning. We'll just leave your mule and your horse in the corral, 'cause neither one of 'em would be worth a shit for the job you're gonna be doing.

"I'll pick out a coupla good cutting horses for you, then have one of the hands ride up there with you. He'll show you what you have to do, then ride the boundary with you till you get the lay of the land."

"Thank you, Casey. I'm sure I'll need all the help I can get."

10

Billy had been living in the shack for almost a month and had seen only one other person: another line rider who lived in a shack along the east boundary. The two men had just happened to arrive at the northeast corner at the same time one day about noon, and had talked for half an hour. The rider, a blond young man who introduced himself as Willy Bouton, and said that he had been working for the Flying W since shortly after the first of the year, was several inches shorter than Free, and appeared to be about the same age.

Although they discussed a variety of things, most of their talk was about mean bulls and crazy cows. Then, near the end of their conversation, Bouton changed the subject: "This line riding has got to be the loneliest job in the world," he said. "What I'm looking forward to is the Fourth of July."

Free, who had been standing on the ground beside his small bay cow pony, stepped into a stirrup and threw his leg over the saddle. "Something special gonna happen on the Fourth of July?"

"Oh, yeah!" Bouton said emphatically. "I guess nobody didn't mention it to you, but I've been told that they have a hell of a blowout down at the ranch house on the Fourth. The way I hear it, Mr. Winter even got drunk last year. The more whiskey he drank, the more he forgot that he couldn't get around like he used to. Kept falling down, then cussing everybody out when they came to help him up. Bob Kenard said the old fart talked for six hours without stopping, and you know what a loud voice he's got. I'm sure glad I didn't have to listen to it."

Billy chuckled again and gathered in the bay's reins. "Nobody mentioned the Fourth of July to me, Willy, so I guess I'll be spending the day riding line."

"Naw, I don't think so," Bouton said, turning his own animal's head south. "Somebody's gonna be riding up to talk to you. From what I hear, every hand on the ranch is liable to ride into San Angelo and tie one on." The two men parted, and it was almost dark when Billy reached his shack. He fed his animals, reheated and ate half a pot of beans, then read himself to sleep by the light of a coal-oil lamp.

Though the days of summer were long and hot, and Billy Free was a very busy young man, he believed that he was fortunate to be where he was. He knew that had it not been for a certain amount of good luck, he might well be in prison now for a crime he knew nothing about. Or he might even be in a Mississippi graveyard. If the Kipling brothers had had their way, it would have been the latter. Billy felt safer right now than at any time since he had left home. After all, who would ever think to look for him in a line shack on a West Texas ranch?

And the shack served his needs very well. Built of rough lumber, with a tin roof that pitched a little too low on the back side for Billy's tall frame, it had a table and two chairs, two bunks with mattresses and plenty of blankets, and a mid-size cookstove that would also serve as a heater in cold weather. And the stove even had an oven in which to bake the cornbread that he liked so well. After learning the hard way that he had to duck his head when he walked under the two-by-fours holding up the roof near the back wall, he had adjusted to living in the shack quickly, and was in fact comfortable enough there.

Thirty yards away there was a pole corral for the horses and a tin-covered shed they could get under when it rained. The small room connected to the shed held tack, feed for the animals, and a few tools, including an ax and a saw. Billy would not be needing the ax for a while, for a stack of dry firewood almost as tall as the cabin was only a few steps from the door.

About halfway between the shack and the shed there was a big spring that supplied drinking water for both man and beast. Billy had to carry several bucketfuls to the horses at least once a day, for the trough in the corral was small. A two-gallon bucket containing a gourd dipper supplied his own drinking and washing water. The bucket sat beside a washpan on a shelf that had been nailed to the outside wall, and Billy washed his face and his dishes in the same pan.

Except for the fact that he rode out in a different direction every other morning, his daily routine never varied. One day he would ride to the northwestern corner of the ranch, intent upon chasing Flying W cattle back on to their home range, then the next morning he would head for the northeastern corner. He rarely had to chase after errant cows, however, for on most days, even though he might ride a mile or so north of the boundary just in case, he saw none.

He now knew that the reason he saw very few cows was simply because they were all farther south, where the grazing was better. He believed that Casey Springer had given him this particular assignment knowing that he would have little to do.

"You won't have any problem handling the job I'll be

turning over to you," the foreman had said. "Sure won't," Billy said to himself each time he recalled Springer's words, "because there ain't no damn cows up here."

Despite the fact that he seldom saw any cattle, Billy earned his keep. His daily search for nonexistent strays always took at least nine hours, and feeding and caring for the horses took another hour. Then, by the time he cooked or reheated his own supper, the day would be gone. Someone had left a box full of books in the cabin, and he had right from the start begun to light the lamp every night and read for a while.

The meeting between the two line riders had taken place during the third week of June, and according to the calendar that hung on the wall behind the stove, on which Billy had been marking off each day with the stub of a pencil, today was the second day of July. He had already marked the date off the calendar, for the sun was rapidly dropping toward the western horizon. He was sitting in the doorway eating a bowl of red beans when Willy Bouton rode around the corner of the cabin leading a pack horse.

"You got an extra bunk for a drifter?" he asked as he jumped to the ground and offered a handshake.

"I just happen to have one," Billy said as he stepped into the yard and grasped the hand. "Got a few beans left in the pot, too."

"That's nice," Bouton said. "Where do I find a bowl?"

Billy pointed inside the shack. "In that little wooden box to the right of the stove. You probably ought to wash it or at least wipe it out good. No telling when it was used last. You'll find a big spoon in that same box."

When Bouton stepped back into the yard, he had a bowl of beans in one hand and a spoon that resembled a small shovel in the other. He squatted on his haunches and leaned against the wall. "I came by to spend the night with you and help you pack up in the morning," he said. "The boss wants us to bring all of the horses and come to the house tomorrow."

"Somebody been up to see you?"

"Casey sent word by Teeter Crum. Said for me to fetch you, then get on down to the ranch house. It's that Fourth of July blowout I told you about."

Although the young men talked till late in the night, both were on their feet at the crack of dawn. Billy built a fire in the stove while Bouton headed for the shed to feed and water the horses. A few minutes after sunup, they poured the last of Billy's molasses over hot flapjacks and washed them down with strong coffee. They headed south a short while later, with each man leading an extra animal. The burden carried by the horse that Billy led was slight, for the packs that were tied on its packsaddle were almost empty. Most of what he had brought north more than a month earlier had been food, and was long gone.

The Fourth of July blowout that Bouton had talked about never materialized on the Flying W Ranch. Three hours after breakfast, the cook prepared an early dinner of roast beef and fried chicken, then took the rest of the day off. Several of the hands had also taken the day off and departed the ranch early, saying they had relatives in the area they wanted to visit.

Casey had told Billy that the ranch had nine men on the payroll, and last night Free had met seven of them. He could tell by their mumbled greetings and the fact that they had all looked over his shoulder while offering a feeble handshake that none of them took him seriously.

Nor did any of the older hands make an effort to associate with Willy Bouton. Both he and Billy Free were obviously considered to be no more than young whippersnappers, mere line riders who were not to be invited into the main circle. At bedtime, the young men staked out two bunks in a far corner of the bunkhouse and directed all of their conversation toward each other.

Casey Springer did not seem to have the same problem as

some of his hands. At the breakfast table, he deliberately walked past several of them and took a seat between the young line riders. Speaking louder than was necessary, he said, "If you boys need anything, don't fail to let me know." Then, speaking even louder, obviously making sure every man in the cook shack heard his words, he added: "You've both been doing a damn good job, and I appreciate it." He laid a white envelope beside each man's plate. "Here's your wages up till yesterday, and I hope you both have a good Fourth of July." He upended his coffee cup, then got to his feet.

"You gonna be around for the rest of the day, boss?" one of the hands asked as Springer neared the doorway.

"Nope. I'm gonna ride into San Angelo some time after dinner and have a strong drink. Anybody who wants to come along is welcome." He smiled and motioned toward Bouton and Free, adding, "Especially my young line riders."

The two youngsters looked at each other with raised eyebrows, then nodded in unison. The question had been settled without a word spoken: they would ride to San Angelo with the boss.

As the foreman left the building, one of the older hands at the end of the table began to speak to another in low tones: "Why d'ya suppose Springer keeps butterin' them two young greenhorns up, Ted?"

The man named Ted chewed a mouthful of food thoughtfully for a while, then swallowed hard. "It's 'cause he knows that they've got feelings just like everybody else, Hank. He also knows that he's liable to need them boys real bad one of these days, and he's just looking ahead. Springer's always looking ahead. That's why he's the boss."

Hank thought on the matter for several seconds, then finally agreed. "I guess you're right," he said. "Either one of them kids looks to me like he could whup his weight in wildcats. That tall one's gonna be a hell of a man when he gets done fillin' out. Take a look at them wide wrists and forearms. Look at them shoulders."

"I've already looked him over," Ted said. "I don't think he needs to do no whole lot of filling out, I figure he's man enough right now."

A few minutes past noon, five riders left the bunkhouse yard headed for San Angelo, a three-hour ride to the southeast. Their specific destination was the Bar None Saloon, across the river from Fort Concho.

Springer, Crum, and Kenard led the pack and the younger men followed behind, each of them riding one of the same horses he had used for the line riding. "You ever been to the Bar None before, Willy?" Free asked after the trip was well under way.

"Sure ain't. I was in Miss Hattie's once, but I just bought one beer and left. I didn't figure I had enough money to talk to any of the girls; I've heard of fellows going in there and blowing a whole month's pay on the same old gal." He began to laugh. "Now, why in the world would a man want to do that? Seems like he'd at least spread his money around a little, so he'd get to know more'n one woman."

Springer fell back beside them at that point and began to talk business. "I want you fellows to exchange places when you go back to work tomorrow. Willy, you turn your cabin over to Billy. Stay with him for two days and teach him the lay of the east boundary, then ride on up and take over the job he's been doing." He smiled broadly, then spoke to Billy directly. "I know there hasn't been much for you to do up on the north boundary, but it'll be a lot different on the east side."

Bouton laughed. "By god that's the truth. Seems like every cow over there decides at least twice a day that she'd rather be living in Louisiana."

"That's all right with me," Billy said. "I'd rather be working than hunting something to do. Hard work makes the time pass faster."

"Well, you'll be at least as busy as you want to be," Bouton said. "Early in the morning is the worst time, 'cause most of the prowling takes place at night. Sam Runyon's spread is to the east of us, and the cows all seem to think his grass tastes better. They know damn well they're not supposed to be over there, Billy, 'cause just as soon as they see you coming, they start hightailing it right back on to Flying W property."

"It's hard to tell just how much any animal really knows," Billy said, "but I've heard people say that a cow is not even capable of thinking."

Bouton took off his hat and wiped his forehead with his sleeve. "I don't know so much about that," he said, shaking his head. "They always seem to remember exactly where the best grass and water is, and they don't have any trouble at all figuring out which side of a hill is gonna be the warmest on a cold, windy day."

Billy rode along quietly for a few moments, then chuckled. "I believe I'll let you win that argument, Willy."

None of the five Flying W men wore a sidearm, though Bob Kenard did carry a rifle on his saddle. Free had left his own rifle leaning in a corner at the bunkhouse, and his gunbelt in a box beside his bunk. He would have no use for either today, for he was only going into town to have a few beers. Might even talk to a woman.

Established at the junction of the north and middle branches of the Concho River in 1867, across the river from Fort Concho, San Angelo quickly became a ranching center for both cattle and sheep. Now, ten years later, it was one of the liveliest towns in Texas. People often jostled each other elbow to elbow along the sidewalks of Concho Street, and wagon traffic had on occasion become so clogged that many of the horses had to be unhitched while, one vehicle at a time, the jam was untangled.

The Bar None Saloon was located on Concho Street. When the Flying W men tied their horses at the hitching rail and entered the building, Billy brought up the rear. Just before he stepped through the doorway, he took one last look up and down the street. He had never seen so many people crowded together. Though the story inside the saloon was the same, Billy saw one vacant table, and Casey Springer was already headed there.

The foreman motioned each of his men to a chair, then headed for the bar. He returned a short while later with a pitcher of beer in one hand and a bottle of whiskey in the other. "Gotta go back for some glasses," he said.

Moments later, he placed a glass in front of each man. "Drink up," he said, "it's all on me." He poured himself a drink of whiskey, then set the bottle in the middle of the table without replacing the cork. "If any of you fellows decide that you want something a little stronger'n beer, have at it," he said, pointing to the bottle.

Bob Kenard was the only man who accepted the offer. "I believe I'll take you up on that, Casey," he said as he poured himself a hefty portion of the red liquid.

They sat at the table for the next two hours, and the only times anybody got up from his seat was to buy more beer or go to the outhouse out back. All of them were content to sip and talk among themselves. Sometimes just watching other people was a show. Several young women moved about the room from time to time, making sure they were seen, but they left the drinkers strictly alone. If a man wanted female company, he himself must make the first move.

The number of patrons inside the saloon was nothing close to constant. At one time there might be as many as twenty men at the bar shouting for service, then twenty minutes later, less than half a dozen. At the moment, there were probably about fifteen men in the building.

Each time the beer pitcher on the Flying W table was emptied, it became a different man's duty to carry it back to the bar and buy a refill. When Billy's turn came, he picked it up and headed for the bar without a word.

The men who were left at the table continued to talk among themselves till their conversation was interrupted a few moments later by a loud, slapping sound. Then, looking toward the bar, they saw Billy Free's body fly across a table, then land on the floor halfway beneath another. The man who had no doubt done the punching now stood in the aisle beside the bar with both of his hands balled into fists.

"Don't go bumpin' into me, you son of a bitch!" he shouted loudly as Free hit the floor.

Billy regained his feet slowly, then stood in his tracks for a few moments as if trying to get his bearing. He took a few measured steps forward, his eyes on the man. Still standing in the aisle, the man began to crook his finger at Free. "Come on," he said with a smirk. "Come on, you son of a bitch."

Billy came on. He moved so quickly that his opponent appeared to go into shock. Free hit him with a flurry of punches so fast that the onlookers had difficulty following them. Then when the man tried to fall, Billy held him up by the throat with one hand. "What did you call me?" he asked loudly. "Son of a what?"

But the man was already unconscious.

Billy dropped him to the floor, then kicked him in the head.

The Flying W men were there now. Forming a half circle around Billy, they stood looking down at the unconscious man, a dark-complected six-footer who appeared to be about thirty years old.

"I didn't bump into him, Casey," Billy said, sounding almost apologetic. "He slid off his stool without looking behind him and bumped into me." Pointing farther down the aisle, where one of the bartenders stood holding an empty pitcher while the other was busy with a mop, he added, "Knocked that pitcher of beer right out of my hand."

Billy had hardly finished speaking when a man who very much resembled the one on the floor spun him around by the shoulder and shoved a gun in his face, the barrel only inches from his nose. "Kick my brother while he's down, will you?" he said loudly. "By god, I'd have shot you right off if you'd been wearing a gun on your hip." He backhanded Billy across the mouth. "I'll shoot you anyway if you raise a hand toward me." He slapped Free again, harder this time, then stepped backward. He made a sweeping motion with his gun barrel, then spoke to the Flying W men as a group: "All of you get away from here so I can see about my brother."

Casey Springer leaned closer to Free's ear. "Let's get out of here, Billy."

Moments later, the five men pointed their horses toward the Flying W. Billy had been the last one to mount, for he had stood beside his horse for several moments wiping blood from his split lip with his bandanna, eyeing the front door of the saloon as if he wanted to renew the hassle. Even after they were under way he continued to look back over his shoulder occasionally.

"This is about the hardest thing I've ever done, Casey," he said. "I mean, letting that bastard slap me around like that."

"I know," Springer said, "but you played it smart. Trying to fight that gun with your bare hands would have gotten you killed. He would have gotten away with it, claiming self-defense. They're the Poe brothers, Frank and Foster, and the county sheriff is their brother-in-law. Frank is the youngest; he's the one who pulled the gun and did the slapping.

"Their oldest sister is the former Ophelia Poe, and she's been married to Sheriff Bill Fink for the past fifteen years or so. I reckon Fink must be afraid of her, 'cause he never does arrest her brothers no matter what they do. Hell, Frank got away with cold-blooded murder right here in town last winter."

Billy rode quietly and thoughtfully for several minutes, his eyes focused between his horse's ears. Then, speaking to no one in particular, he said, "He might have gotten away with killing somebody, but he ain't got away with slapping me yet."

II

Billy had been on the east boundary for a month now, and thanks to Willy Bouton, who had ridden line with him for the first three days, knew the area well enough to handle his assignment with ease. The line cabin was exactly like the one Free had lived in up north, except that it had a small porch. The porch was where he usually spent the last few minutes of daylight each day, sitting in the cabin's only chair as he watched the day slowly turn into night.

The small structure was located on Snake Creek, which turned and twisted much like its namesake. So much so that if a man headed directly south from the cabin, he would cross the creek four times while traveling only a few hundred yards. The clear-running stream doubled back on itself repeatedly, and at times appeared to wander aimlessly as it meandered along in its never-ending search for the path of least resistance. And though its course alternated between the Flying W and the Slash R ranches at least a dozen times, it was dependable year-round, and the only source of good drinking water in the immediate area.

True to the forewarnings he had received, line riding on the east side of the ranch turned out to be a twelve-hour-a-day job, and Billy usually ate his lunch in the saddle. He was pleased with the constant activity, however. Idleness gave him too much time to think about home, and the reason he happened to be in Texas to begin with. He was well aware of the fact that he had so far drawn a lousy hand in the game of life, but he also knew that a man must play whatever cards he was dealt. And there would probably always be people like the Kipling brothers and the Poe brothers around.

He felt no remorse whatsoever about shooting the Kiplings, and since his run-in with Frank Poe, he had undertaken a new line of defense: for more than three weeks now, he had been practicing the fast draw. Unloading his gun as soon as he became fully awake every morning, he would stand beside his bunk for the large part of an hour, whipping the big Peacemaker from its tied-down holster and bringing it up to an imaginary target. Then he would practice for another hour just before going to bed at night. Sometimes he even made a few fast draws during the daytime if and when a lull in his cow-chasing chores occurred. The blisters that had appeared on his gun hand the first day had burst on the second, and eventually turned into calluses.

He could see a big improvement in his speed from one week to another, and had decided right away that he was considerably faster early in the morning, right after a good night's rest. That fact might very well be worth remembering some time in the future, he told himself.

He had met Whistler Willingham, who worked for Sam Runyon's Slash R Ranch, during his first week on the east boundary. Twenty-five years old, dark-haired and of medium height and weight, the man said that he had been given the nickname because he usually whistled while he worked. He was quick to inform Billy that he had been riding Runyon's west boundary for more than a year.

Although he was an experienced ranch hand, and could have handled a wide assortment of other assignments, line riding was the job that he himself had requested, Willingham said. He preferred being alone to sleeping in a crowded bunkhouse, and appreciated knowing that he could prepare his food exactly the way he liked it, any time he wanted it. And, he added, unlike conditions in most bunkhouses, he could keep his living quarters clean. His cabin was located on Snake Creek, half a mile south of the one occupied by Free. The two men had visited each other after work a few times and talked till late in the night.

Billy could usually tell when he was about to be visited by Willingham, for he could hear the man whistling long before he arrived. Such was not the case today, however, for Whistler had ridden up the hill quietly and brought his horse to a halt in the front yard. He now sat his saddle soundlessly, watching the activity before him.

Completely oblivious to the rest of the world, Free was standing on the west side of the cabin practicing with the Peacemaker. Having just made fifty fast draws with an empty gun, he now loaded five shells into the cylinder of the weapon, then set up a six-inch block of wood. He walked backward for at least forty feet, then stood for a moment with his eyes glued to the target. When he snatched the Peacemaker from its holster and fired from the hip, the block flipped end over end several times; then as soon as it settled to the ground, a second shot sent it flying off again. "By god, that's mighty good shooting!" Whistler said from his position in the yard. He kneed his animal forward, adding, "It's just about as good as a fellow's likely to see around these parts."

Billy turned quickly, surprised that someone had been able to ride up on him completely unnoticed. "Hello, Whistler," he said, "you almost scared me. I didn't hear you coming like I usually do." He nodded toward the wooden block, adding,

"I've been able to hit what I shoot at for most of my life. I'm just trying to learn to do it quicker."

Willingham dismounted. "What you've been doing there ain't exactly slow," he said. He tied his mount to the hitching rail, then pointed to the wooden block. "Put it back up there," he said, "let me see if I can hit it."

Free obliged, then returned to the cabin and stood beside Willingham, who moved his Colt up and down a few times to make sure it was riding loose in its holster, then spread his legs and bent his body slightly forward.

Billy did not actually see Whistler's draw. What he did see was a sudden blur of movement beside him, a belch of flame from the barrel of a six-gun, and the wooden block go flying through the air.

Free was dumbfounded. He stood quietly for a long time, staring at the stump on which the target had been resting. He was silently trying to understand how any human being could move so quickly. Not only had Willingham drawn with lightning speed, but his shot had been right on target. The block of wood had neither flipped end over end nor veered to either side. It had moved straight backward for several feet, indicating that it had been drilled dead center. Finally Billy turned to face the shooter. "Beats any damn thing I ever saw, Whistler," he said.

Willingham ejected the spent shell from the cylinder of his Colt, then replaced it with a live one from his cartridge belt. "I don't try that more'n a few times a year nowadays," he said, "but I used to work at it several hours a day. The year I was sixteen I spent all summer quick drawing and dry firing. I didn't have any money to buy shells back then."

Billy stood shaking his head as he realized how far he himself still had to go. "How in the hell did you ever get so fast, Whistler? I mean, how do you move so fast and still concentrate on your target?"

"Concentrate?" Willingham chuckled. "Hell, that's it right there. The fact is, you don't concentrate. Concentrating takes up too much time, a whole lot more time than you're likely to have if you ever get in a tight spot where you really need that gun.

"It's something that's awful hard to explain, Billy. I suppose different men do it different ways, but I really don't believe that I actually look at my target. Maybe I do glance at it, but I think that mostly I just try to sense its location. If your mind knows exactly where the target is, your hand will put the slug there. You just have to keep on practicing till your mind and your hand start working together."

Billy nodded. "Makes sense, Whistler, and I think you explained it so it's easy enough to understand." He pointed toward the shack. "You had supper? You want some coffee?"

Willingham shook his head. "No coffee," he said, "and I've already had my supper."

They seated themselves on the edge of the porch and continued to talk. The subject of their conversation changed several times during the next half hour, but Billy wanted to know more about the quick draw. "Do you think I'll ever get as fast as you, Whistler?" he finally asked.

Willingham nodded. "Of course you will. You're already off to a good start, because you can hit what you shoot at. Being able to put 'em where you want 'em is by far the most important part of the whole shebang. I once knew a fellow who could draw a gun quicker'n a cat could blink, but he couldn't hit the broad side of a damn barn.

"He later moved off to El Paso, and I've often wondered what became of him. I'd be willing to bet that if he ever got into a gunfight, he's dead now." He sat quietly for a few moments biting his lower lip, then added, "You need a different type of holster, Billy. I've got an extra quick-draw rig down at my cabin that I'll give to you."

"Well, I'll certainly practice with it," Billy said quickly, "but you don't have to give it to me. I've got the money to pay you whatever it's worth."

Willingham shook his head. "I'll bring it by before sunup

in the morning, and I don't want any money. I'm gonna give it to you because you need something more practical for what you're trying to do. That holster you've got is all right, but whoever made it didn't expect to ever have to get a gun out of it in a hurry." Without another word, he untied his horse, mounted, and rode south.

Willingham returned before sunup next morning, arriving just as Billy was leading his horse from the corral. "I think you'll like this a little better," Whistler said, handing over the gunbelt and holster without dismounting. Then he reached into his saddlebag and handed Billy a small blue can. "I finally remembered you saying a few days ago that all your lard had gone rancid, so I brought you a little of mine. This stuff is in good shape, because the supply wagon was up to my cabin just three days ago." Then, not waiting for Billy's reaction to the gifts, Willingham whirled his mount and rode east toward Slash R property.

Billy stood watching till Whistler disappeared. Then he set the small can of lard on the porch and began to inspect the gunbelt. Deciding that it was practically new, he looked in the direction Willingham had ridden, then shook his head. The man had given him something that he could have easily sold for good money, and Billy would not forget it.

A short time later, he was standing behind the cabin with his new gunbelt buckled around his middle and the holster tied to his right leg with rawhide. Right from the very first draw, he knew that his speed had increased tremendously. He emptied the holster several times, then nodded in satisfaction. Whistler had given him something nice, all right.

Whistler had given him something that would take up every minute of his free time for the rest of the year.

On the night of December thirtieth, Billy lay on his cot in the bunkhouse reading by the light of a coal-oil lamp. He had joined the regular cowhands almost three months ago and had been readily accepted by them all. During the first week of October, Springer had sent a man to the line shack to replace him, saying that Free should report to the ranch house for regular duty. Billy had come down to the bunkhouse that same afternoon, and stowed his things in a wooden box at the head of the cot that had been pointed out to him by Bob Kenard.

Now, noticing that it had already grown dark outside, he laid the book aside and raised himself up to a sitting position. Seated on the cot, with both feet on the floor, he sat thinking. He was happy with his job on the Flying W, and even happier with the fact that, only yesterday, Casey Springer had told him that he had learned fast and progressed nicely; that his work was satisfactory on every count.

Billy was also happy that 1877 was about to come to an

end, for it had been the worst year of his life. Just one more
day. Tomorrow was New Year's Eve, and earlier today the
ranch hands had drawn cards from a poker deck to see who
would go to town and who would have to remain on the
ranch. Those who drew the highest-ranking cards would be
off for the day. The others must work as usual.

Billy had assured himself a seat on a San Angelo bar stool
when he pulled the ace of diamonds from the deck. Willy Bouton, Teeter Crum, and Bob Kenard had also drawn high cards,
and all of them would no doubt be celebrating along Concho
Street. Casey Springer, being the boss, was of course excused
from the drawing. When asked if he was going to town, he
simply smiled, then left the bunkhouse. However, every man
present believed that the foreman would indeed welcome in
the new year from San Angelo.

During Billy's last week on the east boundary, Whistler
Willingham had watched him practice with the Colt for close
to an hour, then proclaimed him fast—very fast. "You're as
fast right now as you're ever gonna need to be," Whistler
had said. "Fact is, I don't see how you or anybody else could
ever hope to get much faster." He watched Billy draw the
weapon twice more, then added, "Yep, you've got it all figured out, Billy. That's all there is to emptying a holster, just
make sure you don't shoot too quick if you ever have to face
another gun."

"Now, I don't mean to say that you can wait around forever, because even if a man's a whole lot slower on the pull
than you are, it ain't gonna take him all day to line up on you.
So even as you make your own draw you've got to keep track
of what he's doing. Then the instant you're sure of your target you've got to fire, because you certainly don't want to give
him a free shot at you."

Billy voiced his gratitude to Willingham for the free advice, and thanked him once again for the gift of the gunbelt.
"This holster's made all the difference in the world, Whistler,
and I certainly appreciate it." That had been the last time he

saw Willingham, for two days later Free had been ordered to leave the line shack and move into the bunkhouse. He had grown to like Whistler very much, and regretted the fact that he had not had a chance to say good-bye to him.

Every night during the three months he had been living in the bunkhouse, Billy had spent at least an hour practicing the fast draw. Shortly after dark every evening, he would ease out behind the barn or maybe in one of the stables, anyplace where he would be out of sight of the others, and pull his weapon fifty times or more. ·

Back in early October, Willingham had expressed the belief that nobody was likely to get faster than Free was at that time. With perseverance and consistent practice, Billy had proved to himself that Whistler had been mistaken, for he knew that he was much faster right now than he had been three months ago.

Bob Kenard was originally from the Houston area and had been on the Flying W for almost five years. A dark-haired six-footer who was about thirty years old, he had more or less taken Billy Free under his wing immediately. He had shown Billy to a cot beside his own the very first time Free walked into the bunkhouse. Later, as Billy began to learn his way around the place he noticed that Kenard was always somewhere close by, ready and willing to show him what needed doing and the easiest way to do it.

Kenard was a likable man who was usually laughing about one thing or another and seemed to know a thousand jokes. Tonight he walked around the bunkhouse for a while, then stopped beside Free's cot.

"Mind if I sit down?" he asked, observing Western protocol, which dictated that no man ever took a seat on another man's bed without first asking permission.

Billy moved his gunbelt off the bed and put it in a box on the floor. "Help yourself, Bob," he said. He pointed to the book he had been reading earlier. "I read two chapters in that thing, but I don't like it much. Too mushy."

Kenard seated himself. "I never was much of a reader," he said. "I suppose that's one of the reasons I ain't very smart." He pointed to the gunbelt in the box, then changed the subject. "I know you never did know it, but I've seen you practicing with that gun." He sat shaking his head for a moment, then added, "It's sort of like watching a show, Billy. I mean, it ain't nothing but a blur."

Billy pulled off one of his boots and shoved it under his cot. "You've been spying on me, huh?"

"Nope. I just happened to be in the stable next to the one you chose to practice in. I didn't want to interfere, so I just leaned against the wall and kept quiet." He dropped the subject and sat quietly for a few moments, then got to his feet. "I reckon it's time for me to turn in," he said. He pulled down the covers on his own cot, then began to undress. "Good night, Billy."

Free dropped his other boot to the floor. "Get yourself a good night's sleep, Bob. You've got to help the rest of the Flying W hands try to drink the town dry tomorrow."

Kenard grunted, then blew out the lamp. Both men went to sleep quickly.

At midmorning next day, Free, Kenard, Crum, and Bouton were standing at the corral saddling their horses when Springer walked from the barn. "Don't you fellows drink it all before I get there," he said, pointing toward town with his thumb. "I won't be more'n a couple hours behind you."

Billy laughed. "We'll save you some," he said, tightening the cinch. He was saddling his own horse this morning, for, with the exception of a short run once in a while, the black had been loafing in the corral for most of the year.

"Billy's a beer drinker, Casey," Teeter Crum said as he mounted one of the dozens of cutting horses owned by the Flying W. "He won't be drinking up any of that stuff you like." He kneed his animal forward a few steps, then sat waiting on the others. "I'm ready when y'all are," he said.

A blond, muscular twenty-five-year-old from North Carolina, Crum had been on the ranch for about three years. And though he stood several inches shorter than the average man, he had balked when some of the ranch hands began to call him "Shorty." He very quickly expressed his dislike for the nickname and refused to answer to it. After being scolded a few times, none of the hands had ever again used the derogatory handle when referring to Crum, for he was a man who was liked and respected by all who knew him.

At one in the afternoon, the four men rode down Concho Street and stopped at the Sombrero Restaurant, which, according to Whistler Willingham, served the best Mexican food in Texas.

"Order the stuffed peppers with red chili sauce," Whistler had said. "If you like Mexican food, that's the best thing you're gonna find on this side of the border."

"I don't know whether I like it or not, Whistler," Billy had said. "I don't think I've ever actually eaten a real Mexican meal."

All three of the men ordered the stuffed peppers with red chili sauce. The young waiter had promised the food in half an hour, but the wait was much longer.

"Sorry it took so long," he said when he finally set the platters on the table. "I think the cooks must be trying to burn green wood."

Half an hour later, they tied their horses and entered the Bar None Saloon. Billy stopped just inside the door and spoke to the others: "If you fellows'll stake out a table somewhere, I'll get a pitcher of beer from the bar. I don't know about the rest of you, but I need to put out the fire in my throat. That red chili sauce feels like it hasn't gone all the way down yet."

His friends agreed and headed for the center of the room, selecting a table that was, for no apparent reason, slightly sequestered from the others. Billy was there soon after, and poured four glasses full of beer before taking his seat. He had just taken his first sip when he noticed that the saloon had suddenly grown quiet. Sensing the presence of someone off to his left, he turned his head in that direction.

With a silly-looking smirk on his face, Frank Poe stood leaning against a nearby post, a six-gun hanging on his right leg. He pointed to Billy with the forefinger of his left hand. "You just don't give a damn whose private table you take a seat at, do you, boy?"

When Free did not answer, Poe raised his voice to a shout and continued to point. "Can't you see that that table's sitting off by itself there, right where me and my brother want it? Don't you know that nobody sits there unless they've been invited by one of us?"

Billy ignored the man and took another sip from his glass.

"Hey, boy!" Poe shouted, even louder now. "You hear what I'm saying? Are you gonna get your ass up and move to a different table?"

"I'm gonna get up," Billy said, then slowly got to his feet and turned to face his antagonist, "but I'm not gonna move to a different table." Knowing exactly what was about to happen, Free spread his legs, leaned his body slightly forward, and locked his eyes onto those of Frank Poe. Then he stood frozen, waiting.

The wait was not a long one. Frank Poe slapped his leg very quickly, but took a shot in the face from Billy's Peacemaker before he could bring his own Colt into firing position. He grunted loudly, dropped his gun, and died.

A shot rang out from the opposite side of the bar, and Billy Free fell. A gaping chest wound turned his blue shirt crimson.

Foster Poe was around the corner of the bar quickly, pointing and yelling. "I shot that man in self-defense, and everybody in this room knows it! He picked a fight with my brother Frank and shot him, then he was gonna come after me.

"Yessir, I was gonna be next. He planned the whole thing, and he'd done told half a dozen people exactly how he was gonna do it." He paused to look around the room in search of a friendly face. "Hell, I reckon you all remember him beating me up last summer for no reason a-tall. Done it right here in this saloon."

He walked to his brother's body and checked it for a pulse. Then, pushing up one of the eyelids, he spoke to the corpse: "I got him for you, brother," he said. "I got him, and he's done for." Then he pointed to Billy's crumpled form, which lay partly underneath a table. "That son of a bitch right there won't never shoot nobody else," he said. Then he walked toward the front of the building.

Bob Kenard had checked Billy's pulse and knew that, although unconscious, he was still alive. Kenard was afraid to make his discovery known, however, for he feared that Foster Poe would finish the job. When Poe finally left the building, satisfied that he had killed Billy Free, Kenard knelt and stuffed the end of Billy's bandanna in the wound, hoping to stop the bleeding.

Sheriff Bill Fink was close enough to hear the shots, but Dr. Ross Blanding was closer. A tall, stoop-shouldered man, the doctor examined Frank Poe, then Free.

"This man's alive!" he shouted quickly. When he asked for three men to carry Billy up the street to his office, the Flying W hands volunteered.

"Handle him easy so he don't start bleeding again," the doctor said as Crum, Kenard, and Bouton carried Billy toward the front door.

Sheriff Bill Fink met them just as they stepped out onto the street. "Who's that you got there, and where you going with him?" he asked, moving in front of them to block their way. "I have to investigate these shootings, you know."

Dr. Blanding spoke quickly: "What we've got here is an injured man, and where we're going is to my office, where all of my equipment is. Get the hell out of our way, Bill Fink, or I'll have the circuit judge and maybe the governor on your ass for interfering with my attempt to save a human life." When the lawman seemed to take too long to think it over, the doctor said: "Git!"

The sheriff walked past them and into the saloon. The three men carried Free on up the street to the doctor's office, which turned out to be an unpainted two-room affair at the end of the block.

"Put him on that cot in the back room," the doctor said, holding the front door open.

The doctor's assistant opened the second door and pointed to the cot. Once Billy was on the bed, Kenard bent close to his ear and began to call his name. He got no reaction. The young, blond-haired assistant, who no doubt possessed at least a little medical knowledge himself, already had a scissors in his hand cutting apart what had once been Billy's favorite shirt.

Dr. Blanding spoke to the Flying W hands as a group: "As soon as Benny gets that shirt off, I want you fellows to turn the patient over on his stomach, then get out of here." He pointed toward the front room. "Plenty of soft seats in there if you want to wait around." Moments later, the three men turned their friend over as gently as possible, then left the room.

Though the doctor's building was narrow, it was lengthy, with the front steps very near the sidewalk and the back room reaching all the way to the alley. A wooden bench that had long since lost most of its cotton padding faced the office window, offering a wide view of the traffic on Concho Street. The Flying W hands seated themselves there to await the doctor's prognosis.

They had been sitting on the bench for about twenty minutes when Sheriff Fink opened the front door and stepped into the office. With a ruddy complexion and brown hair turning white around the temples, he was a skinny man. He stared at the men distastefully for a moment, then pointed toward the door separating the two rooms.

"Blanding in there?" he asked gruffly.

When the men nodded quietly, the lawman stepped into the back room and closed the door. A loud conversation immediately erupted on the opposite side of the door, but the men on the bench, though they were listening very closely, could make out none of the words. However, Bob Kenard soon made the announcement that, whatever the argument was about, he believed the doctor was winning. His voice was by far the loudest.

A few minutes later, the sheriff walked back into the office noisily, leaving the door to the sickroom standing open behind him. He stood looking through the window for a moment, then turned to face the Flying W hands. Pointing to the closed door, he spoke loudly: "That man back there's gonna be a whole lot better off dying where he's at, 'cause it beats the hell out of hanging.

"Frank Poe's dead, and I'm charging Billy Free with first-degree murder. I'm on my way right now to get the warrant."

Bob Kenard was on his feet. "Sheriff, Frank Poe picked that fight, and all Billy did was defend himself." He motioned to Bouton and Crum. "All three of us were sitting there, and we'll swear to it. And there's something else: Foster Poe lined up on Billy and bushwhacked him from halfway across the room. You gonna do anything about that?"

"Bushwhacked?" Fink asked, a silly grin appearing on one side of his mouth. "Bushwhacked, you say? Now, that ain't exactly the way I heard it. The way I heard it was that Billy Free rode into town for the sole purpose of killing the Poe brothers. He made his brag to several people that he was gonna kill Frank for slapping him last summer, then he was gonna shoot Foster, too. No wonder Foster put some lead in him. Hell, he done it to save his own life."

Kenard shook his head several times. "No, no," he said emphatically, "that ain't the way it happened at all. Billy Free didn't even know either one of 'em was on the premises. Even after he shot Frank in self-defense, he still didn't know that Foster was in the building."

Fink chuckled softly. "Well, you three can swear to that shit if you want to, but I've got at least a dozen witnesses who'll testify that Free walked into the Bar None Saloon today with killing on his mind."

After another hour, the doctor and his assistant walked into the office. "He's gonna be out for another day or two," Blanding said, "but he's gonna live." He tossed a small piece of lead into the air and caught it, then shoved it into his pocket. "We dug out the bullet."

Kenard spoke for the trio: "We appreciate everything you've done, Doctor, and don't you worry none about your fee. It'll be taken care of."

Blanding chuckled. "Well, that certainly would be something different," he said. "Right now, I want all of you fellows to get on out of here. You can visit the patient some time later on, 'cause he's gonna be here for a while. Sheriff Fink's gonna be wanting to transfer him across the street to the jail, but he ain't taking him nowhere till I say so. And that ain't gonna be no time soon."

"Thank you again, Doctor," Kenard said, "and we won't be forgetting it." With Crum and Bouton close on his heels, he opened the door and stepped out onto the street.

13

Billy Free had been in Dr. Blanding's sickroom for five days, and at least one of the Flying W hands had visited him every day. He was conscious and talking now, but so far the doctor had not even allowed him the luxury of sitting up in bed. Today was Casey Springer's turn to visit, and he had just spent an hour with the patient. When his visit was over, Casey closed the sickroom door and stepped into Blanding's office. "He seems to be doing all right, Doctor. Do you know how long it's gonna be before he can get around?"

Blanding did not answer right away. He stood staring at the wall for several seconds, seeming to be contemplating some kind of difficult decision. "Be a while yet," he said finally. He pointed to the sickroom. "Of course, I can't keep him back there forever. The sheriff's got that murder warrant, and he's already wanting to move him over to the jail.

"I guess I can stall Fink for a few more days, but then I'm gonna have to turn that man over to him." He was thoughtful for a few moments, then added, "I'm surprised that some of Billy Free's friends ain't done come through that back door late at night and took him outta here. Door ain't never locked." He gave Springer a quick glance out of the corner of his eye, then continued, "I reckon if some of them fellows did take it on themselves to move him, they could just pull a spring wagon up to that door about two o'clock in the morning and do it. Hell, they could have him and be gone within a minute or two.

"Now, if somebody actually did decide to steal the patient, I reckon they'd steal that little tin box of salve and that stack of bandages, too. The dressing on that wound oughtta be changed every day. And I suppose they'd be sure to take that laudanum there on the table, so they could give him a little of it every few hours to ease his pain." He seated himself behind his desk. "Yessir," he said, spinning his chair around to look out the window. "I'm surprised as hell that some of his friends ain't already done that."

Springer stood quietly for a few moments, then spoke over his shoulder as he turned back toward the sickroom. "Pardon me, Doctor, but I need to discuss one more thing with the patient. I won't be but a minute."

14

★

Three nights later, at two o'clock in the morning, a light wagon entered the alley behind Concho Street. Drawn by a team of black horses, the vehicle moved through the darkness slowly. The wagon box contained bedrolls and blankets, along with cooking utensils and a month's supply of groceries. The two men on the seat were both armed to the teeth. The team came to a halt at the back door of Dr. Blanding's office, and Bob Kenard jumped to the ground. Teeter Crum remained on the wagon seat, the reins in one hand and a six-gun in the other.

When Kenard turned the knob and gave a slight push, the door opened soundlessly. He stepped inside and closed the door, then moved away from it quickly. He stood against the wall for a few moments waiting for his eyes to adjust to the dark room.

"You awake, Billy?" he whispered after a while. When he got no answer, he tried again, a little louder this time. "Billy, this is Bob. Are you there?"

"I'm here," Billy answered softly. "I saw you come in, but I had to make sure it wasn't Foster Poe coming to finish me off. I'm straight across the room from you, just walk in the direction you're facing till I touch you."

Kenard moved quickly, for he could now see well enough to discern Billy's outline. When they touched hands, Free said, "I'm already dressed except for the fact that I don't have a shirt." He laid the bandages, the salve, and the laudanum in Kenard's hands, then added, "I've been told to take these things along. Now, if you'll just let me lean on you, we can get out of here."

Two minutes later, Billy lay stretched out in the wagon box under a blanket. Kenard climbed to the wagon seat and picked up his rifle. "Let's get out of Bill Fink's county, Teeter."

Crum picked his way out of town at a walking gait, then whipped the team to a fast trot. They were back on Flying W property shortly after sunup, and stopped at a spring long enough to make coffee and heat up some of the stew Kenard had brought from the cook shack. Crum let the tailgate down and Billy, wearing a shirt that the men had brought, took a seat in the back of the wagon, his long legs touching the ground. He had insisted on feeding himself and apparently needed no help.

He had been wearing his gunbelt when he left the sickroom, and his Colt was now resting in its holster. Crum had handed the weapon to Billy the instant he got in the wagon, for he suspected that they might very well have to fight their way out of town. Now Billy emptied his bowl, then sat sipping coffee. "Where in the hell are we headed, Teeter?" he asked.

"Up on the North Concho," Crum answered, "just a few miles across the county line. Casey's the one told us about it, then me and Bob rode up and looked it over. It's the perfect place for you to hide till you heal up, Billy. I mean, you just ain't gonna have no damn company unless you want it. The old cabin ain't much, but I believe the roof'll still turn water. The weather's been a whole lot warmer than usual so far this winter, but even if it does turn cold it ain't gonna hurt you none." He pointed to the wagon box. "Two buffalo robes and a stack of blankets there, and you've got that fleece-lined coat."

They stayed on Flying W range till they crossed the county line. Then Crum spent the next two hours picking his way through a thick infestation of mesquite trees, for with the area being completely uninhabited by humans, roads were nonexistent. The rough terrain and meager amount of yearly precipitation made the land unsuitable for farming, but at least one man had insisted on learning that fact the hard way.

Seth Conner had built a cabin there a generation ago, and had toughed it out for four years. During each of those years, with the help of his wife and his two young sons, he had put a crop in the ground in early spring, then watched it wilt and die as he prayed for the rain that seldom came. Then during his last year, when it seemed that his prayers had finally been answered and he got enough rain to raise a decent crop, the Indians had picked him clean, even stealing one of his mules. Conner had thrown up his hands and headed for San Antonio shortly thereafter, and had never been heard from since.

It was to the old Conner cabin that Crum and Kenard had brought Billy Free. Crum brought the wagon to a halt on the hill above it, then pointed down the slope. "I'll guarantee you that Bill Fink don't even know this place exists," he said. Billy pulled himself up to a sitting position and followed Crum's point with his eyes. The two-room cabin, the upper portion of which now leaned about two feet south of its foundation, stood fifty yards away, partially hidden by tall weeds and a stunted willow. The small house had been built with rough scrap lumber, some of it with the bark still on. It had a roof made of cypress shingles, however, and as Crum had predicted earlier, probably would not leak.

A few moments later, Crum brought the team to a halt at the front door. He jumped to the ground, then spoke to Free: "Just sit here in the wagon till we get all this stuff inside." He

pointed to a bulging pillowcase. "Everything you had in that
box beside your cot is in there, including the ammunition for
your Colt and your Winchester." Then, with Billy's rifle in
one hand and the pillowcase in the other, he disappeared inside the cabin.

When Kenard lowered the tailgate, Billy got to his feet
and stood holding onto the wagon box. Dr. Blanding had
warned him against overdoing it, but had been quick to sug-
gest that he stand on his feet and even walk a little as soon as
he could bear the pain. And there was much less pain right
now than there had been one day ago. Free believed that he
could actually feel the healing that was taking place in his
chest, and he had no intention of lying around any longer
than was absolutely necessary. Inactivity made a man weak,
and weakness was an affliction that he could ill afford.

An hour later, Crum headed back to the ranch in the
wagon, leaving Bob Kenard behind. Teeter would return two
days from now with both of Billy's animals, and a saddle
horse for Kenard. It had been decided right from the start that
Bob would remain in the cabin till the wound healed, and
Billy could get around well enough to take care of himself.
Even now, Kenard had a fire going in the fireplace, waiting for
a bed of coals on which to make coffee and cook a pot of
beans.

Billy motioned toward the fireplace. "Do you think there's
any chance of somebody seeing smoke coming out of the
chimney?"

Kenard shook his head. "No. This wood I gathered up is
mighty dry, so there ain't gonna be no whole lot of smoke.
Wouldn't make much difference down here in this hole, anyway. It'll scatter to the four winds long before it reaches
ground level. I'd be willing to bet that it can't be seen from
three hundred yards away."

A short while later, they were sipping coffee while a pot of
beans simmered on the fire. Free was sitting on a rolled-up
buffalo robe with his back against the wall, and Kenard sat

cross-legged in front of the fireplace. Neither man had spoken for several minutes. Then Kenard refilled his cup, and, choosing a new subject, opened another conversation: "I've been wondering about something for a long time, Billy. I mean, I fully expected you to outdraw Frank Poe, 'cause I'd already watched you practice in that stable. But back last summer, I was truly amazed at how quick you whipped Foster Poe's ass. Where'd you learn to fight like that?"

Free stared at the wall for a while, taking his time about answering. "It might be that I just came by it naturally," he said finally. "People always told me that my daddy was a good scrapper, so maybe that had an effect on me. I really couldn't say for sure. Anyway, I got plenty of practice growing up. You see, my daddy was killed in the War, and my momma had some mental problems.

"Then the year I turned thirteen, some of my schoolmates started making fun of me, laughing about me not having a daddy, and saying that my momma was crazy. I fought with all of them, Bob. The first year I fought with every boy who said it, and the second year I clobbered anyone who looked like he even thought it. They all eventually quit making fun of me, but by that time I already had the reputation of being a scrapper. I had to fight a lot after that, 'cause there was always somebody coming around wanting to try me."

Kenard nodded. "I understand what you're saying," he said, "and I guess it's been that way since the beginning of time. When a man gets a reputation for being good at something it becomes an open invitation to challengers." He pointed to the big Colt, which was lying on the floor within easy reach of Billy's right hand. "Don't you suppose it's gonna be the same with that?"

"I don't have any way of knowing the answer to that question," Free said, "but I certainly won't do anything to encourage it." He handed Kenard his empty cup and waited for a refill, then added, "That's not to say that I intend to let Foster Poe get away with drilling this hole in my chest."

Kenard nodded. "I already had that much figured out, but you be careful when you take that joker on, Billy. He's done ambushed you once, and he'll do it again if he gets a chance."

"I know that, Bob." Billy had unrolled the buffalo robe and stretched out, his head resting on a folded blanket. "What I haven't quite been able to figure out is how he managed to sneak up on me the first time. I mean, I usually pay more than a little bit of attention to what's going on around me, but I sure didn't see him."

"Didn't none of the rest of us see him either. If we had, we'd have shouted a warning to you." He inhaled the last of his coffee, then dashed the grounds into the fireplace. "Looking back on it, I reckon I first noticed him at the exact same instant he fired on you. He was holding his Colt with both hands and aiming down the barrel with one eye closed, just like somebody shooting target practice."

Free had his boots off now. He spread one of his blankets over his feet, then lay down again. "Just like somebody shooting target practice!" he repeated loudly. Then he closed his eyes wearily.

Moving around as quietly as possible, Kenard filled one of the cooking pots with water from the spring, which was located about fifty feet from the door. He spent the next hour gathering deadwood and stacking it against the building. Then, one armload after another, he carried dead leaves, grass, bark, and twigs inside the cabin and piled it all in a corner. Some years it actually rained in this area during the wintertime, and he wanted to make sure Billy had plenty of dry kindling.

Just as darkness closed in, Kenard eased into the cabin and lighted a lantern. Seeing that Free was awake, he made no effort to be quiet as he pulled the pot off the fire. "I reckon these beans are done," he said. "Do you need some laudanum to deaden the pain first, or are you ready to eat now?"

Billy chuckled. "I never did believe in a man taking any

kind of medicine unless he absolutely has to," he said. "I think the beans'll do me a whole lot more good in the long run than the laudanum will. Anyway, it's already getting so I don't feel much pain unless I try to move."

Kenard was busy dishing up beans. "Hell, that's the answer to the problem, then," he said. "Just quit moving."

Free accepted one of the steaming bowls and set it on the floor to cool. "The doctor warned me about that," he said. "Doc says that I ought to start moving around just as soon as I can, even if it hurts. He says that if a man lies in bed long enough, he'll get so damn weak that he can't even get up to take a shit in the morning. I believe every word of that, Bob."

"Me, too."

After each of the men had eaten two helpings of beans, Kenard put the empty bowls in a pan of water to soak. Then, noticing that Free was asleep again, he spread his own bedroll and blew out the lantern. He pulled a blanket up under his chin, and the sound of Billy's light snoring soon put him to sleep.

15

★

Instead of two days, which had been the original plan, it was four days later that Teeter Crum showed up. Free and Kenard had just eaten half a pot of rabbit stew and were standing beside the spring when Crum rode down the slope leading two saddled horses. Billy's mule, with its packsaddle in place, trotted along behind one of the saddlers.

Billy pointed up the slope. "Hey," he said loudly, "I believe that's my saddle on that damned filly. I wonder why he didn't bring my black."

Kenard began to laugh. "He didn't bring your black because he got a chance to bring you something a whole lot better." He too was pointing up the slope now. "Hell, Billy, that's Miss Muffet!"

Miss Muffet! Billy repeated to himself. The name meant nothing to him. He stood quietly as Crum rode to the spring and dismounted. "Sorry I didn't get back when I expected to," Teeter said, "but Springer was a little bit leery about me rushing off. Sheriff Fink's already been out to the ranch asking questions, and we thought some of his bunch might still be around somewhere watching.

"Casey thought it might be best if most of the ranch hands didn't know where you are, so we didn't tell them. I left the ranch before daybreak and kept a careful watch on my back trail all day." He pointed over the hill. "Ain't nobody coming back there."

Billy nodded and took a seat on a stump beside the spring. He sat watching as Kenard and Crum put the saddles and the packsaddle inside the cabin, then picketed the animals farther down the slope. He got a good luck at Miss Muffet as she was led down the hill, and was hardly impressed. Aside from the facts that she was taller and her legs were a little longer and slimmer than the average filly, she appeared to be quite ordinary.

There was one thing about her, however, that did strike him favorably: she was the exact same color as a mouse. Seeing her at a distance would be extremely difficult, even while using a spotting glass during daylight hours. At night it would be impossible. She would also be hard to see on a rainy day, for she was almost the same color as the rain.

Billy was still sitting on the stump when Kenard and Crum returned to the spring. Crum took a drink of water, then rehung the community cup on the willow limb. He fished around in his pocket for a moment, then laid fifty dollars in Billy's hand. "Casey said that you had nearly a month's pay coming, and he threw in a twenty-five-dollar bonus; said he had no doubt that you were gonna be needing it."

Billy pocketed the money. He sat quietly for a while, then spoke to Crum: "Did Casey say anything about my horse? Did he say why he sent that filly up here wearing my saddle?"

Crum and Kenard looked at each other blankly for a moment, then both men chuckled softly. "He sent Miss Muffet to you because he wants you to stay alive, Billy," Kenard said. "He don't want somebody running you down and putting a rope around your neck."

Billy pointed down the hill. "So Casey thinks that filly'll outrun 'em all, huh?"

Crum decided to answer the question himself: "He knows damn well she'll outrun 'em all. He knows that there ain't a horse in three counties, male or female, that'll catch Miss Muffet." He seated himself on the ground and leaned his back against the big rock. "Actually, I don't suppose you could really call Miss Muffet a filly," he continued. "At least not in the usual sense of the word.

"You see, she's already five years old, and she never has come into heat a single time. Old Coot Samuels says she never will come around; that some of her organs are either missing or not working right, and that she ain't never gonna have a colt. Coot knows more about horses than other any man I can think of, and so far he's been right.

"The only reason you ain't seen her or at least heard somebody talk about her is 'cause she ain't been around since you showed up. Mr. Winter's brother-in-law's been keeping her over at his place for nearly a year, but he sold out a few days ago and brought her back home.

"I reckon she ain't really even supposed to be in the world. I mean, the fact that she was ever even born was an accident. Nobody planned it, 'cause her mammy was just an old plowhorse that was sometimes used to pull a wagon to town. One day one of the hands parked the wagon in the alley behind Concho Street and, just like he'd always done, took the mare out of the traces and tied her to a hitching post. A man who was supposed to have seen it said that somebody's thoroughbred stallion got loose and nailed her right on the spot. It must have happened that way, 'cause she foaled exactly eleven months later.

"Harvey Soledad was the one who named the foal Miss Muffet. He was an educated man who read everything he could find. That corner of the bunkhouse where he slept looked like a library, and he kept a book in his hand at least three hours a night. One time when he was feeling like talking, he told me the history of that name. He said that way back in the sixteenth century, there really was a little girl named Miss Muffet.

"He said that her daddy, Dr. Thomas Muffet, had dedicated his entire professional life to the study of spiders, and wrote the nursery rhyme 'Little Miss Muffet' for his daughter, whose given name was Patience." Crum chuckled, then added, "I asked Harvey what the hell a tuffet was. You know, that thing Miss Muffet was supposed to be sitting on. He said that there was no such word; that the doctor just made it up so he'd have something that rhymed with Muffet."

Billy smiled. "Do you believe all that?" he asked.

Crum wrinkled his brow. "I don't have no reason not to. I reckon Harvey Soledad read about half of the books ever written, and he told me that was fact, not fiction." He got to his feet and headed for the cabin, adding over his shoulder, "I wouldn't talk Miss Muffet down too much if I were you, Billy. The less you say, the fewer words you're gonna have to eat after she takes you on the fastest ride of your life."

"All right," Billy said, getting to his feet, "I guess you've got me convinced. When you get back to the ranch, tell Casey that I appreciate him sending her up."

While Crum and Kenard were busy reheating the stew and carrying on a conversation between themselves, Billy took a pan and a change of clothing and headed for the spring. He washed himself as best he could, then removed the dressing from his chest for an inspection. He decided immediately that he would not replace the bandage, for the wound had scabbed over well enough to provide its own protection.

Moving slowly and very carefully, so as to aggravate the wound as little as possible, he slipped into a clean shirt and a new pair of jeans. Then, after washing his feet in the spring's runoff, he put on a new pair of wool socks that he had been carrying in his pack for the better part of a year. A few minutes later, he hung his mirror on a nail at the side of the cabin and shaved his face.

"I almost didn't recognize you without that beard," Crum said when Billy walked back into the cabin. "You figuring on going dancing?"

"Yep," Free answered, pouring himself a cup of coffee. "One of these days I'll probably be doing exactly that." He seated himself on his bedroll and leaned against the wall. "These long winter nights are gonna seem even longer after you fellows leave, Teeter. It sure would have been nice if you'd thought to bring me some books to read."

Crum pointed to Billy's saddlebags. "Always look before you speak, young man. There's three books in each one of them bags."

Moments later, Billy sat with his saddlebags in his lap. He looked each of the books over, then stacked them beside his bedroll. "Please forgive me, Mr. Crum," he said jokingly. "I now declare you a man who thinks of everything."

Half an hour later, Crum sat his saddle in front of the cabin door. "It'll be dark by the time I get back to the bunkhouse," he said, "and that's just the way I want it. Bill Fink might have somebody watching the ranch, you know. The way all of the buildings are situated down in that hole, it would be mighty easy to do. Casey sent several riders to circle the place a few times, but none of them saw anybody.

"Speaking of Casey, he says that the idea of you ever working for the Flying W again, or anywhere else in Tom Green County, is completely out of the question. He sent his regards and said to tell you to hunt some new country." He bent over and offered a parting handshake. "I reckon that would be my own advice too, Billy. Just get on out of this area and start over somewhere else." He pumped Free's hand one last time. "I probably won't ever see you again, but it's been nice knowing you." He released the hand and pointed down the hill, adding, "You take good care of Miss Muffet, now. You do that, and she'll take care of you." He kicked his horse in the ribs and rode over the hill at a trot.

16

★

Five days later, Bob Kenard mounted his own horse and spoke many of the same words used by Crum. "I've told you exactly how to locate Foster Poe," Kenard said as the two men shook hands, "but don't go rushing into it. Knowing that you're still running loose, he's gonna be acting a whole lot more cautious than usual, 'cause he's already seen the way you can handle a gun. The longer you wait around, the braver he'll get. Just take your own sweet time, and don't go into town looking for him under any circumstances." He released Free's hand, then slapped the horse's neck with the reins. "Goodbye, Billy," he said. Then he was gone.

Free stood in the yard long after Kenard had disappeared, wondering if he would ever see the man again. Probably not, he decided, then headed down the hill to bring his animals to water. When both had drunk their fill at the spring, he hitched them to a post in front of the cabin and tied on their nose bags.

He was well aware of the fact that the meager amount of nutrition in the dead grass they were eating was woefully inadequate, and knew that he would eventually have to figure out a way to come by more grain. Even though he fed each of them only a small portion once a day, the hundred-pound sack of oats that Crum had brought from the ranch was already half gone.

He curried the animals while they ate, then backed off to get a better look at Miss Muffet. He walked around her repeatedly, hoping to spot whatever it was that supposedly made her so special. Even after several minutes of close inspection, the long, slim legs and the small, round hooves were the only things he saw that even suggested that the filly might be a speedster.

Teeter Crum had said that she could run all day, but if she had big, strong lungs, where in the hell were they? Her chest was not broad. In fact, it appeared to be a little narrower than most. Billy shook his head. Nope, she did not have oversized lungs. He patted her on the rump and smiled, finding a little humor in what he was thinking: maybe she could run all day because she just didn't use as much air as ordinary horses.

He began to practice with his six-gun again that same afternoon. Though the quick movement of his arm and shoulder caused him some pain, it was nothing close to unbearable, and after only an hour, he believed that he was emptying his holster as quickly as ever. Afterward, when he opened his shirt and inspected his wound, he saw that the scab had already fallen off, leaving a bright, red welt in its place.

The wound was healing rapidly, he decided, and now he must get his body back into condition. He believed that the small amount of pain he had felt today had been mostly the result of his allowing his body to go to sleep. Starting tomorrow, he would exercise for long periods each day, then practice the quick draw for two hours every night. He chuckled to himself as he looked toward the picket line that he had moved to the north side of the cabin, where the grass was somewhat better. About two days from now he would be ready to try out the great Miss Muffet, he was thinking.

He felt so good when he awoke next morning that he decided not to wait two days. Today he would put the renowned filly to the test. As he did every morning of late, he stood beside his bedroll for several minutes doing bends and exercises, then kindled a flame in the fireplace. By the time the sun came up he was washing down a breakfast of johnnycake and warmed-over beans with strong coffee. When he was finished, he dropped his cup, spoon, and empty bowl into a pan of water, then got to his feet.

He carried his saddle into the yard, then came back for his Winchester. He leaned the rifle against the outside wall of the cabin, then threw Miss Muffet's bridle over his shoulder and headed up the hill to the picket line. She accepted the bit eagerly, then, no doubt anticipating a good workout, snorted loudly as she was led down the slope.

Before Billy had even finished mounting, he knew that Miss Muffet was a different type of animal from those he was used to riding. Unlike all of the other saddle horses he had known, who always began to fidget around the instant a rider put his weight into the stirrup, the filly stood deathly still. Even after he threw his leg over the saddle, she failed to move a muscle. When he laid the rein against her neck and touched her belly with his heels, however, she moved instantly, heading down the slope at a fast trot.

After about two hundred yards the slope leveled off into a meadow that was more than a mile wide. Once there, Billy put his heels to the filly again, and the response was immediate. Free had always believed that he had ridden some fast horses back in Mississippi, and in fact thought that his own black gelding was pretty fast. Miss Muffet very quickly proved him wrong on both counts.

After only a few leaps the filly was going all-out, and Billy, who had lost his hat to the wind, smiled and leaned over her neck. He pulled up at the far side of the meadow and sat shaking his head as he stroked and petted the animal. Though the speed and smoothness of the ride he had just taken had left him in a state of disbelief, he had also noticed something else: Miss Muffet had carried his one hundred seventy pounds at a full gallop for at least a mile and a quarter and was still breathing normally.

Never before had he seen a horse make such a hard run without panting, and a few of them had even sounded like they might not live out the day. No doubt about it, the filly not only had an unbelievable amount of top, she also had plenty of bottom. He patted her neck again, then headed back up the meadow to retrieve his hat. Riding along at an easy canter, he suddenly thought of Bob Kenard and Teeter Crum. They had known exactly what they were talking about when it came to Miss Muffet. So had Casey Springer.

Billy rode to the cabin and unsaddled the filly, then watered her at the spring. A few minutes later, he tied on the nose bag and curried her shaggy winter coat while she ate. According to Crum, Casey Springer had said that Billy might very well be needing a speedy mount at any moment of any given day. Free nodded at his thoughts as he dragged the currycomb across Miss Muffet's rump one last time. Springer had damn sure supplied the correct remedy for the speedy-mount problem, he was thinking.

17

★

During the third week of February, Billy decided that it was time for him to move. His wound had healed completely, and he felt as good as he could ever remember. His animals were also in good shape, for they had been eating grain both morning and night. Twice during the past few weeks Free had ridden twenty miles northeast and bought grain from a farmer, telling the man that he was a new homesteader who had come west too late in the year to put in a crop of his own. On each occasion he had left the farmer's crib with two large gunny-sacks full of shelled corn on his mule.

He had given Miss Muffet a good run every day, and she had surprised him with regularity. By now he was convinced that she was nothing close to ordinary horseflesh; that she surely had something in her blood that other horses did not have. The mere fact that her sire had been a thoroughbred fell far short of being an acceptable explanation for her excessive speed, for Billy had ridden a few thoroughbreds in Mississippi, and none of them had even come close to the filly.

And those thoroughbreds had been brought into the world by the careful breeding of handpicked, full-blooded racing stock, while Miss Muffet had been nothing more than the accidental offspring of a lowly wagon mare. Billy was hoping to someday run across someone who was an expert on horseflesh. Then he might get an understandable answer to the riddle.

At two o'clock in the afternoon, he mounted the filly and tugged on the mule's lead rope. He rode to the top of the rise, then headed southeast, toward the Flying W Ranch. He was deliberately leaving at this time of day because he wanted to arrive at the bunkhouse well after dark. He would tell Springer that he was leaving his mule in the corral for a while and would pick the animal up at a later date. As of today, he was on a mission, and it was possible that sometime very soon he might have to move much faster than the mule could run.

All afternoon he rode at a walking gait, staying among the trees as much as possible. And each time he came to a hill he rode around it rather than over it, for skylining himself, even for a moment, was out of the question. Though he intended to take nothing for granted, he seriously doubted that Bill Fink or any of his underlings would be prowling around on Flying W property.

Foster Poe, however, was another matter. He was the man who had started it all by picking a fight in the saloon last summer. He was also the man who had ambushed Billy and put a bullet in his chest. Therefore, if he was a man of even average intelligence, he would surely know that Free was not likely to take it all lying down. With all of this in mind, Billy had long ago decided to expect the unexpected from Foster Poe. There was simply no telling what the man might do.

By nightfall, he was in an area that he knew well, about two miles northwest of the ranch house. He dismounted beneath the canopy of a large oak and tied his animals to a nearby bush, for he needed to kill at least two hours. If he waited till all of the Flying W hands had gone to bed, he could ease inside the bunkhouse and have a muted conversation with Casey Springer, whose cot was just inside the door. Now, with his back against the oak and his Winchester lying across his lap, he sat down to wait for his friends in the bunkhouse to get sleepy.

Three hours later, he crept into the bunkhouse and knelt beside Springer's cot, careful to stay out of arm's reach. The foreman was awake instantly after Free whispered his name. "That you, Billy?" he asked softly.

"It's me, Casey. I need to talk with you outside." He left the building quickly and returned to the corral. Springer joined him there a short while later. "Are you getting too brave for your own good?" the foreman asked, "or do you know something the rest of us don't?"

Billy shook his head. "I don't know anything new, Casey. But my chest has healed up real good now, and I think it's time for me to get this thing with Foster Poe over with once and for all. I've come to believe that if I don't find him, he'll find me. And he'll do it when I least expect it."

Springer moved into the long shadow created by the barn, then stood leaning against a corral post. "You're probably right, Billy," he said. "Do you know how to find Poe without calling attention to yourself?"

"I think so. What I plan to do is—"

"Don't tell me what you're gonna do," Springer interrupted. "If I don't know anything about it, I won't have to lie to anybody."

"Makes sense," Billy said quickly. "I'll hush about Foster Poe." He stood quietly for a while, then began again: "I had three reasons for coming by tonight: I wanted to leave my mule in the corral, because I think he'd just hold me up; I wanted to thank you for sending Miss Muffet to me, 'cause she's about the fastest thing on four legs; and I wanted to ask you for a sack of food for my saddlebags. I thought maybe you could get me something from the storeroom that I won't need a fire to fix, 'cause I can't afford to take a chance on the smoke."

Without a word, Springer reached for Billy's saddlebags and headed for the storeroom. "Put the mule in the corral," he said over his shoulder, "and hang your packsaddle on that sawhorse in the corncrib. There's a lantern hanging just inside the door if you need it."

Billy did as he had been told, then stood in front of the barn waiting. He could see that Springer had lighted a lantern in the storeroom and was obviously selecting what he put in the saddlebags with care. Free then glanced at the bunkhouse, which was plainly visible in the starlight. No light shone through its windows, proof enough that if any of the hands knew he was on the premises, they had decided to mind their own business.

When Springer returned to the corral he laid the bulging saddlebags across Billy's forearm. "Enough stuff here to last you a couple weeks," he said. "I put in some mesquite-smoked ham, several tins of fish, two blocks of cheese, jelly, crackers, and about ten pounds of jerky. Can you think of anything else?"

"No, no," Billy said as he placed the bags in front of his saddle. "I've got plenty to eat now and a good, warm bedroll; about all a fellow really needs to get through the world." He stepped into the stirrup and threw his leg over the saddle, beginning to pat the filly's neck. "And I especially want to thank you for sending Miss Muffet to me." He sat his saddle quietly for a few moments as if trying to think of something else to say. Finally he raised his arm to wave good-bye. "So long, Casey," he said, then touched the filly with his heels and disappeared into the night.

He rode in a southeasterly direction toward River Road, so named because it ran northeast out of San Angelo, parallel to the Concho River. This particular trip was the direct result of a long conversation with Bob Kenard. "If you stake out River Road and keep a good eye on it," Kenard had said, "sooner or later you're gonna spot your man.

"While you were lying up in Dr. Blanding's office, I talked with at least a dozen men who know Foster Poe well. It seems to be common knowledge that he's almighty friendly with a widow named Willadean Ball, and that he spends at least one night a week in her home. She lives in a big white house on the south side of the road, about ten miles northeast of San Angelo.

"Now, the widow Ball is a good twenty years older than Poe, so most of the men I talked with are convinced that he's only after her money. She's bound to be loaded, 'cause she's Pete Ball's widow, and he was one of the richest men in Tom Green County. It don't take anything more than a little common sense to figure out that he intends to fleece the old gal in the long run.

"You yourself know how easy it is to get a woman in San Angelo, Billy. They're up and down Concho Street all day and all night. Some of them are still in their teens and good-looking as hell, and they're all hunting a man. Foster Poe wouldn't have any problem bedding one of them, so why in the hell would he ride twenty miles round trip to sleep with a fifty-year-old woman who, by all accounts, wasn't pretty even when she was young?" He was quiet for a while, then answered his own question: "Money, old buddy. An unbelievable amount of money."

Kenard had also come by the information that Poe rode a big gray gelding, and that his nighttime visits to the widow Ball's house always occurred early in the week, usually on Monday or Tuesday. It was obvious that Poe had other fish to fry on weekends, for none of the snoops that Kenard had talked with had ever seen his big gray in the widow's corral on a Saturday or a Sunday.

After hearing which days of the week were the most likely ones to offer a face-to-face meeting with Foster Poe, Billy had deliberately chosen a Sunday night to put his plan into action. Now, still riding at a fast walk and holding to his southeastern course, he knew that by now he should be nearing River Road.

The starlight was not bright enough for him to read the face of his watch, and he dared not strike a match, but his internal clock told him that it had been at least four hours since he left the Flying W corral. When his calculating was done, he had decided that it was very close to two o'clock in the morning. He still had five hours left before sunup, plenty of time to take a nap if he could find a good hiding place along River Road. He kicked Miss Muffet to a trot, and within the hour was sleeping soundly in the middle of a large stand of bushes and saplings.

At daybreak, he opened his eyes and sat up on his bedroll, eager to see if the place he had chosen looked as good in the daylight as it had at night. The answer was no, but it would serve his purpose. By parting two small limbs and peeking between them, he had a very good view of the road fifty yards away. Anyone in the road looking in his direction, however, would have a problem distinguishing one thing from another, for the bushes and saplings, most of which still hung on to their dead leaves, would give off an appearance not unlike that of a solid wall.

He pushed his blanket aside and got to his feet. He had slept with his boots and his fleece-lined coat on, for he had needed them to keep warm. Even now, the temperature was uncomfortably cool, but building a fire was out of the question. He stomped his feet a few times, then walked over and began to pet Miss Muffet, who was tied to a sapling twenty feet from his bedroll.

He felt a twinge of guilt where the filly was concerned, for she would probably have to stand in the same spot all day long. There was not a single blade of grass here for her to eat, and she would have to wait till after dark for a drink. She would not suffer from the lack of water, however, for he had allowed her to drink her fill from the river just before leading her into the thicket.

A short while later, trying to decide what to eat for breakfast, he sat on his bedroll looking over the food Casey had put in his saddlebags. He finally settled on the mesquite-smoked ham, which was fully cooked and smelled very good. He cut off several slices with his pocketknife, then sat eating ham and crackers, washing it down with water from one of his canteens. He was almost through eating when he noticed Miss Muffet staring at him. Each time he put food in his mouth, her big eyes followed the movement of his hand like a begging dog.

Billy sat returning her steady gaze, sorry that he had nothing to feed her. Then his eyes came to rest on the bag of crackers. Would she eat one of those? Maybe, he decided. Weren't they made from grain? A moment later, he held one under the filly's nose. After sniffing it carefully and fumbling it clumsily with her lips a few times, she ate it with relish, then nudged his arm for another.

And she got it. In fact, Billy fed her at least half of the crackers in the bag. He stopped only because he believed that they would make her thirsty, and he had no intention of taking her to the river in broad daylight. Though she would surely be less recognizable than the majority of the saddle horses in the area, for no one had ever ridden her to town, the big Flying W on her hip could hardly be missed at close range.

Her rider was a wanted man, at least in Tom Green County, and since it was widely known that he had once been employed at the Flying W Ranch, Billy believed that, in the minds of most, the mere sight of that particular brand on the filly's hip would immediately tie her to him. Which was something that he simply could not afford, especially this morning. Indeed, going to the river for water before dark was not even to be considered. He would neither expose himself nor his mount, but would continue to lie low till his situation demanded action.

Later, he sat on his bedroll trying to figure out exactly where he was in relation to the widow Ball's house. Kenard had said that she lived ten miles from San Angelo. Billy estimated that he had camped approximately eight miles from town last night, which meant that the widow lived two miles northeast, and on the same side of the road as his present position.

He rose to his knees and poked his head through the bushes, looking left then right to determine how far he could see up and down the road. About half a mile in either direction, he decided, far enough that he would have plenty of time to saddle the filly if he needed to. If not, he would lead her deeper into the thicket, for the farther she was from the road, the smaller the chance of her giving away his position by whinnying if another horse came by.

Though Free was somewhat surprised at how lightly traveled the road was, especially on a Monday, a few horses, most of them pulling wagons or buggies, did come by as the day wore on. At midmorning, two young boys had ridden up the road toward town, then returned in the afternoon with several packages tied on their saddles. They talked and laughed loudly as they passed, while Billy stood in the brush holding the filly's nose with both hands to keep her from neighing.

An hour before sunset, he poked his head through his leafy cover and looked up the road. It was then that he saw the buggy. Drawn by a blaze-faced black and coming down the road at a trot, it would pass his position within the next two minutes, for it was less than three hundred yards away.

Moments later, he stood holding Miss Muffet's nose, disappointed that he had let the vehicle get so close before becoming aware of it. Though he had been checking out the road to the west every few minutes, he had no doubt failed to see the buggy because he had been looking directly into the late-afternoon sun.

Because he needed a wider view of the road, he had broken off a few limbs earlier in the day. Now, with one hand on the filly's nose and the other on her bridle, he stood watching and listening as the sounds of hooves and wheels striking the hard earth gradually grew louder.

As the buggy finally came into view, Billy suddenly stiffened and tightened his grip, for the driver and only passenger was none other than Foster Poe. Riding comfortably on a cushioned seat, he held the reins in one hand and appeared to be feeding himself with the other. Even as he passed he poked another bite of whatever he was eating into his mouth.

Billy stood still till the buggy was at least a hundred yards down the road. Then, in what might have been record time, he saddled the filly and tied on his bedroll, then shoved his rifle in the boot and picked up his saddlebags. He led the animal to the edge of the thicket and stood for a moment checking out the area in all directions, then mounted and took out after the buggy, which was by now several hundred yards down the road.

He pushed Miss Muffet to a canter, riding parallel to the road rather than on it, hoping that the grassy earth would muffle her hoofbeats. Though he knew that it was difficult for a man driving a buggy to hear anything other than the sounds made by his own horse and vehicle, Billy was taking no chances. He unsheathed his Winchester and levered a shell into the chamber. He intended to use the rifle if Poe should suddenly discover that he was being followed, for the buggy was still well out of range for his Colt.

It turned out that he did not need the rifle, however, for Poe continued down the road at a trot, apparently in a world of his own. When Billy neared the vehicle, he shoved the rifle back into its scabbard, then drew and cocked his Colt. He kicked the filly again, and three jumps later, was abreast of the buggy.

Clearly startled, Foster Poe turned the color of ashes as he stared into the barrel of the big Peacemaker, for he also recognized the man holding it.

"Pull up!" Billy shouted.

The order was carried out immediately, and Free was suddenly face-to-face with the man who had tried to kill him from ambush. "How do you do, Mr. Poe?" he asked, a hint of a smile playing around one corner of his mouth. "Have you bushwhacked anybody else lately?"

"Wha . . . uh . . . I—"

"Cat got your tongue?" Billy interrupted. With his own Colt still trained on Poe's face, he pointed to the gun on the man's hip. "Now, I suppose a fellow who likes long odds would say that you've got a chance to win this argument, Poe. All you've got to do is draw that gun and kill me before I can pull this trigger."

"Why, tha . . . that ain't no . . . no chance a-tall," Poe stammered.

"It's a whole lot better than the one you gave me, fellow," Billy said, his Colt pointed at the wide spot just above the man's nose. "And the cold hard fact of the matter is that, good or bad, it's the only damn chance you've got." He sat quietly for a moment, then added, "I'm waiting, Poe."

Poe got his gun out of its holster, but Billy shot him between the eyes before he could lift it.

Dismounting hurriedly, Billy holstered his weapon. He tied the filly to the front wheel and walked to the other side of the buggy. Collecting the dead man's Peacemaker, he tucked it behind his own waistband. He decided it was all right to keep it: Poe had twice tried to kill him with it. He would carry it in his saddlebag, fully loaded. A man never knew when he might need extra firepower. One thing was for certain: Foster Poe would never need it again.

He unhooked the traces from the whiffletree and hung them on the hames, then led Poe's horse forward, allowing the buggy shafts to fall to the ground. He unharnessed and unbridled the animal, then turned it loose, all of which took less than two minutes. Then he mounted Miss Muffet, and with daylight fading fast, headed for the Flying W to pick up his pack mule.

18

★

The town of Fort Stockton had come into being because of the military post of the same name. On the Butterfield Overland Mail Route, at the crossing of Old San Antonio Road and the Comanche War Trail, the fort had been established in 1859. The town sprang up immediately thereafter, and very soon became an important supply and shipping point for farmers and cattlemen.

And though it was directly in the middle of what many Eastern writers had referred to as an arid wasteland, Fort Stockton had water in abundance, for several large springs nearby flowed year-round. Because of the springs, the location had been popular with the Indians long before any white man arrived.

Nor were the outlying areas as desolate as they appeared, for the Leon and the Comanche Rivers offered ample water for the raising of livestock. A few miles to the west was Coyanosa Draw, and to the north, the big Pecos River, both of which provided drink for the large herds of cattle belonging to numerous Pecos County ranchers. While it was widely known that producing one cow required at least fifty acres of land in this particular area, and that a higher ratio would surely amount to overstocking, many ranchers nonetheless owned thousands of cattle, for it was not uncommon for a man to claim a hundred thousand acres or more.

Six weeks after dispatching Foster Poe, Billy Free rode into Fort Stockton. He turned Miss Muffet and his pack mule over to the hostler at the livery stable, then took a room at a small hotel halfway down the block. He washed himself as best he could from the pan of water provided by the establishment, then changed his clothes. He did not shave his face, for he had decided that a beard would make him harder to recognize. A few minutes later, he took a seat on a bar stool in the Grey Mule Saloon, which had long been the town's leading dispenser of red-eye.

There were three drinkers in the saloon at the moment, all of them seated at the far end of the bar. Billy ignored them and spoke to the tall, skinny, gray-haired bartender. "Can I get a small pitcher of beer?" he asked.

"Smallest pitcher I've got'll set you back fifteen cents," the bartender said, then raised his eyebrows.

Billy nodded and was served quickly. He laid the money on the bar, then picked up the pitcher and the glass and walked to a table near the wall. Before seating himself he turned his chair to face the front of the building, where he had an indistinguishable view of the street through a window that had obviously not been washed in several years.

Staring through the window at nothing, he sat sipping beer and recalling events of the past six weeks. He had returned to the old Conner cabin immediately after his final showdown with Foster Poe, and had remained there for the next five weeks. Bob Kenard had turned up there a week ago, and brought Free up to date on a few details.

"Sheriff Fink don't know for sure that you've even been back in Tom Green County, Billy," Kenard had said. "As a matter of fact, he don't even know that you're still in Texas. He showed up at the ranch right after the last Poe brother died, wanting to know if you'd been around. He don't have a witness or any other kind of proof that you shot Foster Poe, but he's convinced that you did. He said that Poe had been an upstanding citizen and that you were the only man in the county who disliked him."

Billy sat shaking his head. "Upstanding citizen, huh?" He frowned and spat into the yard, as if suddenly having a bad taste in his mouth. "Then I suppose he's gonna charge me with it."

Kenard nodded. "I believe he already has. At least he told Casey that he had two separate murder warrants against you."

Kenard's visit to the cabin had lasted little more than an hour. He had already mounted, ready to head back to the ranch, when he suddenly snapped his fingers. "Damn," he said, reaching into his vest pocket. "I almost forgot, and Casey would have never let me hear the end of it." He leaned over from the saddle and handed Free a folded piece of yellow paper. "He sent you this bill of sale for Miss Muffet." He chuckled, then added, "Actually, what it amounts to is a bill of swap, not a bill of sale."

And a bill of swap it was. Consisting of only two lines, the paper stated that an even trade had been carried out between Billy Free and Casey Springer: one mouse-colored filly for one blaze-faced black gelding. The paper was dated two months ago, and signed by Casey Springer. "Tell Casey that I appreciate this," Billy said, refolding the document and shoving it into his pocket. "In fact I've wondered a few times just how I'd go about proving ownership of the filly in case I ever needed to. Of course that hasn't happened yet, 'cause nobody has seen me riding her."

Kenard nodded. "Well, it never will be a problem now, 'cause you've got all the proof you need." He pointed to the sun hanging no more than two hours above the western horizon. "I've got to be on my way, Billy. Even now, it's gonna be dark before I get to the bunkhouse. Teeter and Casey both asked me to give you their regards, and tell you that they wish you well." He offered a military salute, then rode over the hill.

Billy moved out the next day. Rolling up the buffalo robes and extra blankets and leaving them in the corner of the cabin, he also left his extra cooking and eating utensils against the day when he might return. He packed his mule with only the bare necessities—including a gunnysack containing fifty pounds of shelled corn. Mounting the filly, he headed southwest, having no idea where he was going.

He held the same course for the next week. When he could find good cover he picketed his animals and slept during the day, then traveled at night. The moon had provided as much light as he needed for the first few nights, but had then disappeared to the other side of the world, leaving him in total darkness. Then he began to travel during the daytime, and this afternoon, not knowing where he was until he read the sign at the edge of town, came upon Fort Stockton.

Now, as he poured his third glass of beer from the pitcher, he began to pay more attention to the interior of the Grey Mule Saloon. Though the establishment had only two customers at the moment, for two of the drinkers at the bar had departed, Billy believed that it could comfortably seat at least a hundred men. The forty-foot-long bar with stations for two additional bartenders suggested that, even if the building was packed, which probably occurred often, especially on military paydays, a man would have no problem getting served when he wanted a drink.

A fiddle and a long-necked banjo lay on top of a piano near the rear wall, and a small hardwood dance floor was closer to the center of the room. The two doors along the back side of the building probably led to cabins where a man could enjoy female companionship for a price, Billy was thinking. And though no women were present in the saloon just now, he had no doubt that they would show up shortly after nightfall.

When he finished his beer, Billy carried the empty pitcher to the bar for a refill. As he waited, he heard the sound of the batwing doors opening. He glanced toward the front of the building and immediately recognized his friend Willy Bouton, the man who had taught him the most about line riding.

"Hey, Willy!" he called, waving. He motioned for Bouton to follow him.

At the table, they pulled out chairs. "I didn't expect to ever see you again, Willy," Free said, as he poured two glasses of beer. "Where you headed? Did you quit the Flying W?"

Bouton took a sip of his beer. "Quit more'n a week ago," he said. "Reckon I just got tired of doing the same old thing. Spent two days in the Bar None Saloon in San Angelo, then decided to hit the trail. I guess I'll just keep wandering about for a while yet, then try to catch on with another ranch just before I run out of money."

"Same with me. I don't have any particular place in mind either. I hated to leave the Flying W more than anything I've ever done, but I didn't have a choice in the matter. I had to get the hell out of Tom Green County."

Bouton sat shaking his head. "Ain't no reason that you can't go back to Tom Green County right now, Billy. All that stuff about the Poe brothers is over and done with. Even the sheriff says so. Bill Fink told me that he had made a mistake when he charged you with two counts of murder. He says that he has since learned that you shot Frank Poe in self-defense, and that you couldn't have killed Frank's brother, Foster, because you weren't even in the county at that time. Fink says that he has already withdrawn the charges, and that the circuit judge nol-prossed both cases."

Billy had been listening to every word, his mouth open. "Did I hear you right, Willy? Did I hear you say that Fink dropped the charges? Are you saying that I'm free to travel just anywhere I take a notion?"

"Absolutely. Everybody in town's talking about it. They all know that the judge killed the warrants."

Billy sat thoughtful for a few moments, then asked, "Did you hear Bill Fink say all that with your own ears, Willy? Did he say it directly to you?"

"Yep. Actually, he did a little more'n that. He sat right down at my table and had a drink with me. He talked about it for a long time, and he looked me right in the eye when he said that he'd made a bad mistake in bringing charges against you. He said that he had just listened to the wrong people the day you shot Frank, and that's the reason he got that warrant. He says he'll try to make it up to you if you ever come back to Tom Green County."

Billy sat staring into his beer glass and shaking his head. "It's all just so hard to believe," he said finally. "After all these months of hiding out and sneaking around, suddenly it's over." He took a sip of his beer and set the glass down on the table noisily. "Suddenly I can go anywhere I take a damn notion."

"That's right, Billy," Bouton said quickly. "No doubt in my mind that Casey Springer would jump at the chance to put you back to work on the Flying W. In fact, I think you'd be smart to go back there right now, 'cause ranching jobs are hard to come by at this time of the year. If you decide to do that, I guess I'll ride back to San Angelo with you. Sam Runyon at the Slash R has offered me a job just about every time he's ever seen me, and I think I'd like to work for him."

Free nodded. "You probably would like working for Runyon. One of his line riders, a man named Whistler Willingham, told me that the Slash R feeds better than any other ranch in West Texas. Said the bunkhouse has cots with springs and good mattresses, too. He said that the boss, who calls himself the ranch manager rather than the foreman, treats his hands like men, and even asks some of 'em for advice occasionally."

"I've heard all of that, too," Bouton said. "Let's just do

that then, Billy. You go back to the Flying W and I'll go to work on the Slash R."

Billy drained his glass, then sat staring through the window quietly for a while. "I guess it's settled, then," he said finally. "I liked the Flying W more than anyplace I ever worked, and it'll be a pleasure to go back." He extended his right hand across the table for a handshake. "We probably won't ever see each other unless we make it a point to, so let's make a deal right now and shake on it: on the first Saturday afternoon of each month, we'll meet at the Bar None Saloon."

Bouton pumped Billy's hand. "That's a deal," he said. "On the first Saturday of each month, we'll meet at the Bar None, rain or shine."

Free smiled, then pushed the empty pitcher across the table. "Your turn to buy," he said.

19

★

They rode out of Fort Stockton at ten o'clock next morning, heading east by northeast. Three large counties lay between Pecos and Tom Green Counties, and the trip would take about five days. Free allowed the filly to choose her own pace, which turned out to be a fast walk. And though the gray mule preferred to move a little slower, the animal had never been one to fight the lead rope, especially when the burden he carried was light. Today, aside from Billy's bedroll and some extra blankets, the packsaddle contained only the bare necessities for traveling.

Bouton kept abreast on a long-legged bay gelding, whose saddlebags were filled with tinned meats and other goods. "I don't like to live any leaner than I have to," Bouton had said this morning. He had insisted on waiting around till the she-bang opened for business, then bought a little of everything that would fit into his saddlebags, including several tins of fish.

An hour out of Fort Stockton, Bouton mentioned Miss

Muffet. "I've seen that filly around the Flying W lots of times," he said, "but I never did ride her. I've been told plenty about her, though. Everybody says she could outrun an antelope."

Billy chuckled. "I doubt that, Willy." He rode on for a few steps, then added, "I believe the antelope would have to crowd what would normally be a year's work into the race, though."

Staying with the main road, they traveled steadily throughout the day. Though they had plenty of drinking water in their canteens, they came upon none for their animals until they reached the Pecos River, where the thirsty beasts very quickly drank their fill.

After fording the river, the men made camp on the east bank, for the sun was now less than two hours high. They staked their animals out on decent grass, then began to look for something to burn. Deadwood was far from plentiful, but after walking the riverbank in opposite directions for a hundred yards or so, each man brought an armload back to the campsite.

Billy broke several dead sticks over his knee, then picked up his coffeepot and headed for the river. He called to Bouton from the water's edge: "If you'll sort out whatever we're gonna eat for supper, I'll build a fire and put the coffee on!"

An hour later, the men had a meal that was far superior to the usual trail fare: smoked ham, sardines, boiled eggs, two kinds of cheese, and a bag of chocolate cookies.

"I don't suppose many men would complain about a meal like this," Billy said as he dashed his coffee grounds aside and picked up the pot to refill his cup. "The plain old truth is that it's a hell of a lot better than the one we paid two prices for in the hotel restaurant last night."

"Sure it is," Bouton agreed, "and I've got enough stuff in my saddlebags to feed us like this all the way to San Angelo." He refilled his own coffee cup. "I've always made it a habit to eat good unless I'm plumb broke, and it ain't all that hard to do if you play your cards right.

"If a man has just a little bit of money, he don't have to live like a damn tramp just because he's traveling." He slapped his knee and began to laugh. "Hell, if you look pitiful enough, just about any of these old women working in the restaurants'll give you a whole sackful of food for a dime. They'll do it for nothing if you act like a poor, helpless man who don't even know how to boil water."

Free poked another cookie into his mouth and washed it down with coffee. "I don't think I could ever bring myself to ask for a handout," he said.

"That's not what I'm saying, Billy. You don't ask for a handout a-tall, you just try to look and sound like you need one. First, you buy a meal, then you spend a few minutes telling the old gal how good it was. You tell her how hard it is to find good food like hers, and how difficult it is to prepare a meal of any kind on the trail.

"Tell her that you're a traveling man with a long way to go, and nine times out of ten she'll volunteer to fix you a sack of vittles. She might not charge you anything, but even if she does, she'll likely let you off for the price of one beer."

Billy picked up the empty coffeepot, intending to wash it out in the river and fill it with water for morning coffee. "Sounds like you've figured out a way to get through the world a whole lot cheaper than the rest of us," he said. "What do you do, buy about one meal a week when you're on the move?"

"One or two."

Free kicked dirt over the remaining coals as darkness settled in. Then the men stretched out on their bedrolls. Billy lay awake for a long time, thinking. Stopping in Fort Stockton had surely been the luckiest thing he had ever done, he decided. Otherwise, he would not have run into Willy Bouton and would have had no way of knowing that Sheriff Fink had finally learned the truth about the shooting of Frank Poe, that he had dropped all charges and now welcomed Billy back into the county.

It was sure going to be nice being able to ride anywhere he wanted to once again, walking down Concho Street as free as a bird, stopping in any of the establishments he chose to. He had no doubt that Casey Springer would put him back on the payroll, and he was already looking forward to seeing and talking with all of his friends at the Flying W. He would head there immediately after he had a talk with Sheriff Fink, thanking him for tearing up the murder warrants.

Free was just about to doze off when Bouton spoke from his bedroll ten feet away: "You know, Billy, I've just been lying here thinking. I don't believe that it's very smart for us to keep riding down the middle of this road like we've been doing all day. It could be that not everybody knows about Sheriff Fink dropping his charges against you, and a lot of people might think you're still wanted for murder. Didn't you notice that most of the men we met today looked at you kind of funny?"

Free thought it over quietly for a few moments. "I don't suppose I did," he said finally. "Of course I didn't pay all that much attention to anybody."

"Well, I looked 'em all over pretty good, especially them two we met in that wood wagon about an hour before we got to the river here. That one-armed man on the passenger side seemed to take a mighty strong interest in you, kept peeking over at you out of the corner of his eye, then looking down between his legs. With me sitting up higher than him I could plainly see that he had a Peacemaker lying on the floorboards, and I strongly believe that he was thinking about using it."

"Well, I'll be damned," Free said. "I guess that just goes to show how much a man's eyes can miss when he's happy with the world. Are you saying that you think we ought to quit using the road and travel cross-country?"

"That's exactly what I'm saying. I just don't trust people a whole hell of a lot, and I'm afraid somebody might try to shoot you down hoping to get in good with the law, or maybe collect some money. And the closer to Tom Green County we get, the more traffic there's gonna be on this road.

"I know this area like the back of my hand, and it's not only safer to travel cross-country to San Angelo, it's a whole lot closer. The road crooks around every little hill and thicket, but we can ride straight through on horseback."

"Makes sense," Billy said drowsily. "You just lead the way and I'll follow."

Billy awoke shortly after dawn next morning to find that Bouton was already busy kindling a fire. "I guess I'll let you handle the coffee chore this morning," Free said, pulling on his boots. He fished around in his pack till he found soap, a razor, and his little mirror, then got to his feet and headed toward the river. "The first thing I'm gonna do today is shave off this beard," he said over his shoulder. "Now that I don't need to hide behind it, I don't see any reason to put up with the itching."

20

Three days later, they forded the Middle Concho River, only a few miles west of the Tom Green County line. "No more than two hours of daylight left," Billy said, "so we'll spend the night here and get an early start in the morning." He smiled broadly and pointed east. "We'll eat supper in San Angelo tomorrow night."

Bouton nodded and began to strip the saddle from his mount. "That's right," he said, "and we'll be there long before suppertime."

They picketed their animals no more than thirty yards away, for good grass was now plentiful along the river. Free made a pot of coffee, and after they had eaten another good supper, Bouton announced that he had plenty of food left for breakfast, which would be their last meal on the trail.

When darkness closed in, the two men spread their bedrolls ten feet apart and stretched out. The hour-long conversation they usually held after retiring did not take place tonight. Free himself could think of nothing to say, and supposed that Bouton had the same problem. They had already discussed about everything either of them knew, anyway, Billy was thinking. There was simply nothing left to say. He tossed and turned a few times, then slept soundly.

When he opened his eyes next morning he realized immediately that the early start he had mentioned would not happen, for it was already well after sunup. He pulled on his boots, then stood up and buckled on his gunbelt. Though Bouton was nowhere in sight, Billy supposed that the man might be hunting a rabbit, for the Winchester that Willy laid across his saddle every night was nowhere to be seen. Knowing that he was a crack shot with the rifle, Free expected Bouton's hunt to be successful. He raked up a pile of dead grass and bark, then began to kindle a fire. It took plenty of heat to properly cook a rabbit.

Squatting on his haunches and facing the west, Billy was still working on the fire when he heard Bouton approaching behind him. "I didn't hear any shooting," Free said over his shoulder, "so I guess you didn't spot any game."

"You guessed right," Bouton said.

Still facing the west, Billy continued to arrange several sticks of deadwood over the flickering flame. With the sun coming from the east, and well above the treetops now, he could see Bouton's shadow on the ground. Suddenly the shadow grew longer, then pressed the butt of a rifle against its shoulder. The barrel of the weapon was pointed straight at Billy's back.

Free read the situation quickly and correctly. With the quickness of a cat he sprang to his left, twisted his body, and drew his Colt all in one fluid motion. The big Peacemaker spat a foot of flame, then tore out Bouton's throat, just as the man fired his rifle. The slug from the Winchester, which Bouton had obviously intended to put between Billy's shoulder blades, kicked up dirt twenty feet beyond the fire.

Still on the ground leaning on one elbow, Billy recocked his Colt and lay watching as Willy Bouton twitched a few times, then lay still. Unconsciously, Free finally rose to a sitting position, but he did not get up right away. He sat staring at the body as the full comprehension of what had just happened began to gnaw at his very being.

Willy Bouton had claimed to be his good friend for almost a year, and this morning the son of a bitch had tried to shoot him in the back. No doubt there had been a reward posted, and Bouton had decided to claim it. Everything he had told Free about the sheriff dropping the charges had been false. The tale had been invented for the sole purpose of getting Billy to ride almost back to San Angelo of his own accord before the bushwhacking took place. After all, transporting a dead body 170 miles in warm weather would present a problem.

Even when Free finally got to his feet he did not holster his Colt. He stood with the cocked weapon in his hand, staring across the river at the distant ridge. At this moment, Billy was the most dangerous man in Texas, for his faith in mankind had suddenly been shattered. He would never trust another man completely, and even now he was making himself a promise that he would never again knowingly allow anything on two legs to get on his blind side.

He finally holstered his weapon and walked forward with the intention of going through Bouton's pockets, having little doubt as to what he would find. When he reached into the vest pocket, he pulled out a folded piece of paper on which someone had sketched a figure bearing his own likeness. "One Thousand Dollars!" the flier proclaimed in large lettering, then went on to promise that the money would be paid to anyone who delivered one Billy Free, dead or alive, to the sheriff of Tom Green County, Texas. A full and fairly accurate description of Free appeared directly below the sketch.

Billy felt as if his heart had fallen into his stomach. He stood for at least two minutes staring off into space, then spoke aloud: "Son of a bitch!" Moments later, he decided to go through the rest of Bouton's pockets. He found a money pouch and counted its contents, then shoved the money into his own pocket. "Two hundred ninety-six dollars," he said to the corpse. "Nowhere near as much as you were gonna get for killing me, but I'm sure I can find something to spend it for." He dragged the man's body, saddle, and bedroll into the thicket, then, once he had transferred all of the food to his own pack, threw Bouton's saddlebags and his rifle in the same direction.

He kicked dirt over the breakfast fire, for food was the last thing on his mind at the moment. He had his pack put together for traveling within ten minutes, then walked to the grassy meadow for Miss Muffet and his mule. He took the halter off Bouton's horse and turned the animal loose. He would put the halter, the picket pin, and the rope in his own pack, for a man never knew when he might need some extra equipment.

Half an hour later, he tied his animals to a small bush and stood looking into the thicket where the body lay. He was sick at heart and stomach as well, and the violent rage, anger, and fury that he felt was almost uncontrollable. Somehow he got the idea that he might feel a little better if he cut out both of Bouton's eyes. He took out his pocketknife and walked to the edge of the thicket. Then, after looking down at the body for a moment, he changed his mind. He refolded the knife and shoved it back into his pocket, for he had suddenly been seized by a completely different urge. While the sightless eyes of the corpse stared up at him glassily, he unbuttoned his fly and spent the next several seconds pissing into Willy Bouton's open mouth.

21

Billy came face-to-face with other people only twice during the next month, then only because he ran short of food. He had bought no grain for his animals, for good graze was abundant in every direction. He had ridden only at night for the first few days after the Willy Bouton incident, then had begun to move about whenever he wanted. Some days he did not ride at all. If he happened to wake up liking a particular location, he might simply sit around in the shade all day watching his animals crop the plentiful green grass.

On the days that he did travel, he rode leisurely, always holding to a southeasterly course. He knew that several large ranches lay in that direction and thought that he might eventually gain employment with one of them. He was in no hurry to find work, however, for he was not exactly short of funds. He still had more than four hundred dollars in his pocket, enough money to see him through the year if he was prudent with his spending.

Knowing that he was at least three hundred miles from

San Angelo, he had pitched his sleeping tent beside the Lavaca River and taken up temporary residence. He spent most of the daylight hours loitering near the water or sitting under the canopy of a large willow, enjoying the cool breeze that usually played around its trunk. Once he had taken off his boots and waded into the river, searching between the rocks in the shallow places for a fish that he might catch with his hands. He was unsuccessful, and knew that he would buy hooks and fishing line at the very next opportunity.

On the fifth morning, because he was beginning to run short of supplies, he decided to follow the river till he came to a settlement of some kind. He left his bedroll and his cooking and eating utensils in the well-hidden tent. He had come to look upon the small thicket as his temporary home, and fully expected to return before nightfall.

Ten miles south of his campsite, he came upon the small town of Edna. The settlement had been built on land granted by the Mexican government through Stephen F. Austin in 1824. As a commissary for Italian laborers on the New York, Texas, and Mexican Railway, it had first been called Macaroni Station, but had later been named Edna and selected to be the seat of Jackson County.

He rode into town from the east and stopped at the livery stable. He watered Miss Muffet and the pack mule, then bought each of the animals a bucket of oats, taking a seat on an upended nail keg and watching till they finished eating. He paid the liveryman for the grain, then led the animals down the street and tied them in front of a store whose sign suggested that it sold just about anything a man might need.

The moment he stepped inside the building he decided that the sign out front was no idle boast, for he could see that each of the aisles was filled with a wide assortment of goods. He had no problem buying everything he had come to town for, and the lady even boxed up two dozen eggs for him, wrapping each one individually so it would not break while being transported on his pack animal. She also had the smoked ham that he had hoped to find, along with red beans and tinned fish. He bought a can of lard, a sack of cornmeal, two boxes of crackers, a bag of coffee, some cookies, and a small jar of hard candy, then rounded out his purchases with a package of fish hooks and a ball of fishing line.

As the proprietress stood at the counter tallying up the charges with a pencil, she was joined by a dark-haired girl who could have been anywhere between fifteen and twenty years old. The older woman nodded toward the young lady. "My niece," she said. "Her name is Bess."

Billy offered his best smile and nodded. "Hello, Bess," he said.

With a pencil tucked behind her ear, suggesting that she had been in the rear of the store taking stock of merchandise, Bess stood beside her aunt smiling broadly. After a moment she laid the pencil on the counter and looked Billy squarely in the eye. "You're the best-looking man I've ever seen in this store," she said boldly, then began to gather up some of the things he had bought. "Here, let me help you with this stuff." She picked up several of the bags, then nodded toward the front door. "You got a wagon out there?"

Billy stood in his tracks silently for a while, then began to shake his head slowly. "Got a pack mule," he said finally.

She nodded toward the door again, giggling softly. "Well, come on and show me where to put all of this."

He picked up the remainder of the bags and followed the girl to the hitching rail. "Just put everything down on the boardwalk till I figure out exactly how I'm gonna balance it all on the mule," he said. "Your aunt did a good job of wrapping these eggs, but I'd still better be sort of careful with them."

The girl continued to stand beside him as he loaded his merchandise on the mule's packsaddle, handing him each particular bag as he called for it. Even after he was done and had thanked her profusely, she showed no inclination to return to the store. She was not a tall girl, standing at least a foot shorter than Billy. Nor could her face be called beautiful. Even while she was standing behind the store counter, he had decided that her face was somewhere between pretty and plain. Her blue eyes were smaller and had shorter lashes than those of most females, and her nose, cheeks, and forehead were unevenly sprinkled with freckles.

Her body was another matter, however. He had become aware of her flawless backside while he was following her out of the store, and noted that she wiggled only a little as she walked. Then, outside on the boardwalk, where the light was much brighter, he very quickly became convinced that Miss Bess had a body the likes of which a man usually saw only in pictures. Still standing on the boardwalk, her waspish waistline and well-developed bosom easily discernible through the form-fitting clothing she wore, she was watching every move that Billy made. "I noticed that you bought hooks and line," she said, still smiling. "Where do you do your fishing at?"

Free chuckled. "No place in particular," he said. "Creeks, rivers, lakes; any old place where I happen to see a fish jump." He untied his animals, then threw his leg across his saddle. "Thanks again for your help, Miss Bess, and I enjoyed talking with you." He headed the filly down the street at a walk, adding over his shoulder, "Maybe I'll see you again some time."

He was halfway down the block when he heard the girl call out loudly: "You won't see me again unless you try!" He turned in his saddle just in time to see her step back into the store and close the door. He stopped his animals at the side of the street and sat scratching his chin. It was obvious that Miss Bess wanted to know him better. For a little while he thought about making it easier for her, then decided against it. Though he believed himself to be safe in this particular town, he was nonetheless a wanted man with no place to light, and the last thing he needed at this point was another friend. Friends could sometimes send a man to the graveyard faster than enemies, a cold, hard fact that Free had learned from Willy Bouton.

After a few moments Billy shook his head and rode on down the street. When he reached the end of the block, intending to buy himself a cold beer, he tied his animals to one of the two hitching rails in front of a small saloon. Four saddled horses, all wearing the same Circle K brand, stood at the opposite rail.

He pushed open the batwing doors, then stood for a few moments enjoying the cushiony feel of the sawdust beneath his feet. As soon as his eyes adjusted to the dim lighting, he returned the bartender's greeting with a wave of his arm, then took a few steps forward.

The bar appeared to be completely square, with stools on all four sides. Four men, most likely the riders of the four Circle K horses outside, were seated on adjacent stools at the back of the bar, facing the front doorway. Billy took a stool about midway down the west side of the polished counter, where he also had a good view of the door.

The bartender, who was obviously of Mexican descent, was there quickly. "What'll you have, my good man?" he asked in perfect English.

"I'll have a beer," Billy said, taking off his hat and laying it on the stool to his right. "On second thought, just bring me a small pitcher." The man complied, then returned to the front of the bar, where he also seated himself on a stool.

With his eyes more or less straightforward, Free drank the first glass of his beer quickly, for he had been thirsty. The second glass disappeared more slowly, however, and by the time he had emptied it, he had seen a sign of friendliness from all four of the men at the back of the bar. He had begun to look around the room after a while, and each time he caught the eye of one of the men, that man had nodded a greeting. Billy returned all of their greetings with a smile and the lifting of a forefinger.

Half an hour later, a shabbily dressed middle-aged man pushed open the batwings and stepped inside the building. He stood weaving from side to side for a few moments, then stumbled into a table, almost knocking it over. He finally steadied himself by holding on to the backs of two chairs. Then, suddenly taking on a look of total sobriety, he walked straight to the bar, his path of movement a literal beeline. He seated himself on the east side of the bar, directly across from Free and a few stools to the left of the Circle K men. "Gimme a shot of liquor, José," he said to the bartender. He laid a gold eagle on the bar noisily. "Make it a double," he added. "I've got money." He refastened one of the galluses on his worn-out overalls, then sat waiting for his whiskey.

The bartender complied with the order, then scooped up the ten-dollar coin. He returned with the man's change a few minutes later, saying, "Behave yourself now, Dewey; don't drink any more than you can handle." With that, he turned his back and went about his duties.

Dewey stared at the bartender as the young man shuffled to the end of the bar, but he said nothing. In fact, he did not speak for the next hour, except to order his second and third drinks. Each time he was served, he would sit gazing hungrily into the oversized glass for a while, seemingly captivated by the sight of the auburn-colored liquid. Finally he would drink the liquor in one or two gulps, then sit quietly staring at the empty glass.

As the afternoon wore on, one or another of the men at the back of the bar initiated small talk with Free. None of them asked him a single question, however, and their conversation pertained only to cattle, crops, and the weather. When Billy ran out of things to say, the Circle K men sensed it, and did not address any more of their remarks to him. They continued to talk among themselves, however, and occasionally laughed heartily. At the moment the man who appeared to be the oldest of the four was telling the others about something humorous that had happened to him while he was in the army.

Just as the listeners' laughter subsided, the man named Dewey, obviously drunk by now, spoke up loudly from midway down the bar: "The army? The army, you say? By god, I was in the army, and I damn sure didn't see you!"

The room grew quiet instantly. The man who had told the story glared at Dewey for a few moments. Then his look softened, and a hint of a smile appeared at the corner of his mouth. The Circle K men sat silently for a few moments. When nothing else was heard from Dewey, the conversation at the end of the bar gradually resumed.

But Dewey was not done yet. He inhaled the last of his drink and set the glass down noisily, then pointed across the bar toward Free. "That your mouse-colored mare at the hitching rail?"

Billy nodded curtly.

Dewey sat quietly for a while, appearing to be in deep thought. "Just been sitting here wondering," he said finally. "A fellow told me one time that any man who really is a man wouldn't go riding around the country on a mare."

Billy did not speak right away. He drained the last of his beer from the pitcher into his glass, then said, "I ride the mare because the mare's what I've got." He drank the beer in one gulp, then added, "Are you questioning my manhood?"

Dewey was staring at his empty glass again. "Ain't questioning nobody's manhood," he said slowly. "Ain't questioning nothing."

Billy sat at the bar for only a few minutes longer, then pushed himself off the stool. He put on his hat, then raised his arm in a farewell salute to the men at the back of the bar. "I enjoyed the conversation," he said. "Good luck to all of you." He offered the same salute to the man on the opposite side of the bar. "You, too, Dewey. Take care of yourself, now."

While the Circle K men waved good-bye, and the man named Dewey stared through glassy eyes that probably did not see, Billy spun on his heel and headed for the front door, bidding the bartender adieu as he passed.

As he stepped through the doorway and onto the boardwalk, he came to a sudden halt, for there, sitting on a wooden bench that would have usually been occupied by nosy whittlers and gossipy old men, was the girl named Bess. "I saw your animals there at the rail," she said, her wide smile revealing rows of near-perfect teeth. She pointed over her shoulder to the saloon. "I didn't figure you'd be in there very long, 'cause you just don't look like a man who spends a whole lot of his time drinking."

He turned to face the girl, then attempted to speak: "Well . . . I guess I don't really . . . I mean—"

"I've been wondering why you didn't invite me to go fishing with you," she interrupted, then crossed her arms and leaned back to wait for an answer.

Billy found his tongue. "It never crossed my mind. You see, I don't ever know when or where I'll be fishing, 'cause I move around a lot. Besides, it's not my practice to ask young girls to go to the river with me."

She giggled softly. "All right, I'll do the asking. Will you take me fishing with you?"

He exhaled loudly and looked up the street toward the store, then began to scratch his chin. "Stuff like that is not something a man just up and does, Bess. Anyway, you must belong to somebody; I mean, you're bound to have a family somewhere that wouldn't like the idea of you tramping up and down the river with a stranger."

She shook her head. "I don't have anybody but Aunt Esther, up at the store. She's the one who told me that I'd be crazy to let you get away." She slid down the bench and began to pat the place where she had been sitting, a clear invitation for him to seat himself there.

Billy looked up and down the street once again, then took the seat. "I can't stay in town much longer," he said. "I need to be in my camp before dark."

She tugged at his sleeve playfully. "You got a woman in that camp?"

He shook his head. "No, no woman." He was quiet for a while, then added, "I don't have a woman anywhere."

"Well, I've heard people say that it ain't natural for a man to be alone. I think somebody that was real smart once said that every man needs a good woman beside him."

Billy chuckled. "Are you a good woman, Bess?"

She sat thinking quietly for a few moments, for she had taken the question in its literal meaning. "I never have had a chance to find out," she said finally. "Never met a man that I wanted till now."

Billy sat repeating her words to himself. Had he heard her right? Hadn't she just as good as said that she was still a virgin, and that she had been saving her body all these years just waiting for him to come along? "How could you be wanting me, Bess?" he asked after a time. "You don't know me; don't even know my name."

"Names don't mean anything except maybe at mealtime; don't have a thing in the world to do with what kind of person somebody is. Would a coyote be any nicer if we called him a sheep?" She tugged at his sleeve again, adding, "I was about to ask what your name is, though."

He nodded, recognizing the wisdom in her words. "My name is Billy," he said, "and I don't know that you and I ought to go anywhere together. To tell you the truth, you don't look old enough to make your own decisions about going fishing with a man."

She began to speak loudly, then gradually softened her tone: "I happen to be eighteen years old, sir, old enough to make my own decisions about anything. And you don't have to take me with you. Just tell me where you're gonna be fishing at, and I'll come there by myself."

No woman had ever been so straightforward with Billy, and he sat thinking on the matter for a while. The offer seemed too good to turn down and he knew that he would enjoy the girl's company in his camp, but he had no intention of being the man who escorted her out of this town. Maybe there was another way. "You got a horse?" he asked finally.

She nodded. "Got a mare at the livery stable."

"Well, if a girl happened to ride west to the Lavaca River, then north up the east bank, she'd run right into my camp after about ten miles." Without another word, he got to his feet and untied his animals from the hitching rail. He threw his leg over his saddle, then yanked on the pack mule's lead rope. As he headed down the street, he heard Bess call after him: "You can look for that girl tomorrow! She should be there sometime around noon."

22

Billy slept till well after daybreak next morning, then lay on his bedroll for another hour. He was thinking of the girl named Bess and wondering if she would actually visit his camp today. After a while, he decided that she probably would. She had certainly not been bashful about saying that she wanted to spend some time on the river with him, and he seriously doubted that catching a catfish was the uppermost thing on her mind.

He finally slipped on his boots and got to his feet, then began to kindle a fire. Still thinking of Bess, he nodded and smiled as he touched the small pile of dead grass and leaves with a match. She would be here, all right, and he had no doubt that she would be thinking of something other than fishing. The thought gave him a warm feeling, for he knew that he would accept whatever he was offered. The idea that he might soon be lying with Bess was more than a little pleasing, for he had never before even seen a body as enticing as hers, much less touched one. In fact, it had been much too long since he had been with any woman, he decided, as he laid several larger pieces of deadwood on the fire.

He watered his animals and moved them to new grass, then put on the coffeepot and set about fixing himself some breakfast. He placed his skillet on the hot coals and dropped in a few slices of smoked ham, then sat peeling eggs that he had boiled over last night's campfire. A few minutes later, he sat leaning against the big willow enjoying his meal.

Once he had washed his skillet, dumped the grounds out of his coffeepot, and filled it with water for the next time, he set off into the thicket looking for two branches or saplings that were small enough, long enough, and straight enough for fishing poles. Though he suspected that he would need only one, for the girl had neither looked nor sounded like a fisherwoman, when he came out of the thicket he had two long, slender branches that were perfect for the job.

He tied fishing line on one of the poles, then searched around till he found a rock that was the right shape and size to use for a weight. With the rock tied on the line, he added a fish hook, then picked up a piece of cheese and headed for the river. He would test the fishing while he was waiting for his guest; might even catch something for dinner. Seating himself on the bank, he squeezed a gob of cheese onto the hook and dropped the line into the water, allowing the weight to carry it to the bottom.

The ripple on the water had no more than settled when Billy felt a hard tug on the line. With his pole bent halfway to the water, he began a sweeping motion that he hoped would tire the fish out quickly. He was not concerned about breaking the line, for the label claimed that it would hold a forty-pound fish. Suddenly there were two more quick, hard jerks, then the line went slack. Moments later, when he inspected it, he found that the line had not broken. The fish had simply managed to throw the hook.

He sat on the bank rolling another ball of cheese onto the hook, thinking about the size of the fish he had just lost. In excess of twenty pounds, he believed. He was glad that the monster had gotten away, for he had no use in the world for it. Most of it would have gone to ruin long before being eaten. Besides, the meat of a catfish that size was mushy and mighty poor eating. Therefore, even if he had caught the fish, he would have released it alive. Finally, hoping to hook up with something in the two- or three-pound range, he gave the ball of cheese one last squeeze, then dropped the line back into the water.

He sat watching the line for the next two hours, but it did not move again. Many things crossed his mind as he sat fishing, but he dwelt longest on the fact that he was tired of loafing, that he needed to find a job. When he finally grew tired of baiting an unproductive hook, he put on one last gob of cheese and tied the line around a bush that he knew would hold any fish in the river, then got to his feet and walked back to his camp.

He had made a decision: Some time within the next few days he would mount Miss Muffet and visit some of the area ranches asking for work. Maybe he would find out where the Circle K was and try there first, for he remembered that the men whose horses wore that brand had been very friendly toward him in the saloon yesterday.

Deciding that it was time to move his animals to new grass, he put a piece of hard candy in his mouth and headed for the meadow. He moved the mule first and had just staked Miss Muffet out fifty yards farther up the hill when he saw a rider approaching from the south. He began to walk back toward his camp leisurely, as he realized that the newcomer was also headed there. Finally he stopped in his tracks and waited.

The oncoming animal continued at a trot, then slowed to a walk as it grew nearer. Astride a blaze-faced chestnut mare, dressed in tight-fitting brown pants and a tan blouse that threatened to pop its buttons, the girl named Bess halted the animal, dismounted, and closed the distance between herself and Billy Free in what seemed like one fluid motion. She threw her arms around his neck and when she had pulled herself up high enough, kissed him on the mouth wetly. "You taste sweet," she said when she finally came up for air.

He smiled. "The kind of sweetness people buy at the store," he said, holding the half-melted piece of hard candy out on his tongue for her to see.

In an instant she had closed her mouth over his tongue and ended up with the candy. "I'll see if it makes me as sweet as it made you," she said, then crunched it a few times and swallowed.

They stood locked in each other's arms for a long time, continuing to kiss each other wetly. Billy knew that the time had come, that passion had already taken them both over. He held her to him tightly, knowing that she could feel his swollen manhood pressing against her. "It's time, Bess," he said finally.

"Yes, Billy," she said softly, speaking into his chest. "Yes, it is."

Without another word, he led her into the thicket, where his bedroll was already spread out and waiting. The girl took off her blouse and stood squarely before him, as if to give him a better look at her beautiful bosom and arouse him further. Billy kissed her, then put his hand on one of her breasts and his mouth on the other. All the while, she was busy unbuckling his belt and unbuttoning his trousers.

Once both of them were completely naked, Billy picked her up in his arms and kissed her passionately, then very gently laid her down on his bedroll. Remembering that this was going to be the first time for Bess, and knowing that he would have all afternoon and maybe even all night with her, he was in no hurry. He began to run his hands over her perfectly proportioned body very slowly, quite confident that she was enjoying it at least as much as he was.

When he began to kiss her all over, touching her body in

one sensitive area after another with his wet tongue, she quivered slightly, then began to murmur, making indistinct sounds not unlike those made by a kitten. "Do it now, Billy," she said softly. A moment later, she spoke much louder. "Now, Billy! I don't care how much it hurts. Do it now!"

Kissing her soft belly one last time, Billy covered her small body with his own, then slid between her legs. And though he carried out the act as deliberately and as tenderly as was possible, he could tell by her grimace and distorted facial expression that he was causing her intense pain. She never complained once, however, and toward the end, as his up-and-down motion reached a greater point of intensity, she began to nibble on his shoulder and cling to him even tighter, following every movement of his body with her own. Finally, after a quick series of deep thrusts, it was over. Both parties lay still for a while. Then he began to kiss her lips, face, and eyes. "Did it hurt much?" he asked.

She stuck her tongue out at him and did not answer the question.

Afterward, they lay on the bedroll talking for an hour, then made love again. This time it took them much longer.

When they had mutually decided that it was time for them to get up and put on their clothes, Bess finally voiced a complaint: she was so weak that she could hardly dress herself, she said. "That's hard work, little girl," he offered, pointing to the bedroll and chuckling softly.

Suddenly remembering that Bess's mare had been left unattended on the hillside, Billy slipped on his boots and left the thicket at a fast clip. Then, as soon as he had a better view, he very quickly saw that there had been no reason for concern. Fifty yards up the hill, with her reins lying on the ground in front of her forefeet, the well-trained mare was standing in the same tracks as when Bess had dismounted.

Good girl, Billy said to himself as he headed up the hill. He led the mare to his camp and stripped the saddle, then rubbed her back down with a handful of grass. After digging around in his pack till he found the rope and the picket pin that had once belonged to Willy Bouton, he watered the mare from the river, then staked her out near his own animals.

When he returned to camp he found that Bess had already rolled up his bedroll and tied it. Taking her action as a hint that she did not want to lie on the bedroll again right now, Billy kissed the top of her head and walked to the fireplace that he had long ago fashioned between several large stones. "What do you want for dinner?" he asked as he squatted on his haunches and began to kindle a flame.

Standing directly behind him, she squeezed his shoulders and kissed his ear, then began to run her fingers through his hair. "At the moment I don't feel like I'll ever want to eat again, but I know I need to. I didn't eat any supper last night or any breakfast this morning; too excited about coming up here to see you, I guess." She kissed the back of his neck, then walked away, adding over her shoulder, "Just fix anything you want to. I'll eat anything you will."

They ate dinner an hour later, with smoked ham being the main course. Then they retired to the riverbank, where they sat down beside the limp fishing line. After a while, Billy cut the line loose from the bush with his pocketknife and retied it to the fishing pole. He pulled it out of the water once to see if the cheese was still on the hook, and, seeing that it was, dropped it back into the water.

After a few moments Bess reached for his hand and placed it against her cheek. "You never did tell me your last name," she said. "My full name is Bessie Mae Noble."

"Pretty name," he said quickly. Then, feeling a twinge of guilt, he added, "My name is Bill Jones, so you can just keep on calling me Billy."

She touched her lips with her fingers and blew him a kiss. "I love you, Billy Jones," she said, then turned her head quickly, as if embarrassed at hearing herself use those words.

Now that he had her talking, he wanted to learn more. "Where do you live?" he asked. "Do you work at your aunt's store every day?"

"I live with Aunt Esther a quarter mile west of town. It's that little white house off by itself on the north side of the road. You rode by it twice yesterday, but you probably didn't pay it any mind."

"I saw it, all right. The house and yard looked so well-kept that I remember wondering what type of people lived there."

"Well, now you know," she said. She chuckled softly, then continued. "I'm sure Aunt Esther would like to be rid of me. She's always pointing out men who need wives to me, reminding me of all the good things this one or that one could give me if I'd just go after him.

"The truth is, she don't really need me at the store, at least not badly enough to justify the five dollars a week that she pays me. That's top money for a working girl, Billy." She was quiet for a moment, then began to laugh aloud. "Of course I'm not saying that it's top money for all working girls. I've been told that whores can make as much as twenty dollars a night. Can you imagine that? Twenty dollars a night?"

"Sure, I can imagine it," he said with a grin, nodding his head several times. "If I had been born a girl, that's probably what I'd be doing right now."

She dropped his hand and slapped his leg playfully. "You wouldn't do any such thing, Billy Jones."

He rebaited the fish hook one last time, and dropped the line back into the water. Then Bess snuggled against his chest and began to talk again: "When I told you yesterday that I didn't have anybody but Aunt Esther, I didn't really mean that I didn't have anybody. I've got a mother who ran off to El Paso with a drunk eight years ago, and I've got a sixteen-year-old brother who's been working on a ranch for the past year. His name is Lenny, and he comes to see me every time he's in town. In fact, he spent several hours with me just last week."

Billy nodded. "A ranch is a good place for a young man to work," he said. "If he wants to save his money it's an easy thing to do, 'cause there sure ain't much out there to spend it on. It's also a good place to stay out of trouble. I've done some ranch work myself, and I enjoyed all of it. In fact, for several days now I've been thinking about going job-hunting myself."

Realizing that local work was the surest way to keep him in the area, Bess spoke quickly: "Job-hunting?" she asked. "You're looking for work? Maybe you could hire on over there where my brother works. It's only about twelve miles from Edna."

"What's the name of the outfit?"

"The Circle K Ranch," she answered. "Ben Karo is the foreman, and his father is the owner. My brother says that the food and the living quarters are good, and that it makes no difference whether a man is a new hire or a long-time resident, Ben Karo treats them all the same."

Billy nodded. "Maybe I'll be having a talk with Ben Karo before long."

She slid into his lap and kissed him. "You could do it tomorrow, Billy. You could go over there in the morning, then be back here at your camp in the afternoon. I'll ride up here about dinnertime, and have a pot of beef stew waiting for you when you get here."

"You say you'll ride back up here tomorrow?" he asked. "Hell, I thought you might be gonna spend the night with me."

"Not this time, Billy, although I'd sure like to. I told Aunt Esther the truth about where I was going, but I did promise her I'd be back home before dark." She got to her feet and stood looking across the river, shading her eyes with her hand. "Judging from the position of that sun, I believe it's time for me to be on my way."

Determined not to show his disappointment, Billy got to his feet. "If you expect to be home before dark it is." He kissed her forehead. "Finish buttoning up your blouse while I saddle your mare."

A short while later, he lifted the girl into the saddle. "I'll have a talk with Ben Karo in the morning," he said, "then come back here and sample that beef stew you promised. What's the best route to the ranch?"

She pointed with her forefinger. "Easiest way would be to just ride over that hill and keep going southeast till you reach the main road, then make a left turn. About a mile after you cross the Navidad River, you'll see the ranch road leading off to your right. There's a sign there."

He nodded and patted her butt; then she kneed the mare down the hill. He stood watching till she was out of sight, then walked to the riverbank and reclaimed his seat. As he sat staring into the river, he was thinking of how glad he was that he had met Bess and how much he had enjoyed her visit today. After a little more thought, he decided that this might very well have been the happiest day of his life.

Not that he had actually ever had all that many happy days. Most of his life had been little more than a drab existence: working from daylight till dark to grow enough corn to feed the mule and the hogs and enough cotton to buy staples for his mother's cabin. Then there was the wood-cutting detail. The kitchen stove had to be fed, and the fireplace burned mountains of split oak in cold weather.

Even in the wintertime, when some people seemed to think farmers spent their time resting, there was always new ground to clear, not to mention the few hours spent almost every day tramping the hills and hollows in search of game for the pot. It was a never-ending cycle. Someone had once said that a farmer had to spend every waking hour of his life working just to survive. Billy knew this to be true, for he had worked in the fields ever since he could first remember. Then, as he moved into his teens and his mother's illness came along, it seemed like the whole world fell on his shoulders.

Billy Free had carried that load for more than six years, till his brother Toby grew old enough to share, and eventually carry, the burden. Being a full-grown man, Billy had early last year decided that it was time for him to leave the nest and turn the reins over to fifteen-year-old Toby. He had found a good job up in Jackson and was scheduled to start on it during the first week of May. However, during the last part of April, Will Kipling had come down the road accusing Free of murdering a deputy sheriff.

Had it amounted to no more than a mere accusation, Billy could have lived with it and took his chances in court. When Kipling decided to storm Amy Shelton's cabin, however, the man had taken his life in his own hands. Being the oldest of the woman's two sons, it had fallen to Billy to remove the oversized bully from the doorway. He had used the big Peacemaker to do the job, and he had been on the run ever since.

All of these things passed through his mind during the span of less than a minute as he sat daydreaming and unconsciously watching the fishing line. With his thinking temporarily back to the present, he stretched his arms over his head and looked about him in every direction, then yawned and allowed his mind to wander again.

He had heard the old saying that life was fair in the long run, that everything eventually fell into place and balanced out. He believed that whoever was the first man to utter that crock of shit needed to be dumped into an ice-cold lake, for he himself was a perfect example that life was anything but fair.

Was it fair that he'd had to leave his home and run for his life because of Will Kipling's unfounded accusations? And the Poe brothers, who had both tried to kill him for no reason at all—was that fair? And was it fair that a crooked sheriff named Bill Fink was circulating a wanted poster charging Billy with two counts of first-degree murder? Murders that in reality had never even happened? He sat shaking his head at his thoughts. He had long ago concluded that life was nothing close to fair, and that nobody but damn fools expected it to be.

He rekindled his fire an hour before sunset and warmed

up leftover food and coffee for his supper. When he had finished eating, he kicked dirt over the coals, then walked to the meadow and moved his animals to a new patch of grass for the night. Then, as darkness closed in, he lay on his bedroll thinking of Bess Noble. He was glad that she had been honest enough to display her feelings right from the start. Otherwise, he would have ridden off and left her standing behind that store counter without ever knowing anything about her except her name.

"I told Aunt Esther more than two years ago that I had never seen a man that I really wanted," Bess had told Billy this afternoon. "I also told her that if and when I did, I would not hesitate to make my feelings known." She was quiet for a moment, then blushed a little as she added, "Then when I saw you standing at that counter looking like a million dollars, I knew that it was time for Bess Noble to get bold."

Bold. She had been bold and she had been honest, and Billy was glad. This afternoon, she had said that she loved him, and he had believed her. With a smile on his face, he turned his head on the folded blanket that he was using for a pillow and was asleep quickly.

23

Billy arrived at the Circle K Ranch at ten o'clock next morning. He rode past the bunkhouse, then on to a hitching rail at the edge of the big ranch house yard. Being reluctant to dismount without first being invited to, he continued to sit his saddle. He had seen no sign of human life, even though his arrival had been repeatedly announced by a pair of redbone hounds who were even now yapping at him from underneath the front porch.

After helloing the house twice and getting no response, he turned his mount and headed out of the yard at a walk. "Howdy!" he heard someone shout from behind him. He stopped quickly, and turned to recognize the oldest of the Circle K men he had talked with in the saloon two days ago.

"Howdy," the man repeated as he walked around the corner of the house at a brisk pace. "I was down yonder at the hog pen where I couldn't hear you if you've been calling out. I could hear them dogs, though, and anytime they raise that much cain, somebody's around." He took a few more steps, then stopped and began to chuckle. "I guess I recognize you now. You're the fellow we talked with in the saloon the other day; the one old drunk-ass Dewey tried to dress down for riding a mare."

Billy dismounted and tied the filly. "That's me," he said. "Good morning."

The man appeared to be about forty years old. Of medium build, with dark hair graying at the temples, he had the leathery complexion of a man who spent a major portion of his time outdoors. He took a few more steps, then stood leaning against the hitching rail. "My name's Ben Karo," he said. "Is there something I can do for you?"

"I hope so," Billy answered, his smile constant. "I've been loafing about as long as I care to, so I'm looking for work."

Karo was slow to answer. He took a brier-root pipe from his vest pocket and tamped it full of tobacco, then struck a match on the hitching rail. He blew several puffs of smoke to the wind, then asked, "Have you worked on a ranch before?"

"Yes, sir."

"Have you ever been on a trail drive?"

"No, sir. I've never driven cattle more than a few miles at a time."

Karo took another deep drag from his pipe and blew a cloud of smoke through his nose, then began to chuckle. "A few miles at a time? Hell, that's all there is to a trail drive. You just keep driving 'em a few miles at a time till you get 'em where they're going."

Billy nodded and said nothing.

"I can certainly use you if you want to sign on for a drive," Karo continued. "We contracted to deliver eight hundred head to a man in Colorado, so we've got to be getting 'em on up there. No bulls, no steers. The herd'll be nothing but brood cows. This fellow intends to breed the Longhorn strain out of them with some Hereford bulls that he's shipping in from back east." He struck a match to get the fire started in his pipe again, then added, "The job'll pay thirty-five a month, and I reckon it'll last about ten or twelve weeks. What do you think?"

"Sounds good to me," Billy answered, "and I'm ready and willing. When does the drive begin?"

"Be about a week or ten days yet. The hands are busy sorting and separating right now, isolating the breeders that're gonna be heading north. You got a place to stay, or do you want to move into the bunkhouse?"

"I've got a camp not too far away that I'm happy with," Billy said, untying his mount as he spoke. "I can show up here again any time you say."

Karo stood scratching his chin for a few moments. "I reckon that with the addition of you, I've got a full crew lined up now," he said finally. "If you'll meet me right here in the yard one week from today, I'll put you on the payroll. Don't let me down, now, 'cause I'll be counting on you."

Billy nodded. "You can count on me, sir. I'll be here."

"My name is Ben," Karo said with finality. "Just Ben."

"All right, Ben," Billy said.

With raised eyebrows, Karo spoke again: "I reckon you've got a name, too, huh?"

Free swung into the saddle. "The name is Bill Jones," he said, then clucked to Miss Muffet and rode out of the yard.

24

★

When he dismounted at his camp four hours later, Bess
Noble leaped into his arms. "I've thought of nothing but you
all night and all day," she said, kissing his face all over. When
he placed her back on her feet, she pointed to the iron pot on
the fire. "I brought some beef from town and made that pot
of stew I promised you."

"Good," he said. "And I'll certainly be ready when it is."
He pointed to her mare, which, still wearing the saddle, was
tied to a bush a few yards away. "Let me take care of your
mare," he said, "then I'll tell you about my trip to the Circle
K." He stripped the saddle and watered the animal, then led
her to the meadow, where he staked her out a few yards from
his mule. Then he returned to camp to care for Miss Muffet.
Before putting her on a picket rope, he would feed her a good
portion of grain, for she had put in a hard day's work.

When he had finished his chores, Bess informed him that
it would be at least another hour before the stew was done.
"Good," he said, reaching for her hand. He led her into the

thicket and to his bedroll, where he undressed her and made passionate love to her for the most part of an hour.

When they had re-dressed, Bess walked to the fire to check on their supper. "This stuff is done," she said, stirring it with a large wooden spoon. "I believe it's gonna be good, too."

"I have no doubt whatsoever," Billy said, beginning to dig bowls and spoons out of his pack. A few moments later he handed a bowlful of stew to the girl, then filled his own. He leaned back against the tree and took a bite, washing it down with water from his canteen. "This is delicious, Bess." He took another spoonful, then repeated himself. "Delicious. I suppose I could have made a pot of coffee to go with it, but . . ." He chuckled. "I was busy with something else."

She blushed, but it passed quickly. "You were going to tell me about your trip to the Circle K," she said.

"So I was," he said, then ate several more bites of stew. "There really ain't a whole lot to tell. I met the foreman, Ben Karo, and he hired me."

She set her bowl down quickly and crawled into his lap. "Oh, Billy," she said, kissing his lips hard. "I'm so happy that you've found work close by. Now we can see each other almost as often as we want to. Maybe someday . . ." She grew quiet instantly, then sat biting her lip.

Billy held her tightly for a long time. "Yes, baby," he said finally. "Maybe someday."

She stayed in his camp this night and every night for the next week. In fact, she returned to Edna only once during that time, and she was back in his camp six hours later.

She had cried when he told her that he was not going to work on the Circle K Ranch itself, but was going on a three-month trail drive. "It's going to seem like an eternity," she had said. "I don't know that I can stand it."

"It'll seem the same way to me, Bess, but I gave the man my word, so I've got to do it."

During the late afternoon of the sixth day, they stood beside the big willow saying their good-byes. Bess had to leave immediately in order to get home before dark, and tomorrow morning Billy would have to report to the Circle K Ranch to begin the long drive north. He stood holding her mare and expressing his regrets at their upcoming separation. "If I had been in love with you the day I rode to the Circle K, I never would have agreed to go on the drive," Billy was saying. "It wasn't till a few days later that I got to where I couldn't stand the thought of leaving you. The feeling just crept right up on me before I knew it."

He put his arms around her and held her face against his chest. "It's just something that we'll both have to live with. I love you, baby, and I'll be back before winter sets in. Then we'll go to California, just like we've been talking about for the past few nights. We'll get married out there somewhere and raise a family in that California sunshine we've heard so much about."

As he lifted her to the saddle, he saw a tear roll off her cheek. "I love you, Billy Jones," she said chokingly. "I love you more than anything else in the whole wide world." Then she was gone.

25

★

The sun was three hours high when Free arrived at the Circle K Ranch next morning. Three men, one of whom was Ben Karo, stood in front of the bunkhouse talking. Billy nodded a greeting, then dismounted and tied Miss Muffet and his pack mule to one of the hitching rails. "I was about ready to give up on you, Jones," Karo said, speaking in a gruff tone of voice that belied Billy's earlier impression of the man. "Around here when we say morning, we mean the time period between daybreak and sunup."

"Sorry," Billy said. "My camp was located ten miles up the Lavaca River. I saddled up and loaded my mule in the dark this morning, and was on my way two hours before daybreak. It's a five-hour ride at a walking gait, and I never push my animals unless there's a good reason for it."

The foreman's easygoing manner that Billy remembered from last week had disappeared completely. In fact he even looked like a different man. "Reason?" he asked loudly.

"What do you call a reason? Hell, you had a job waiting, fellow."

Billy stood quietly for a few moments, fighting to control his emotions. "We didn't even discuss what time of the morning you wanted me here, Mr. Karo, so I decided that nine o'clock ought to be about right. I had a job waiting, all right, but I damn sure don't intend to start it off by getting my ass chewed out about something that don't amount to a hill of beans." He pointed with his thumb. "If you insist on making a big thing out of it, that road there runs both ways."

A barrel-chested young man standing beside Karo spoke to the foreman quickly: "It would leave us a man short, Ben, and I don't know who in the hell we'd get this late in the game. Took us nearly a month to come up with the crew we got."

Karo's facial expression changed instantly. He began to smile, then patted Billy on the back. "We're mighty glad to have you no matter what time you got here," he said in a soothing tone. "Welcome to the Circle K. You're on the payroll as of right now." He turned his head slightly and spoke to the two men behind him. "Our new hand here goes by the name of Bill Jones, fellows." Then he pointed to the man who had spoken up earlier, saying, "Bill Jones, this is Bert Sampson, and he'll be your trail boss. The man beside him is Bailey Eddings."

Billy took a few steps and shook hands with both men, reaching for the hand of the trail boss first. Standing about five-ten, with a solid build, Sampson appeared to be about twenty-five years old. He had dark eyes and coarse brown hair that stuck straight out from both sides of his head, all the way from his temples to the brim of his hat. The powerful muscles of his arms and upper body were noticeable even through his shirt, and he had the overall appearance of a man who would be hard to handle in a scrap.

Bailey Eddings offered a firm grip and a toothy smile. "Welcome, Bill," he said, pumping Free's hand a few times. "It's good to meet you." He was a six-footer who weighed about one-eighty, and appeared to be in his late twenties. "I expect you and me to get along just fine," he continued. "I can tell by hearing you talk that you're a product of the Southeast, and me being from Alabama, that accent sounds mighty close to home."

Billy nodded and released the man's hand.

Then, as if suddenly deciding that Bert Sampson could handle things from here on, Ben Karo chose this moment to be elsewhere. Nodding to the young trail boss, he shrugged, then headed for the main house.

Sampson motioned across the road to the barn and the pole corral, then spoke to Free: "You can leave your pack mule in the corral there till you get back from Colorado. He'll be taken care of right along with the rest of the stock. And you'd better hang your packsaddle in the corncrib out of the weather. You'll see the pegs on the wall just inside the door."

As Billy led the mule across the road, both men were close at his heels. After stripping the packsaddle and turning the animal into the corral, he began to remove a few things from his pack. First came his fleece-lined coat, then his bedroll, followed by two changes of clothing, a pair of moccasins, and several pairs of socks. The last thing was a small sack containing his shaving gear. "I've never been on a trail drive before," he said, speaking to Sampson. "How much of this stuff can I carry with me?"

"I imagine you'll need it all," Sampson said. "I know for sure that you'll be needing that warm coat before you get back to Texas. That Kansas wind can just about cut a man in two, even during the fall."

"How about my saddlebags?" Billy asked.

Sampson nodded. "You can roll 'em up in your bedroll and put 'em in the chuck wagon when we get to the herd."

Billy hung his packsaddle in the corncrib, then carried the rest of his things across the road and piled them at the feet of Miss Muffet. As the others stood by watching, he placed his coat and extra clothing, along with his socks and the moccasins, on one of his blankets. Then he tied the four corners of the blanket together and hung it on his saddle horn. When he had tied his bedroll behind the cantle and placed his shaving gear in his saddlebag, he spoke to Sampson: "I'm as ready as I'll ever be."

Sampson nodded and the three men mounted up. "The herd's about an hour's ride from here," the young foreman said, pointing. "We started bunching 'em up on Buffalo Creek more than a week ago, and we've been adding a hundred head or so every day since then. They're getting harder to hold now that they've eaten up everything in sight." He chuckled, then added, "Of course, I'm not gonna worry much if this herd loses a little weight on the trail, not like I did when I was doing business with buyers at Dodge City. We're not selling this bunch by the pound, they're all brood cows."

They rode past the main house and the hog pen, then waded a shallow branch and headed north. Not another word was spoken till they reached the herd. Then Sampson tied his mount to a front wheel of the chuck wagon and spent several minutes talking with the cook, a bearded, medium-sized man who appeared to have been around for at least half a century.

"That cook's name is Hub Weatherford," Eddings said as he and Free tied their mounts and seated themselves on the ground. "But that long white beard of his earned him a nickname so long ago that hardly anybody remembers what his real name is. The only handle he answers to nowadays is Santa."

"That figures," Billy said, nodding. "The name fits."

While their horses grazed on picket ropes a short distance away, several men lay on the ground leaning on their elbows, resting themselves while they had a chance. Each of them knew what lay ahead during the coming weeks, either from firsthand experience or because he had been forewarned by other drovers. A few minutes' rest would be difficult to come by later on. And getting a good night's sleep would be completely out of the question, for aside from the task of keeping the cattle moving in the desired direction all day, each of the riders must devote an additional two hours a night to guard duty.

And that was only when things were going well.

26

During the first week, by which time the cattle usually became trail-broke, or at any other time when the animals seemed especially restless or skittish, each man would spend half the night with the herd. Then, after sleeping for four hours or less, he would be back in the saddle at daybreak. After no more than a week or two, such a schedule would begin to take its toll on a man. Indeed, of all the hardships encountered by cattle drovers, lack of sleep was probably the complaint heard most often. More than one man had been known to doze off and fall out of his saddle during a long day's drive, and at trail's end, it was not unusual for a cowboy to sleep for twenty-four hours.

Billy was still leaning on his elbow when Sampson stepped in front of the men and began to talk: "I know that nobody likes a speech," he said loudly, "and I don't reckon I could make one anyhow. But on every drive that I've ever bossed, I've always said a few words at the beginning. They all turned out all right, so I just decided to make it a habit." He twisted and turned a few times, clearly uncomfortable with this role. "I'm sure you all know that I expect every man to carry his own end of the log," he continued, "so we can just skip that part of it.

"Now, let me tell you exactly where we're going. A man named Joseph Beard owns a spread in northeastern Colorado, just west of the Nebraska line. He bought eight hundred head of breeders from Mr. Karo, and it's our job to deliver the goods. We'll be leaving here with eight hundred forty head of cows and a few old steers to lead 'em. Of course I don't expect to get there with all of 'em.

"We're bound to have at least some of the usual problems, but Mr. Karo didn't skimp on manpower. There's an even dozen of us, and I'm not bragging when I tell you that I have on two separate occasions trailed three times as many cattle, with half as many men.

"We've got plenty of horses, and every man can change mounts as often as he needs to." He paused for a moment as if to take a deep breath, then pointed northeast. "We'll travel the old Bill Johnson feeder trail for the first ten days or so. A few miles north of San Antonio it runs into the Western Trail, and we'll follow the Western Trail almost to the end of our destination." He stood smiling for a few moments. "Dodge City is as far north as I've ever been, so from there on, I'll be looking at new country along with most of you.

"We'll use two point riders, two swing riders, two flank riders, and two men riding drag. The point men, who will be Bailey Eddings and Bo Carson, will maintain their same positions for the duration of the drive. Everybody else will rotate, with every man moving up one position each day. Not only will he move up one position, but he will change sides, so that when we get to Colorado, each man will have eaten about the same amount of dust." He paused again, then waved his arm in a sweeping motion toward the loafing riders. "As soon as the cook finishes dinner, I want all four of you to eat up, then relieve the men guarding the herd." That said, he headed for the woods to relieve himself. "We'll put 'em on the trail shortly after daybreak," he said over his shoulder.

During the afternoon and night, Billy was introduced to every member of the crew. Aside from the trail boss, the cook, and Bailey Eddings, Free shook hands with Bo Carson, Rusty Oglethorpe, Hank Dew, Jim Fleming, Kirby Ewing, John Rocker, Joe Bullard, and Lenny Noble. Young Noble had been assigned the position of nighttime horse wrangler, more often called the nighthawk. Although Free talked with Lenny for a while, he made no mention of the fact that he knew the boy's sister. And maybe he never would. He would make that decision later.

They began to move the herd northeast two hours after sunup next morning. At the drovers' first attempt to move them out, the cattle had begun to mill, creating a problem that lasted for more than an hour. Finally, with the four steers in front and some of the older cows directly behind them, the herd began to move toward the top of the hill. After several minutes, with the point men and the swing riders pressing them constantly, the herd gradually narrowed to four animals abreast and took on the appearance of a trail drive.

The trail boss rode far out in advance of the herd, and Carson and Eddings both rode point, as they would for the entire trip. Carson, who had first asked for two volunteers to ride drag, had then assigned the others to their positions as swing or flank riders. All of which would not be necessary again for the duration of the drive, for every man would simply move forward one position each morning.

The chuck wagon, with the cook driving a four-horse team, also traveled well in advance of the herd, off to the trail boss's left. The two could quite easily carry on a conversation if the need arose. Off to the right and also in front of the herd was the remuda. Joe Bullard was the daytime horse wrangler. Miss Muffet was traveling with Bullard's bunch this morning, for having no idea what she did or did not know about herding longhorns, Free had chosen to ride a small bay that knew the job well.

Then he and Kirby Ewing had volunteered to ride drag.

Lenny Noble's job as nighttime horse wrangler required that he be awake all night every night, and though he was at the moment riding in the chuck wagon, lying atop the soft bedrolls and grabbing a few winks, that luxury would surely be short-lived. A nighthawk got even less sleep than anyone else on a trail drive, for in addition to watching the horses all night to keep them from straying, he was expected to perform myriad chores for the cook, among them rustling firewood and washing pots and pans.

During the first week, the drovers had only a few problems, and none that they had not anticipated. Most of the cows had been driven before, and aside from the ones who tried to double back to rejoin their weanlings left behind at the Circle K, seemed content to follow the steers all day.

Having been traveled by South Texas herds for the past several summers, the old Bill Johnson Trail was clearly marked, and the creek and river crossings were shallow. None of the streams that the Circle K crew had encountered so far had turned out to be anything worse than a slight inconvenience. At times appearing to be pushing the lead steers, and sometimes actually nosing them forward, the cows had taken to the water eagerly, and though they had already crossed the Navidad, Lavaca, and Guadalupe Rivers, no animal had been forced to swim. Cattle and horses alike had merely waded across on the streams' rocky bottoms.

During the late afternoon of the seventh day, they threw the herd off the trail and onto good grass, then set up camp within seeing distance of the town of Seguin. By the time they had seated themselves in a semicircle around the campfire and the coffeepot, with each man holding a tin plate filled with beans and bacon, twilight had come upon them, and the lights from the town could now be seen.

Bo Carson, a big man with a slight limp who at forty was the oldest of the drovers, threw his coffee grounds over his shoulder and walked to the fire. He motioned toward the lights. "What's that little town out yonder like?" he asked of no one in particular as he refilled his coffee cup. "Any of you ever been there?"

Though several men spoke up at the same time, John Rocker's voice was the loudest. "I've been there a few times," he said. "None of my visits were planned, though. I just went along because that's what the rest of the crew wanted to do at the time. As for what it's like, it's just a wide spot in the road where there's little to do besides drink. Good place to sip a few and move on, but a lousy place to light."

"You don't know what you're talking about, Rocker," Hank Dew said in a sarcastic tone of voice. "The times I was there I remember thinking that it was one of the nicest little towns I'd ever been in." John Rocker exhaled a deep, audible breath, but refused to argue with the man. He scraped the last of the beans from his plate and dropped it into a tub of water, then disappeared into the woods.

Although the drive was young, Hank Dew's disposition had already become a thorn in the side of most of the drovers. A prematurely balding six-footer who appeared to be a couple years shy of thirty, he was forever complaining about one thing or another and never passed up a chance to disagree with somebody.

Billy Free himself had had a few words with the man during the noon stop the day before, when Dew had chosen Lenny Noble to pick on: "I'm gonna tell you something, boy," Dew had said, "and if you don't want a good spanking you damn well better listen. You've brought my horse up last for two mornings in a row now. I want him brought up first. Do you understand?"

Lenny Noble was a slick-faced, soft-spoken youngster who reminded Free of his own brother, Toby. The two were the same age and about the same size, and Billy had decided

early on that at a distance they looked remarkably alike in the
way they carried themselves. "Yes, sir, I understand," Lenny
said in answer to Dew's question. "I don't actually pick out
the ones I bring up first, though. I just get whichever ones are
the easiest to catch."

"Well, like I said, I want mine up here first, and if you
don't want that spanking I mentioned, you'd better make sure
that he's the easiest to catch." He paused to blow on a book
of cigarette papers in an effort to separate them, then continued. "Now, if you don't believe I'll—"

"Leave the boy alone, Dew!" The authoritative command
had come from the man the drovers knew as Bill Jones, and
had been heard by every man present.

Dew's response was equally loud. "You stay out of this,
Jones! It ain't a damn bit of your business!" When Free made
no other comment for the moment, Dew began to snicker,
adding, "What makes you think I'd pay any attention to you,
anyhow?"

Free spoke quickly and loudly: "I don't care whether you
pay any attention to me or not, Dew! I told you to leave the
boy alone, and I meant it. If you start in on him again, I'll stop
your ass."

None of the drovers spoke. Finally Lenny Noble got to his
feet. He walked to where Free sat with his legs crossed, and
reached for Billy's empty plate. "You want me to get you some
more beans, Mr. Jones?"

Free shook his head. "No, thank you, Lenny." He got to
his feet and dropped his plate into the tub, then disappeared
behind the chuck wagon. A moment later, he mounted Miss
Muffet and rode toward the herd to relieve one of the hungry
drovers.

27

★

A few miles north of San Antonio they threw the herd on the well-marked cattle road known as the Western Trail, which at this point led in a true northerly direction. Having been trampled by the hooves of at least a million head of cattle and horses, the earth of the trail had been cut several inches deep and was completely barren of vegetation. Dozens of herds had no doubt passed this way already this year, and judging from the fresh droppings, another bunch was no more than a day or two ahead.

All of the Circle K drovers were glad to finally be on the big Western Trail, even though it was at present a mess. It had rained most of the night before, and water, which would no doubt become a scarce commodity at a later date, stood in every rut. And the hooves of the longhorns immediately turned the water into mud. Though the drovers wore their slickers all day, most of them cursed a little more than usual, for both men and horses were covered with muck that was almost as sticky as glue.

The longhorns had seemed to be in their element, however, and had taken to the muddy trail eagerly. The lead steers
had set a faster pace of their own accord, a pace that the trail
boss allowed them to hold right on through the dinner hour.
Then, three hours before sunset, Sampson stopped in the middle of the road and signaled the drovers to split the herd and
throw it off the trail. Because the animals had not been allowed to graze and the riders had passed up their own noon
meal, the day's traveling was over at least two hours earlier
than usual.

The cows were driven in a circle till they milled down to
a halt and began to graze. Then Sampson joined the drovers
and spoke to each man individually. "I'm sorry about trailing
right on through the dinner hour," he said when he reached
Billy Free. "We'll get an early supper, then start a little later
than usual in the morning. I don't intend to make a habit of
it, but I just couldn't see making a noon stop when everything
was going so good. I mean, a few times I felt like the herd was
gonna run over me, 'cause them cows didn't want to slow
down for nothing." He shook his head and glanced at the sky,
then added, "I'd bet a dollar that we've covered at least eighteen miles today, and it's still a good three hours till dark."

Free nodded, saying nothing, and Sampson rode on to the
next man.

They ate an early supper of johnnycake and beef stew. At
least the cook called it beef stew. Billy thought it was vegetable soup, for he had eaten two bowlfuls and neither saw
nor tasted any meat. He did not openly dispute Santa's decla-
ration, however, for according to traditional trail-drive eti-
quette, a meal was whatever the cook said it was.

Bert Sampson expressed the opinion that, unlike a herd of
four-year-old steers, it was highly unlikely that the brood cows
would stampede at any time during the drive, and for the past
several nights he had assigned only two men at a time to guard
duty. The riders would slowly circle the herd in opposing directions for two hours, usually with one or both of them sing-

ing, then one of them would awaken the two drovers who were scheduled to relieve them.

Though the night guards worked an average of two hours, the last shift of the night could sometimes turn out to be much longer. On days when they set up camp earlier than usual or if the weather was cloudy, the last two men on night guard might have to circle the herd for three or four hours. Nonetheless, they would stay with the cattle till relief came at daybreak.

The sun was still an hour above the western horizon when the cook yelled that supper was ready. Free filled his plate and his coffee cup, then took a seat on a large rock twenty yards from the chuck wagon. Though the remainder of the drovers sat in a semicircle closer to the campfire, Lenny Noble seated himself on the ground beside Billy. The youngster ate like there would be no tomorrow for a few minutes, then spoke around a mouthful of food: "Why do you treat me so good, Mr. Jones? How come you made Mr. Dew quit messing with me?"

Billy was slow to answer, for the fact was, he had no answer. "I don't know, Lenny," he said finally. "It just seemed to me that you were a likable young fellow, and several times I noticed you going out of your way to please somebody else. Besides, I think everybody ought to be treated good."

"Me, too," Lenny said, then picked up Billy's empty cup. "I'll get us some more coffee," he said.

Free finished eating and then took a seat on the ground beside Lenny. Billy had decided several days ago to eventually discuss the fact that he was acquainted with the young wrangler's sister, and right now, with all of the other drovers out of earshot, seemed like a good time. "I knew who you were before I even talked to anybody at the Circle K, Lenny," Free said, speaking low enough that only the youngster could hear. "Your sister told me about you."

The boy swallowed hard. "Bess?" he asked excitedly. "You know Bess?"

Free put a forefinger to his lips to caution the youngster against speaking so loudly, then dropped the volume of his own voice even lower. "I know Bess well. In fact, we're gonna be married when I get back from this trail drive."

Lenny shook his head several times, then sat staring at the ground between his legs. "You and Bess married," he said as if talking to himself. "You're gonna be my brother-in-law." He put his hand on Free's shoulder and squeezed. "That's gonna be real nice."

Billy patted the youngster's arm and smiled broadly. "That's the same way I've got it figured," he said. "Bess and I intend to go farther west, and we thought you might want to come and live with us after we get settled."

Lenny nodded eagerly. "That's gonna be real nice," he repeated.

Billy motioned toward the other drovers. "All of this is really none of their business, Lenny, so let's just keep it between the two of us."

"Yes, sir. You can trust me to keep my mouth shut, Mr. Jones."

"I'd appreciate it if you'd just call me Billy. Especially when nobody else is around."

"Billy," Lenny repeated, smiling. "All right." He was getting to his feet now. "Mr. Bullard's put in a long day, and it's time I relieved him at the horse herd." He dropped his cup and plate in the tub, then mounted and headed for the remuda.

At the first hint of darkness, Billy spread his bedroll beside the rock and stretched out. He could sleep for four hours before it was time for his guard duty. Sleep did not come right away, however, for he had too much on his mind. He was thinking of Bess Noble and wondering if at this very moment she might be thinking of him. He was glad that he had told Lenny about their acquaintance and their plans to be married, and the news had obviously been pleasing to the boy.

But even though he was anxious to start a new life with Bess Noble as his bride, Billy was nonetheless glad that he had signed on for the trail drive. He was learning things that he otherwise might never have known, gaining knowledge every day that might serve him well in the future. Just by listening, he had learned something about the huge margin of profit to be made from longhorn cattle.

With the ten-dollar Texas cows bringing anywhere from thirty to thirty-five dollars a head at the railroad or on the Northern ranges, it should be relatively easy for a man who already had enough money to get into the business, to make a killing. With a trail boss being paid a hundred dollars a month, the cook about fifty, the drovers thirty-five, and grub for a dozen men costing about a hundred dollars a month, the moneymen got off light.

Sampson had said that the overall cost of moving a herd was about a dollar a mile. A dollar a mile! Billy repeated to himself. A thousand dollars for this bunch, since they would be trailing for about a thousand miles. He lay multiplying the figures in his mind for a while, then was shocked at the answer: eight hundred cows, at thirty-five dollars a head, came out to twenty-eight thousand dollars.

Billy was thinking that in truth, all but a thousand of those dollars were profit, since Karo did not and never had owned the land on which the cattle had been raised. He had dragged their ancestors out of the river brakes shortly after the Civil War, then laid claim to at least two hundred thousand acres of public property. With over three hundred square miles of free grazing land, the man had for the past decade been shitting in tall cotton while the original herd presented him with a new generation of free cattle every year.

As far back as 1868, the Circle K had driven cattle up the Chisholm Trail to Abilene, and nowadays sent one to three herds up the Western Trail to Dodge City every year. While listening to conversations carried on by drovers who had been acquainted with the family for many years, Billy had come to understand that the free-cattle-and-free-grass business had turned the Karos, originally dirt farmers of meager means, into a family of great wealth.

Billy held no ill will in his heart for old man Karo; he only wished that he himself could do the same thing. The time was gone when a man could do it all on a shoestring, however. Wild longhorns were scarce in the brakes and thickets these days, and a man would likely have to own, lease, or buy his grazing land.

28

The weather was pleasant for the next ten days, and the drive uneventful. They had camped on the north bank of the San Saba River last night and had traveled for only about four hours this morning when Sampson ordered the herd split and thrown off the trail. "Sure is a pretty day for driving," he said to the drovers after the herd had been circled and brought to a halt, "but we'll hold 'em here till sunup tomorrow. Right now we're gonna have dinner a little bit early, then me and the cook's got a short trip to make.

"We're running low on grub and a few other things, and the town of Brady is no more than three miles from here. Me and Santa'll take the chuck wagon in and pick up what we need. We should be back long before sunset." He pointed to a stunted mesquite. "We'll take the bedrolls out of the wagon and put 'em under this tree. We can reload 'em before we pull out in the morning."

Two of the drovers unloaded the bedrolls. Then after the cook had warmed up and served leftover beans and johnnycake, he and the trail boss climbed to the wagon seat and headed for Brady.

Free sat on his bedroll sipping coffee for much of the afternoon, moving his seat several times as the meager amount of shade offered by the mesquite crawled ever eastward. Then, two hours before sunset, he saddled Miss Muffet and rode to the herd for his turn at guard duty.

He had deliberately left the filly in the remuda for the past few days, using her only to circle the herd at night. There were simply too many ways for a horse to get hurt on a trail drive. Due to the swift starts, quick turns, and sudden stops required of a cow pony, pulled tendons were common, and broken legs not unheard of. Free feared that some such thing might happen to his own speedy animal, so he had decided against riding her during the day. From now on she would be reserved for night duty. Changing mounts every few hours, he would use the fifteen-dollar horses from the remuda for the grueling daytime work.

Free had been circling the herd for less than an hour when he saw the chuck wagon returning from town. As the cook parked the wagon beside the mesquite tree, the trail boss jumped to the ground and mounted the nearest horse. Free halted his animal and sat waiting, for he could clearly see that the young foreman was headed in his direction.

The knowing look on Sampson's face was easy to read as he came to a sliding stop beside Miss Muffet. He sat quietly for a few moments, however, as if concentrating on choosing the right words. "I ran into a United States marshal while I was in Brady," he said finally. "His name is Bill Fink." He reached inside his shirt and handed over a wanted poster, the subject of which bore a striking resemblance to the man he knew as Bill Jones.

The new poster was a little different from the original: the reward had now been raised to two thousand dollars, and the smaller print at the bottom of the page stated that Bill Fink was now a United States marshal, with offices in Tom Green,

Concho, and McCulloch Counties. Billy read the poster with a long face, for he knew that he was at this very moment in McCulloch County.

"I tore that dodger off a post right in the middle of town," Sampson was saying, "and I talked with Fink afterward. He wanted to know the name of every man on this crew and exactly what he looked like. I told him that I wasn't very good at describing people; that my whole bunch looked sort of ordinary.

"Fink says he'll be out here to look the crew over himself some time before dark." He glanced at the sun, then added, "That ain't gonna be long from now." Clearly uncomfortable, Sampson fidgeted about in his saddle, then began to bite his lower lip. "Now, if you're afraid that marshal might mistake you for the man on that dodger, you can just hit the trail before he gets here." He began to fish around in his pocket. "I reckon you ought to have about twenty-eight dollars coming; I can give that to you."

Without a word, Billy held out his hand and Sampson laid the money in it. Free stood in his stirrups and took a long look toward town, then turned his mount toward the chuck wagon, saying, "Good-bye and good luck, Bert Sampson. I don't meet many men like you."

He spoke to no one when he rode into camp, just dismounted and began to gather up his belongings. Moving quickly, he tied his bedroll and blankets behind the cantle, checked his saddlebags to make sure that his extra Peacemaker was close to hand, then shoved his Winchester in the boot.

He had just thrown his leg over his saddle when five riders topped the rise. Coming from the direction of Brady, they rode at a canter and were no more than two hundred yards away. Though he gave the group no more than a quick glance before turning his own mount in the opposite direction, Free had no doubt whatsoever that the man riding in the middle was the newly appointed United States marshal, Bill Fink.

Billy could hear the riders shouting back and forth among themselves, and when he looked over his shoulder he was not surprised to see that they had passed up the drovers' camp in order to follow him. They had now pushed their horses to a hard gallop, hell bent on overtaking the fleeing drover. Deciding to show Fink and his men early on that they were not chasing a plow horse, Free gave his mount some slack in the reins and dug in his heels, sending the signal that Miss Muffet had been waiting for.

The filly pinned back her ears and stretched out, and a short time later, Free could hear the riders shouting to each other again. After several hundred yards the distance between the pursued and the pursuers increased dramatically, however, and the sound of their voices was lost in the wind.

The straightaway was more than a mile long, and Billy held the same gait till he had crossed it. As he took to the timber, a glance over his shoulder told him that his antagonists were several hundred yards behind him, still out on the wide-open meadow. Dismounting behind a clump of saplings, he quickly tied the filly, then yanked his Winchester from the boot.

Resting the barrel of the rifle on a low-hanging limb, he fired a shot a few yards in front of the riders. When they made no effort to even slow down, he fired twice more in quick succession, putting one shot on each side of the middle rider. This time there was an immediate reaction. The man's horse appeared to stumble, then regain its footing. All five of the riders slowed and eventually came to a halt.

With their nervous horses stomping their feet, snorting and turning in circles, the riders held their position, which was now well within earshot of the timber. When Fink cupped his hands around his mouth and began to yell, Free had no problem hearing him. "Come on down here and give yourself up, Billy Free!" he shouted. "We can work this out so nobody gets hurt!"

Free was not about to pass up this chance to read the man

off. He cupped his own hands and shouted back. "You mean so you don't get hurt, you no-good son of a bitch! What I should have done a minute ago was put a slug between your goddamn eyes instead of just trying to scare your horse!" He sat quietly for a few moments, then began to shout again. This time he was not speaking to Fink, but to his companions. "I'm wondering why you other four men let that crooked bastard lead you around."

He replaced the spent shells in his rifle, then sat waiting for a response from somebody in the meadow. When none came, he spoke to them all again. "If any of you men have as much sense as God gave a rabbit, you can see that this chase is over for today. None of you is gonna get any closer to this timber than you are right now. Everybody just go on home before I lose my patience." No one moved.

When he fired another shot into the ground between the two lead horses, one of the animals almost jumped out from under its rider. Then, even as Fink and his men engaged each other in conversation, they were turning their horses and heading back the way they had come. Billy watched them all the way across the meadow. With darkness coming on, he could not tell whether they had stopped at the drovers' camp or kept on going.

29

As darkness closed in, Billy remounted and rode over the hill, picking his way through the woods at a walking gait. He was under no illusion that his antagonists would give up the chase, and he wanted to put some distance between himself and Bill Fink. With the moon being in its first-quarter phase, it would provide enough light for him to find his way, but not enough for the marshal to follow the filly's tracks.

When he rode out of the thick stand of timber on the north side of the hill, he left the woods and headed east. He was now on a grassy plain, and though a thin cloud diminished the amount of light the moon offered, he was nonetheless able to distinguish the outlines of bushes and stumps for a distance of a hundred yards or more. He kicked the filly to a ground-eating trot and held the same gait till he came to a wagon road that ran north and south.

He took to the road without a second thought, for he wanted to mix the filly's tracks with those of as many other horses as was possible. He turned south and pushed the animal to a canter.

Half an hour later he came to a stream that, unknown to him, was called Brady Creek. At the ford, the filly took to the shallow water eagerly. He halted midstream and allowed her to drink as much as she wanted. Sitting his saddle and looking downstream, listening to the animal suck up the life-sustaining liquid, he decided that the creek just might be his saving grace.

Moments later, the filly was traveling in an easterly direction down the middle of the stream, wading water that was anywhere from knee- to belly-deep. Though Billy received a few bumps and scratches after first taking to the creek, as the night wore on and the clouds disappeared, the moon shone bright enough that he could usually avoid contact with the limbs and briars that often hung out over the water.

He stayed in the creek for most of the night, stopping every few minutes to let Miss Muffet blow. Wading water was in itself hard work, and fighting the sticky mud on the bottom of the creek made it even more tiring for the animal.

Billy intended to rest her well tomorrow, however. Even now he was keeping his eye open for a good place to hole up. As soon as he came upon the right spot, he would spread his bedroll and allow the filly to rest and graze till noon. Then he would begin to make his way south leisurely, for he simply did not believe that Bill Fink could track him after such a diversionary tactic as was taking place right now. He believed that once he had left the water, Fink or any other tracker who found his trail would do so out of blind luck.

A few hours before daybreak, he reached the point where the creek emptied into a river that he correctly assumed was the San Saba. He reined the filly to the south bank, where, dodging saplings and feeling her way through the briars and undergrowth, she heaved herself and her two-hundred-pound burden to the top of the steep slope. There she halted of her own accord and stood panting, her sides rising and falling dramatically.

Billy dismounted quickly and began to pet the animal. He had never before heard her breathe so hard. Though she had shown no signs of being winded while in the water, fighting the sticky mud on the creek bottom for so many miles had obviously pushed her close to the limit of her endurance.

He loosened the cinch and talked to the filly softly for a while, continuing to rub her neck and ears. When her panting subsided quickly, he decided that all she needed now was to rest. He led her to a nearby clump of small trees, then stripped the saddle. He tied his two picket ropes together, then led her into the meadow and sank the picket pin deep into the soft earth. With twice as much rope, the hungry animal could reach twice as much grass.

He returned to the thicket and spread his bedroll beside his saddle. Then, with his Winchester and both of his Peacemakers within easy reach of his right hand, he dozed off quickly.

The sun was well above the eastern horizon the next time he opened his eyes, and a glance at his watch told him that it was past eight o'clock. He had slept this late a few times before, but certainly not since he had been working on the trail drive. Like everybody else following the herd, he had not had a good night's sleep since signing on, which was probably the main reason he had suddenly died after taking to his bedroll last night.

He stood up and stretched his neck to check on the filly, then sat back down after he saw that she was contentedly cropping grass at the end of her picket rope. He pulled on his boots, then put on his hat and buckled on his gunbelt, which were the only things he had taken off last night. Then he got to his feet. He knew immediately that he was a hungry man, and that he would very shortly be hunting for something to eat. But first he would see to his animal.

With his Winchester in his hand, he watered the filly, then led her to a new patch of grass and stomped the picket pin back into the ground. Jacking a shell into the chamber of the Winchester, he walked to the riverbank to begin searching for his breakfast.

A rabbit he shot a few minutes later provided a tasty meal, for he had both salt and pepper in his saddlebags. After he had eaten and stretched out on his bedroll again, his thoughts very quickly turned to Bess Noble. Though he knew that few men would call her a beauty, she was a pleasure to be around, and he believed that she loved him at least as much as his mother did. And he loved her, too; loved her and wanted her to be the mother of the children that he hoped to have someday.

During the past several days he had begun to wonder if there really was a place where he and Bess could live out their lives peacefully. With him first being wanted in the East, and now in the central part of the country, California seemed like the only place left. He had been told that, like Texas, California was big; that a man could use any name he wanted and blend in easily. It was truly a land of sunshine, he had been told, and a man was seldom questioned about his past.

Billy did not intend to take Bess to California or anywhere else, however, until after she knew exactly who he was and where he had come from. She must be told about the warrants in Mississippi as well as those in Texas. She must fully understand that Billy Free was a wanted man, and that one lawman or another might hound him for the rest of his life.

If he continually worked his way south he would see Bess within the next two weeks; then he would tell her all of these things. And he had something else that he wanted to discuss with her. Lately he had been thinking that it might be best if he first went to California alone, then sent for her when he got settled. He did not expect her to like the idea, but he would mention it anyway.

Billy's stomach was uncomfortably full, and he continued to lie on the bedroll waiting for his breakfast to digest. "If a full-grown man ain't got nothing but meat to eat, he ort to eat at least two pounds of it every day," he remembered his mother saying, at a time when the only food in the cabin was a deer he had shot. According to her words, he probably would not really need anything else to eat until tomorrow. The rabbit had dressed out about two pounds, and he had eaten it all.

At noon, he saddled the filly and headed southeast. He had decided against going back to the Circle K Ranch for his mule and packsaddle, for he believed that it could be dangerous. There was at least a chance that somebody on the ranch had learned his true identity by now. If so, and they decided to try to collect the reward, he would be greatly outnumbered.

And even if that was not the case, there were other things to consider. First, he would have to explain to Ben Karo exactly why he was not still with the herd, and a good explanation Billy did not have. If he told Karo that he had quit, it would make him look like a no-account who could not be depended on to keep his word. If he said that he had been fired, he would appear to be a worthless drifter who was not even worth his johnnycake. In either case, Karo would probably charge him more for the mule's upkeep than the animal was worth.

Telling Karo the real reason he had quit the herd was out of the question, so Billy would forfeit the mule and the packsaddle. He could probably replace them both for twenty dollars if he kept his eyes open, but for the moment, the last thing he needed was a pack animal. With a U.S. marshal and a posse on his trail, there was no telling when he might have to move out in a hurry. Then if he happened to be leading a pack animal he would have to turn it loose, for there was probably not a pack horse in the world that could keep up with Miss Muffet.

He rode southeast all afternoon, and by sunset was halfway across San Saba County. With neither water nor wood being a priority, he made a dry camp just before dark.

He had filled both of his canteens about two hours ago, and the filly had drunk her fill at the same spring. And since he had no food to cook, no coffee to boil, and the time when a man needed a fire to keep him warm was several months away, he had no reason to be concerned about fuel. He staked the filly out on the long rope, then spread his bedroll fifty yards away.

Due to the fact that he had slept so late that morning, then dozed off again after eating the rabbit, sleep was several hours in coming. Nonetheless, he realized very quickly that he had lucked out in choosing a campsite. One of the good things about camping on a dry plain was that sometimes a man found a spot where he did not have to fight mosquitoes. Tonight he had dropped his bedroll in exactly the right place.

He lay thinking for a long time, wondering what Bill Fink would do next. There was absolutely no chance that he would give up the chase and go on to something else. The federal government was paying him a salary plus traveling expenses, and he could no doubt make the list of expenses read just about any way he wanted it to. He had finally been appointed to a position that at least a few people respected; a position that allowed him to see the country, sleep in the best hotels and eat in the finest restaurants, while billing it all to Uncle Sam. No, sir, Bill Fink was not about to give up the chase, and Billy was confident that he would see the man again.

And Free was not surprised that the man had reappeared in his life on a Monday, for as long as Billy could remember, Monday had been his unlucky day. Both of his stepfathers had died on that day of the week. The first time his mother temporarily lost her mind was on a Monday afternoon. And early one Monday morning during the year he was nine, Billy had fallen out of a tree and broken an arm and a leg.

It was on a Monday night that Will Kipling had barged into Amy Shelton's cabin, leaving Billy no choice but to kill him and his brother. Then on New Year's Eve 1877, which had been another Monday, Billy had been forced to kill Frank Poe in San Angelo. He had also dispatched Frank Poe's brother Foster on a Monday. And on what day of the week had he shot out Willy Bouton's throat because the man had tried to shoot him in the back? A Monday.

In fact, every single bad thing that Billy could remember ever happening to him had come about on a Monday. He thought about all of those things for a long time, then finally managed to push them out of his mind. He was going to be all right, he began to tell himself. Anyway, he had five more good traveling days before Monday came around again. He turned onto his other side and went to sleep.

30

★

He headed south on the Llano road at sunup, and an hour before noon came upon a covered wagon parked at a spring beside the road. He could see the wagon team grazing a short distance away, but saw no sign of human activity. Choosing to ignore it, he had already ridden past the vehicle when a woman's voice called out to him: "Mister! Will you help us, mister?"

When he pulled up and turned his animal broadside, he could see the lady seated on the ground on the far side of the wagon. A man lay beside her with his head in her lap. Billy sat his saddle for a few moments, then kneed the filly back up the road to the rear of the wagon. With his right hand on the butt of his Colt, he raised the flap and looked inside. Then, convinced that no one was in the wagon, he dismounted and tied the filly to the rear wheel. "I apologize for peeking, lady," he said softly, "but I don't trust people near as much as I used to."

"I understand," she said. With graying hair and deep lines in her weathered face, she appeared to be about fifty years old. And although the morning was actually a little on the warm side, she wore a sweater that appeared to be made of wool and an ankle-length dress made from some other kind of thick material. It was obvious that the head she cradled had very recently taken a beating, and she was in the process of smearing salve on the many cuts and bruises. "My name is Emma," she said softly, "and this is my husband. His name is Clint Spalding."

The man was a six-footer who appeared to be a few years older than his wife. He had the same leathery complexion and was clean shaven except for a thin white patch of hair on his upper lip. With a distorted facial expression that indicated he was in great pain, he slowly lifted his gray eyes till they made contact with those of Free. "They . . . damn near . . . beat me to death, son," he said haltingly. "I . . . I reckon they thought I was dead. They—"

"You just lie there and rest, old-timer," Billy interrupted. "Don't try to say anything else." Then he turned to the woman. "Now, who was it that did it, and why?"

"They seemed to enjoy it. One of them, the redheaded one with the rotten teeth, was laughing all the time." She wiped a tear off her cheek, then dabbed at her eyes. "They didn't stop beating on Clint even after they got our money. We would have given them what we had without a struggle, 'cause neither one of us is able to fight."

Billy stood quietly for a while, trying to get the situation straight in his mind. "Can I do something to help?" he asked finally.

"Lord, I don't know. Don't see that there's anything you can do. I guess that when I saw you riding right on by, it just seemed like you ought not to be leaving us here by ourselves. Clint's afraid they might come back."

"They won't," Billy said. "I don't know that they won't come back, but they won't hit your husband again. I'll stay around for a while."

"Well, bless your heart, son. I'll bet you know how to use

that thing on your hip to back up what you say, too." She cushioned her husband's head on a folded blanket, then got to her feet. "Don't suppose you had no breakfast this morning." She began to stir the ashes of the dead campfire. "Probably ain't even had no coffee, since you ain't packing no pot."

Billy smiled broadly. "You're right on all counts, ma'am."

She handed him a blackened coffeepot. "Wash this out over there at the spring and bring back a pot of water. I'll get this fire going again. We had some leftovers from our own morning meal, but the robbers ate it all."

Half an hour later, Billy was eating a late breakfast of biscuits, thick slices of smoked ham, and eggs. He ate till he would have been embarrassed to continue, then sat drinking one cup of coffee after another.

The lady was a talker. Even as he ate, she had been busy telling him exactly who they were, why they happened to be on this lonely stretch of road, and more of their life history than he really cared to know.

She had been married to Clint Spalding since she was sixteen years old, and the union had produced no offspring. Her husband, who was ten years older, was a jack-of-all-trades who had tried his hand at a variety of things over the years. Though he had never stayed with any particular thing for very long, he had nonetheless been a good provider, and the marriage had been a happy one.

Spalding's most recent venture had been a hardware store in Dallas. He had operated the business for more than two years, then sold it at a profit three weeks ago. "We only paid three hundred dollars for that store," Emma was saying. "We got a thousand when we sold it, so I reckon we done all right. We still had over eight hundred dollars after we paid off all of our bills, enough to build us a good house after we got to Fredericksburg.

"You see, my husband's nephew lives at Fredericksburg, and he's been after us to move down there for years. He say's that Clint can pick up enough odd jobs around there to support us, since we'd own our own home and wouldn't have to pay no rent. Of course, we ain't gonna have that house now, not since them men took all of our money."

Billy finished his coffee, then turned the cup upside down on a rock. "Which direction did the men come from, Miss Emma, and which way were they headed when they left?"

She pointed. "They came up the road from the south. Then when they got done with us, they just turned around and headed back in the same direction they came from."

He nodded. "Did either of them ever say anything to give you an idea about where they might be going?"

"Don't know for sure. The redhead did most of the talking, and he started laughing and carrying on like a little kid when he saw how much money was in Clint's poke. He kept throwing one of the double eagles into the air and catching it; talking about how much more profitable robbing old men was than working. Then he began to rattle a handful of the gold coins, saying, 'Ain't none of them Llano poker players gonna bluff me out of a pot today.'" She pointed south again. "I made it a point to remember that, 'cause I know there's a town up ahead called Llano."

"Yes, ma'am," he said, "it's not very far, either." Pointing toward the couple's wagon team, he got to his feet. "I'm gonna water your horses, then move them to new grass."

When he returned to the wagon, he watered his own animal, then mounted. "I intend to find out whether I can help you or not," he said, "so I'm gonna take a ride into Llano."

"You going after them men that robbed us?"

"Maybe. It would help if you can give me a good description of them, I mean something more than the fact that the redhead has rotten teeth."

"Well, the redhead was near about as tall as you, but maybe a little skinnier. He wore a brown vest over a flannel shirt that was about the same color as his hair. The other man was several inches shorter, with dark hair. He wore no vest at all, and his flannel shirt had sort of a bluish tint. Both men wore dark pants and black hats, and both appeared to be under thirty years old." She sat thinking for a moment. "Don't reckon I noticed nothing else."

Billy smiled. "You did fine," he said. "Can you describe their horses?"

"I sure can. The redhead rode a piebald that was a good hand, maybe two hands taller than the average saddle horse. The other fellow was riding a black gelding with four stockings."

"Four? Are you sure?"

She nodded. "Four. And, yes, I'm sure."

Billy nodded, and grunted his satisfaction with the descriptions. As he turned the filly's head, the lady spoke again: "I just thought of one more thing, young man: if you happen to see my husband's poke anywhere, you sure can't mistake it for somebody else's. He made it from the hide of a calf we butchered last year, and he left the hair on it, so it wouldn't slide out of his pocket so easy. On one side, the bottom half of it is brown, and the top half is white. The other side is just the opposite, so if you ever see it, you'll certainly recognize it. Clint said it had six hundred forty dollars worth of double eagles in it, but of course they wouldn't be there now."

"You're probably right, ma'am," he said. "We'll see." He dismounted and led Miss Muffet to the spot where the robbers' horses had stood. Squatting on his haunches, he studied their tracks for a while, then remounted. "You folks just stay right where you are and make yourselves as comfortable as possible. I'm gonna leave now, but I'll be back."

"The Lord'll sure bless you, young man!" the lady called as Free guided the filly onto the road and kicked her to a canter.

31

As he rode along he was thinking that of all the things he had ever gone looking for, the dark-haired robber's horse should be the easiest to find. Black geldings with four stockings were as scarce as hen's teeth; in fact, so scarce that he had never even seen one. He chuckled and rode on. Two hours later, he reached Llano and halted at the edge of town to look the place over.

Situated in one of the more scenic areas of the Texas Hill Country, the town of Llano had first been settled in 1855. The original inhabitants had been plagued by Indians, who stole their livestock and equipment. The housewives were particularly upset with the redmen during the first year, for they even stole their clothing off the line. Nonetheless, the town was well established by 1860, with several stores, saloons, and a hotel.

Now Billy sat his saddle taking stock of the town for only a few moments, then moved off at a slow walk. He rode down one side of the town's only street and back up the other, looking for a wanted poster with his picture on it. He saw none. Even if his picture was posted somewhere about town, he was hoping that nobody would recognize him, for at the moment, he was sporting a full month's growth of thick black beard.

Now, back at the point from which he had started, he turned the filly around and headed down the street again, for he had spotted the big piebald and the black gelding on his first pass. The animals had been standing side by side at the hitching rail of a run-down saloon. When he reached the saloon for the second time, he dismounted and tied the filly alongside the robbers' animals.

He stood for a moment shaking his head, finding it difficult to believe the impudence of the men who rode those horses. They had beaten a helpless old man half to death and robbed him of his life's savings, then ridden only a few miles before stopping to get drunk. Billy believed that most men who had committed such a heartless and dangerous deed would have been more concerned about putting some distance between themselves and their victims. Why had these two halted so quickly? Because the conscienceless, insolent bastards were simply incapable of reason, he decided quickly. He shook his head again, then stepped onto the boardwalk and pushed his way through the batwing doors.

There was more light inside the large building than in most saloons, for there were more windows and the shades were open. Billy could see that two gaming tables had some action farther back in the building, but there were only two customers at the bar: the very same men that he had come here to see. The dark-haired man was sitting halfway down the bar, a mug of beer in his hand. The redhead was close beside him, standing on his right leg with his left knee resting on a bar stool. He had just upended a glass of whiskey.

Billy walked to the bar and seated himself a few stools away from the men. "I'll have a beer," he said to the middle-aged bartender.

"Yes, sir," the barkeep said. He drew a mugful of the

foamy brew, then placed it on the bar and picked up Billy's dime.

"His beer's on me, Delbert," the redhead said loudly. "In fact, everybody drinks on me today."

The bartender nodded. He gave Free's coin back to him, then walked down the bar to collect for the beer. Out of the corner of his eye, Billy recognized Clint Spalding's poke as the redhead pulled it from his vest pocket and extracted a coin. He dropped it on the bar noisily. "Ain'tcha got nothin' smaller'n a double?" the barkeep asked, looking down at the twenty-dollar gold piece.

The redhead smiled broadly, revealing the rotten teeth Emma Spalding had mentioned. He held the poke out and rattled its contents. "Ain't nothing in there but doubles," he said. "I don't carry nothing smaller nowadays." Laughing loudly, he rattled the poke again.

Knowing all of the circumstances behind the man's sudden wealth, Free had seen and heard as much as he could abide. While the bartender was busy explaining to the redhead that he did not have enough money on hand to make change for a double eagle, he also had the black-haired man's undivided attention. Billy seized the moment. He slid off his stool and drew his Peacemaker, then suddenly appeared between the two drinkers. He jerked the dark-haired man's Colt out of its holster with his left hand, then jammed the barrel of his own weapon up against the redhead's ear.

The man stiffened nervously as he heard the unmistakable sound of the hammer being cocked. "Just leave the poke there on the bar!" Billy commanded, his big voice sounding even deeper than usual. "Pick up that double eagle and put it right back in the pouch." When the man hesitated, Free poked him in the ear with the gun barrel, breaking the skin and bringing forth a drop of blood. "If I pull this trigger they'll have to scrape your brains off of that post over there, fellow. Do as I say!" Moving slowly and very carefully, the man complied.

Billy disarmed the redhead. Then with both of the men's weapons tucked behind his own waistband, he pointed to the poke and spoke to the bartender, saying, "These no-good bastards beat an old man damn near to death and took that money off of him this morning. I'm here to get it back." He pointed to the hairy pouch again. "I want you to count the money in that thing. It had six hundred forty dollars in it when they made off with it."

The bartender dumped the coins on the bar and began to separate them one at a time, mumbling to himself all the while. "Six hundred forty dollars!" he said finally, dropping the coins back into the pouch and handing it across the bar to Free. "I reckon by god you must be tellin' it straight," he said. "Otherwise, you wouldn't have had no way of knowin' how much money was in that damn thing."

"That's right, Delbert, and you're my witness if I ever need one."

"Reckon so," the man said, putting a hand to his face to stifle a sneeze. "You damn sure called that money right."

Billy shoved the pouch into his front pocket, then backed away from the bar. "You sons of bitches took advantage of the wrong people this morning," he said, finally making eye contact with both the redhead and his companion. "That man you beat up and robbed is a friend of mine, and if you ever come near him again, somebody'll be hauling your dead asses off to the graveyard." He continued to walk backward toward the front door, adding, "I'll leave your guns in the street at the edge of town, and you'd be wise to make sure that I don't ever see your ugly faces again." The dark-haired man nodded, indicating that he clearly understood.

Though Billy untied both the piebald and the black when he reached the hitching rail, neither of the animals showed any inclination to leave the area. Then when he mounted the filly and headed up the street at a hard run, both of the horses galloped after him for a short distance, then gradually gave up the chase and trotted off between two buildings. When he reached the wagon road, Free slowed his mount to a canter and turned north. He had a present for Clint and Emma Spalding.

"My land!" Emma said when Billy handed over the pouch. "Did you really get our money back? Did you have to kill them?"

"The money's all there," he said, "and I didn't kill anybody."

"My land!" she repeated. "How in the world did you make that redhead give up the poke without killing him?"

"I convinced him that I was gonna kill him if he didn't."

"Oh," she said softly. She pushed the money pouch down inside her thick stocking, then began to talk again. "I don't know why you'd want to go to so much trouble for us, but I sure do thank you. Clint will too when he wakes up and hears the news." She pointed to the iron pot. "I made some johnnycakes and boiled up some brown beans while you were gone. I didn't have no way of knowing whether you like that kind of stuff or not."

Billy chuckled softly. He was very hungry, and the lady was talking about some of his favorite food. "Just point me toward a plate and a spoon," he said, "then watch me."

32

Billy ate his fill, then washed his eating utensils at the spring. "I'll spend the night here with you folks," he said to Emma when he returned to the wagon. He dropped the tin plate, spoon, and coffee cup into a box beside the campfire. "Early in the morning we'll hitch up and head for Fredericksburg."

"Oh," she said. "I didn't know that you were going to Fredericksburg, too."

He shook his head. "I'm not. I just want to make sure that you folks get there all right."

Although she did not appear to be crying, Billy saw a tear roll off her cheek. "The Lord's gonna bless you, mister," she said for what seemed to Free like the tenth time. "Just as sure as we're sitting here, you're gonna get a big blessing."

"It's good to hear that, ma'am." He turned and headed for the meadow, adding, "I guess a good blessing is exactly what I need."

He watered the wagon team and moved them to a new

area, then staked the filly out closer to the wagon. The grass was greener and several inches taller near the spring, and the animal's long picket rope would allow her to drink from the runoff anytime she wanted.

When Billy returned to the wagon, Clint Spalding was awake and seemed to be in much better spirits. He began to talk with no trace of the halting speech pattern he had used this morning. "The wife told me what you done, young man, and I reckon you might be the only fellow in the world who could have done it. We both appreciate it to no end." Grunting with the effort, he turned onto his left side and lay still for a few moments. "Without you, we wouldn't have had a dollar to our name," he said after a while, "so the only right thing for us to do is to split that money with you."

Looking the man squarely in the eye, Billy began to shake his head. "When I was a kid, I was taught not to argue with my elders, Mr. Spalding. But this time I'm gonna have to tell you that you don't know what you're talking about. Splitting your money with me is not the right thing for you to do. The right thing for you to do is to go on to Fredericksburg and build that house you and your wife are gonna be needing."

"Humph!" Spalding exclaimed loudly. Lowering his voice, he added, "Just seems to me like you ought to be rewarded somehow."

"I've already been rewarded," Billy said quickly. "You have no idea how good I felt while I was making that redhead cough up your money. In fact, I don't think I've felt that good about anything else in years." He stirred the ashes and set the coffeepot on the gray coals, then continued, "You just keep resting till you get over that beating; I'll help you get to Fredericksburg."

Billy and Emma ate more beans and johnnycake just before sunset; then she fed some to her husband. When the meal was over, Free kicked dirt over the coals. "I don't think we should have a fire or light a lantern tonight; no reason to call attention to ourselves. If you folks will go to bed in your wagon just before dark, I'll spread my bedroll close by. The moon will provide as much light as I need to watch over everything." He pointed to a sharp rise in the terrain on the other side of the spring. "I'll be in the bushes up on that hump. Don't you worry, now, 'cause I'll be awake."

Emma patted his shoulder. "Bless you, young man."

As the sun dropped over the horizon, Billy picked up the groaning old-timer and carried him to the open tailgate. Then with Emma in the front of the wagon pulling on his arms and Billy standing outside pushing on his legs, they managed to get Clint Spalding into his bed. Groaning again, he turned himself over under his own power to make room for his wife. "Good night, sir," Billy said, dropping the canvas flap. "I believe you'll feel better in the morning."

Once he had tucked his spare Colt behind his waistband, he picked up his bedroll and his Winchester and headed for the bushes. As soon as he found a spot that was more or less level, he spread the bed so that his head would face the wagon. He lay down to find out how much of the area he could see, then began to break off sprouts, small limbs, and undergrowth. When he was done, he had a good view of everything on this side of the hump. Then he moved to the other side and repeated the process. Finally, he decided that, by keeping his head down and walking from one side of the hump to the other every few minutes, he could command a good view of everything within a quarter-mile circle.

Night came on quickly, and though it was as dark as pitch for the first hour, the moon gradually dragged itself above the distant treetops. Careful to keep his head down so as not to create a shadow, he moved from one side of the hump to the other every few minutes. On the side opposite his bed, in the direction of Llano, he could see half a mile, though he could not distinguish one object from another at that distance.

His view of the wagon road was relatively unimpaired, however; there were several short stretches and a few long ones where nothing hampered his vision, and he knew that he could spot a man on horseback long before he came into effective shooting range.

For the next several hours Billy crept back and forth between the north side of the hump, where his bedroll lay, and the south side, where he had the longest and most unobstructed view. He was unable to read the face of his watch in the dim moonlight, and he dared not strike a match. Nonetheless, he knew that it was well past midnight when he saw movement at the top of the hill. From his position on the south side of the hump, he had seen two specks on the road that could very well have been mounted men.

First he saw them, then he did not. It was several hundred yards to the top of the hill, and Billy knew that he had been able to detect their presence only because they had been moving. He also knew that he could not see them now because they had stopped or maybe left the road.

Over the years, Free had practiced and perfected the art of jacking a shell into the firing chamber of a rifle soundlessly. These days he could do it so quietly that the action would not even spook a deer, much less a human. Now, believing that he was about to have company, he eased a shell into the barrel of the Winchester and sat waiting, his eyes darting back and forth between the meadow and the section of road where he had last seen movement. He sat watching for what seemed like an hour, but saw nothing else that aroused his suspicion. Maybe his eyes had deceived him, he was thinking. After all, the moonlight was dim and the distance was long.

It was Miss Muffet who finally pointed the men out to him. He had been casually looking in her direction when she suddenly raised her head and funneled both ears toward the bushy area between the meadow and the road. Billy trusted the animal's instinctive nature completely, for he knew that sneaking up on a horse in an open meadow was next to impossible.

The bushes grew in thick clusters along the edge of the meadow, with a few yards of open, grassy area on each side of every clump. Billy raised the rifle to his shoulder, then sat with his attention focused on the cluster that the filly had unwittingly pointed out.

Then he saw two men on foot, as first one, then the other darted between two clumps of the leafy vegetation. He held his fire, for the bushes were already beginning to thin out. Very soon the intruders would be sitting ducks, for before reaching the wagon, they would have to cross a fifty-yard area that had no cover whatsoever. And they obviously intended to come all the way to the wagon, for each man had been carrying a handgun instead of a rifle. Billy took a deep breath and waited.

When they finally reached the extent of their cover, both men stepped into the open. Bent over at the waist, they trotted a short way, then stopped and began to carry on a muted conversation, nodding back and forth to one another. They came on a few more steps, then stopped again, with the taller of the two beginning to point with his gun barrel, obviously giving last-minute instructions to his partner.

Billy waited no longer. Taking a bead on the gun at the end of the tall man's outstretched arm, he fired. And though he did not see the gun leave the man's hand, he heard the rifle slug hit metal and knew that he had scored a bull's-eye. The tall man let out an oath, then grabbed his right hand and whirled back toward the bushes. Free's second shot went between the feet of the shorter man, who must have been a fast runner, for he passed his partner on the way back to cover. Billy sent two quick shots after them, making sure that he fired over their heads, then left the thicket in a hurry.

Figuring that they had surely pinpointed the position of his muzzle flash by now, he ran past his bed, the spring, and was now lying on his stomach on the opposite side of the wagon waiting, but no return fire ever came. Nonetheless, Billy lay in the deep wagon rut for a long time. He knew that he had not killed either of the men, for he had deliberately aimed to miss. He had enough problems already, and although killing them would have surely amounted to self-defense, he had no doubt that it would have put another price on his head. And another lawman on his tail.

At last he heard the sound that he had been waiting for: hoofbeats on the hard surface of the road. He lay still till the sound receded, then got to his feet. He walked to the wagon and spoke through the canvas covering: "Are you all right in there, Miss Emma?"

"Miss Emma slept right through the whole thing," Clint Spalding said. "How are you?"

"I'm fine, Mr. Spalding. I fired all four of those shots myself, but I didn't kill anybody. We were about to have company and I was just trying to discourage them. I figure it was the same two characters who beat and robbed you. I told them not to come around here again, but neither one of them struck me as being very bright."

"Are they gone?"

"I think so. At least I heard hoofbeats going over the hill. I have no idea whether they'll stay gone or not, though. Like I said, I seriously doubt that either of 'em got this far in life because of his ability to think. They both looked mighty stupid to me."

"Of course they are," Spalding said. "That's why they act the way they do." He raised the flap at the rear of the wagon and slid off the tailgate onto his feet. "A man can't stay in that thing forever without peeing," he said. He walked a few steps haltingly, then stopped and unbuttoned his fly. "The wife rubbed my chest, arms, neck, and shoulders with some of that liniment she's always bragging about. By god, I believe it works, 'cause I ain't half as sore as I was."

The two men carried on a muted conversation for a while. Then Spalding suggested that Free get some sleep. "A man can't travel all day and stay awake all night," he said. "It'll catch up with him mighty quick." He climbed back inside the wagon, and Billy saw the flare of a lighted match through the canvas. When Spalding slid back over the tailgate he had a

Spencer carbine under his arm. "Put your bedroll under th
wagon and take a nap. I'll be awake the rest of the night.
looked at my watch while I was in the wagon, and it's alread
after two o'clock."

"Do you really feel up to standing guard?"

"I feel as good out here as I would in there," Spaldin
said, pointing to the wagon. "You just get some rest. Ain't n
body gonna sneak up on me, I've still got good eyes." He pa
ted the stock of the Spencer. "This thing'll shoot a whole l
farther than I can see, too."

Free knew that to be true, for one of his cousins back i
Mississippi owned one of the deadly carbines. One Saturda
afternoon Billy had fired the seven-shot weapon several time
at a long-range target and had been amazed at its accuracy. I
had a bore like a cannon, and the .52-caliber, soft-nosed lea
bullets would certainly not leave a man looking very prett
"I'm familiar with the Spencer," Free said. "It kicks like
mule, but it delivers a hell of a punch from the business end.
He was already headed for the bushes. "I think I'll take you
advice and put my bedroll under the wagon."

He slept fitfully throughout the remainder of the night, de
spite the fact that each time he opened his eyes he could se
that Spalding was alert and on guard, standing somewher
close to the wagon with the Spencer across his shoulder. A
hour before daybreak Billy went into a deep sleep and awok
only after Emma had kindled a fire and begun to prepar
breakfast. The sun was well above the horizon when he raise
himself up on his elbows. "That sure smells good, Mis
Emma."

"Thank you," she said, bending over to stoke the fire. "
reckon it'll taste about like it has for the past thirty-fou
years."

"I guess so," Billy said, knowing nothing else to say. H
tied his bedroll with rawhide strings, then dropped it besid
his saddle. The bedroll, which actually amounted to a thic

quilt doubled and sewn inside a seven-foot-long section of tarpaulin, had been rolled and twisted so many times that it was almost as flexible as cloth, and when rolled tightly, created a surprisingly small bundle behind the cantle of his saddle. And it kept him warm and dry, even if the ground was wet.

He walked to the spring where Clint Spalding sat on a log, the Spencer still in his grasp. "Good morning," Billy said. "Are you feeling better?"

Spalding shook his head. "Seems like the soreness has crept back into me since the effects of that liniment wore off, so I reckon it's gonna be around for a while. I ain't gonna lie down and let it whip me, though. The only way to deal with stiffness is to keep moving."

"I believe you're right," Billy said, "but I think you should be careful not to overdo it." He pointed toward the meadow. "I thought I'd water your team, then hitch up the wagon. If I get that done while Miss Emma's fixing breakfast, we can hit the road right after we eat."

"Sounds all right to me," Spalding said. "I've got it figured to be about forty miles from here to Fredericksburg, so two more days of traveling will put us in there." He pointed to the pile of chains and harnesses beside the wagon tongue. "I reckon I'd be in your way hitching up, so you just go ahead and take care of it. I'll be more than happy to pay you for all this if you'll accept it."

With no further comment, Billy headed for the meadow. He watered the heavy draft animals, and half an hour later, had them hitched to the wagon. Because of her long picket rope, Miss Muffet did not have to be led to water. Even now she was standing in the middle of the spring's runoff ditch. Free led her to the wagon, cinched down the saddle, and tied his bedroll behind the cantle. Then he tied her to a wagon wheel and walked to the campfire, for Emma had just announced that breakfast was ready. "I heard all that shooting last night," she said as Billy stooped over to fill his plate. "I could tell that every shot was coming from your hiding place, though, so I figured that you had somebody on the run."

Free nodded, and sipped at his coffee. "You figured right," he said. "That's what it amounted to. As near as I could tell, it was the same two men who robbed you folks."

"We probably haven't seen the last of them either," she said, reaching for a tin plate. "They'd probably kill their mother for a few dollars." She filled the plate and handed it to her husband. "Men are a strange breed," she continued, shaking her head. "At least some of 'em are. Not only will they kill for money, but they're liable to fly off the handle and start shooting over the smallest thing imaginable. Just like my two brothers-in-law. They killed each other during an argument over a banty rooster, shot each other to pieces down at the barnyard. One of 'em died right on the spot, and the other one early next morning. Can you believe that? Two men dead over a ten-cent rooster?"

Billy did not answer. He could believe it, all right, for he knew of a man in Mississippi who had been shot dead over a five-cent poker bet.

They finished their meal in silence; then Billy washed the cooking and eating utensils at the spring. He kicked dirt over the fire and loaded the grocery box onto the wagon, then helped Clint Spalding to the seat. "Keep a sharp lookout on both sides of the road, sir." He pointed to the Spencer lying at the man's feet. "I'll be scouting pretty far ahead of you, but I'll be within hearing distance if you have to fire that cannon."

Moments later, Spalding drove the team onto the road, both he and his wife seated on folded blankets to cushion the ride. Billy rode past the wagon at a slow canter, then soon disappeared over the hill.

An hour later, at the top of a long hill, the one road split and became two. Though there was no sign at the intersection, Free knew that a right-hand turn led to Fredericksburg, and that the road to the left was what would turn out to be Llano's main street a quarter mile farther on. Wanting to make sure that Spalding took the right turn, Billy rode into the woods and sat waiting for the wagon.

When Spalding reached the fork in the road he did not even look to his left, but continued down the road to Fredericksburg. Billy sat smiling for a moment, then rode past the wagon and disappeared again.

He kept at least a hundred yards between himself and the road during the next several hours, with the only times he touched it being when he crossed it. Riding parallel to it, first on one side and then the other, he continued to ride in a wide half-circle for a closer inspection of every likely-looking ambush point. He was on the west side of the road and had just looked at his watch to see that it was eleven o'clock when he saw a quick movement off to his right.

He hauled the filly up instantly and sat with his eyes glued to a particular brushy area, waiting for whatever he had seen to move again. Though he waited for several minutes without seeing further motion, he held his position, for he was positive that he had seen movement out of the corner of his eye. Had it been nothing more than a deer darting from one clump of brush to another? It was impossible to know at this point, Billy decided, for he knew that peripheral vision was not to be trusted.

He had about made up his mind to move when he saw motion again. And this time it was not out of the corner of his eye. He was looking straight at the piebald and the black as they trotted from behind a cluster of bushes, crossed a small opening, then disappeared again. No doubt about it, the redhead and his dark-haired friend had not given up yet.

A good half mile ahead of Spalding's wagon, the men were headed in the direction of Fredericksburg and were about three hundred yards west of the road. Billy fell in behind them immediately. Each time he lost sight of them he would stop and sit his saddle till he saw them moving again. Keeping his distance and using the clumps of short cedars for cover, he followed them for at least a quarter mile. Then when they turned back toward the road, he decided that they knew exactly where they were. They had reached the point of their intended ambush.

Peeking above the top of a cedar, with his hat in his hand, Billy saw the men dismount and tie their horses to a low-hanging tree limb. Then they unsheathed their rifles and, each of them bent over at the waist, headed toward the road at a fast walk. As soon as they were out of sight, Billy stepped down from the saddle and tied the filly right where she stood. He did not bother with his Winchester, for any fighting he did now would be at close quarters.

Darting from one clump of cover to another, he began to follow the men toward the road, his cocked Peacemaker in his hand. He gave their horses a wide berth, for fear that one of them might whinny. When he topped a small rise, he saw the men disappearing over another one. Knowing that the road was halfway down the other side of the hill the men had just gone over, he began to step lively, for he knew that the Spalding wagon would be along any minute.

When he topped the next hill, he could plainly see both of the men lying behind a fallen log with their rifles trained on the road. The men were no more than twenty yards away and Billy knew that he could take them from where he stood, but he decided to see how close he could get before they became aware of his presence. He began to move forward on his tiptoes. He closed the distance to ten yards and probably could have gotten even closer, but he could now hear the wagon coming. He must move now. "You sons of bitches sure are slow learners!" he shouted loudly.

Both men whirled instantly and died just as quickly. Billy's first shot hit the redhead in the nose, and the second put out his partner's right eye. With nothing more than a loud grunt, they dropped their rifles and fell forward on their faces. Billy turned them over with the toe of his boot and saw that their eyes had now turned to glass.

Free went back over both of the ridges at a trot. He

stripped the saddle from the redhead's piebald, then, without untying the bridle from the limb, pulled it over the animal's head. The big horse whirled about, then headed in the direction of Llano. Billy repeated the process with the black, then headed for his own animal. Moments later, he mounted the filly and kicked her to a gallop. When he entered the road, he could see that Spalding had brought the team to a halt up ahead.

"I heard the shooting," Spalding said when Billy came abreast of the wagon. "Did you finally have to kill 'em?"

Billy ignored the question. He rode forward a few steps, then turned to face the couple. "You folks don't have anything to worry about now, so I believe that you can get to Fredericksburg without any more problems. I'm headed somewhere else, myself, so I'll be leaving you now. Good-bye and good luck to both of you."

Before either of the Spaldings could speak again, the filly had jumped the ditch and was carrying their young friend southeast at a lively canter.

33

★

Three days later, still headed southeast, Billy rode out of the Hill Country. At midafternoon he selected a campsite on the San Marcos River, a short distance from the town of the same name. He had decided to pay the settlement a visit, and thinking that it might possibly be dark when he returned to the river, he gathered an armload of deadwood and dropped it on the spot he had chosen for his campfire. He hoped to find a grocery store on the edge of town, for he was a hungry man. He had eaten only a small cottontail yesterday, and nothing at all today.

He remounted and guided the filly up the slope toward San Marcos. Even from a distance, he could see that a certain amount of thought had been given to the laying out of the town. The business section appeared to be clean and neat, and the residential streets were straight. Huge live oaks shaded beautiful homes that had obviously been erected by master builders.

There had been a time when Billy would have ridden about the town for no other reason than to admire its beauty, but that time was no more. Even though his thick beard covered most everything except his eyes, he dared not show his face to more people than was necessary.

The first building he came to was the livery stable. When he rode through the wide front door and dismounted, he was greeted by a freckle-faced boy who appeared to be in his early teens. "You want me to feed her and put her up for the night, sir?" the young man asked, smiling broadly.

Free handed over the reins and shook his head. "I won't be leaving her overnight," he said. "Just give her a good feed of oats and leave the saddle on. I also need an empty gunnysack if you have one around. I'll pay for it if I need to."

"Pay for a gunnysack?" the boy asked, his smile constant. "Heck, they don't cost us nothing."

"Well, that's good," Billy said, holding out his hand. "I need the sack now, if you will, 'cause I want to pick up some things while the filly eats."

The boy took a gunnysack from behind a grain bin and laid it in Billy's hand. "I don't reckon these things are worth keeping. All of our feed comes in 'em, and don't nobody ever ask for 'em back."

Billy nodded. "Is there a place close by where I can buy a few groceries?"

The boy pointed. "There's a big store two blocks down the street on your right, and there's a little one about a hundred feet from here, right over there on the corner."

"Thank you," Billy said. "I'll try the little one."

He headed for the corner, and half an hour later had enough food to last him several days. Along with a stick of Bologna sausage and a box of crackers, he had bought cheese, tinned meat, and tinned fish. He also bought a can opener and half a dozen cans of soup. As she sacked up his purchases, the middle-aged lady was looking him over knowingly. "You can heat the soup up right in the can if you don't have a pot," she said. She reached under the counter and dropped a spoon into the sack. "Maybe you can use this, too."

He smiled. The lady had him figured out, all right. "Maybe," he said. He paid for his merchandise and headed for the door. "Thank you, ma'am," he said over his shoulder.

At the stable, he tied the gunnysack to his saddle horn, then paid the boy for the filly's oats. "Mighty pretty town you've got here," he said as he threw a leg over the saddle.

"Maybe so," the boy said. "It's the only one I've ever been in, so I guess it's all right."

Billy nodded, then rode the filly through the doorway. He went down the slope at a trot and, just before he disappeared from sight, stopped and turned in his saddle for one last look at San Marcos. He liked everything that he had seen, and believed that under different circumstances, he would have tried to settle right here. The grassy plains were a cattleman's dream, and the nearby Hill Country supported abundant wild game of all shapes and sizes. Then there was the clear, cold San Marcos River, and the many kinds of fishes in its waters for the taking. He sat considering the magnificence of it all for only a few seconds, then turned his mount and continued down the slope.

He built no fire when he reached the river, for nothing that he had bought had to be cooked. He sat under the big live oak for a long time wolfing crackers and chunks of Bologna sausage, washing it down with water from his canteen. Then he opened a can of vegetable soup. Though he supposed that it would have tasted better if he had heated it, he enjoyed it just as it was, and tossed the empty can out of sight in the brush. Then, still a little hungry, he opened a can of sardines and ate them all.

When his appetite was finally satiated, he led the filly to good grass and stomped the picket pin into the ground. Then he carried his bedroll and everything else that he owned to a small thicket thirty yards away. A few minutes later he was stretched out, not even caring if he dozed off before nightfall. If he went to sleep early and then came wide awake at midnight, he would simply saddle Miss Muffet and continue his journey. The stars would guide him on his southeasterly course, even if they did cloud over at times.

He did go to sleep before dark and slept soundly. He was still sleeping like a log when, some time around midnight, he suddenly sat up on his bed, unable to tell exactly what had awakened him. After listening for several seconds he heard it again. It was a sound that he very quickly recognized: the rattle of bridle bits and chains. A moment later, sitting on his bedroll with a Peacemaker in each hand, he heard the creak of saddle leather only a short distance away.

Suddenly a deep, loud voice shattered the stillness of the night, a voice that Billy recognized as belonging to Bill Fink. "The woman at the store and the livery boy both said he came this way," Fink was saying, "so he probably forded the river right here."

"Ain't no other place within a mile of here that's shallow enough to ford," another voice answered. "Every man I know always crosses a stream before he makes camp, so we might as well ford here, then spread out on the other side." He was quiet for a moment, then started to speak again. "I don't reckon nothing I say is gonna carry any weight, but it wouldn't surprise me none if he traveled another four or five miles before he bedded down. The sun was still two or three hours high when he left the livery stable."

"What you say carries a whole lot of weight," Fink said to the man, speaking much softer now. "And you damn well might be right." Then he raised his voice again. "All right, now, let's get on the other side! All of you! Ford the river and fan out!"

The men began to move. They had come so close to his hiding place that Billy could hear their mumbling and the sound of metal horseshoes striking rocks almost as clearly as if they had been in the thicket with him. He crawled forward and peeked down toward the river, hoping to find out how many men were in the party. All of which was to no avail, for a thick cloud blocked off the light of the half-moon.

As soon as the last of the group crossed the river, Billy brought up the filly and cinched down the saddle in short order. Moments later, he mounted and headed back up the slope toward San Marcos at a fast walk. He would skirt the town, then head back into the Hill Country, where he could make life a little more difficult for his pursuers.

Once out of hearing distance of the river, he kicked the filly to a canter, for he wanted to be on the other side of the slope when the cloud moved away from the moon. He was aware of the fact that the cloud might have saved his life, for if the moon had been shining brightly the posse might very well have discovered his hiding place. Or maybe spotted the filly, who had been grazing a little farther down the meadow. The posse! Fink could undoubtedly raise a posse anywhere he happened to be with all his talk of monetary reward.

He had obviously just happened to be in San Marcos when word was passed that a stranger had been seen at the edge of town. The fact that the stranger was a tall young man who rode a tall filly and that he had bought a feed of oats and a sack of groceries and headed right back in the same direction he had come from would be all that Bill Fink needed to hear. He had no doubt been able to raise a posse right on the spot. At least the man that Billy had heard talking with Fink must have been from San Marcos, since he seemed to know the depth of the river for miles around.

Staying with his northwesterly course and riding deeper into rough terrain, Billy was trying to unravel the puzzle. As big as Texas was, and of all the other towns Fink could have been in, had he just happened to be in San Marcos today? And of all the places that Billy could have bought groceries, why in the hell had he chosen the same town? Could it all really have been happenstance? Or just dumb luck? What were the odds against the two men showing up in the same place at the same time? A million to one?

Billy thought on the many possibilities till he began to feel like he might get a headache, then discarded everything except dumb luck. He nodded at the thought. It had been dumb luck pure and simple, and would not happen again in a million years.

He rode deeper into the Hill Country. What he had in mind for the newly appointed U.S. marshal would have nothing to do with luck. He had already decided that he would do whatever he had to do to get Bill Fink off his trail.

34

★

Holding his mount to a walking gait, Billy rode for the remainder of the night. Two hours before daybreak he watered the filly from the Blanco River, then climbed higher into the hills. At sunup, he was more than a thousand feet above the valley floor. Finally halting at an overlook that offered a clear view of his back trail, he dismounted and put the filly on her picket rope.

He sat down beside a large boulder that lay very close to the edge of a two-hundred-foot drop-off, then began to eat some of the groceries he had bought in San Marcos—very expensive groceries, as it had turned out. First he ate some crackers and cheese, then two cans of soup. Then, making sure that they could not fall anywhere near his back trail, he tossed the empty cans as far out into open space as he could.

Looking around him, he decided that he had been fortunate to come upon such a perfect location. He could not imagine a better place to pull up and wait till he learned what was going on behind him. He had little doubt that Fink or somebody else in the posse would finally figure out what had happened back at the river. They would eventually turn around and scout both banks till they struck his trail. Then they would be coming.

But they would not be coming without Free being aware of it. In fact he would know their exact location two hours before they became a threat to him. From where he sat he had only to crane his neck and look down to get a bird's-eye view of the many switchbacks that he had negotiated only a short while ago. Some of them amounted to nothing but narrow, rocky ledges, where the slightest misstep could send both horse and rider into the treetops a hundred feet below. Knowing that to remain in the saddle could be risky business, Free had dismounted and, at a snail's pace, led his animal to the top.

Anyone following him would have to approach the zigzagging goat trail in the exact same manner, and Free would be waiting. From his perch at the summit, he would have the posse members in plain view as they scrambled up the rocky mountainside. And for the last hour, they would be in range of his Winchester.

He grew restless after a while and began to walk around. Fifty yards off the trail he found a seep, where several inches of water had accumulated between two large rocks. After first testing the water by tasting it from a cupped hand, he lay down on his stomach and drank all he could hold. A few minutes later, the filly drank the puddle dry. Billy led her back to her graze, knowing that if it turned out that he had to spend the night on the mountaintop, he could expect the seep to provide both him and his mount with another bellyful of water in the morning.

Back at the boulder, he surveyed the area below for several minutes, but saw no sign of life. He was not surprised, for he knew that somewhere along the line the posse would have had no choice but to stop and wait for daylight. Tracking a horse with no more light than a half-moon provided was tedious at best, and could sometimes be impossible. Billy expected it to be at least midafternoon before he saw them, for he could not imagine them doing anything other than waiting at the river till morning so they could see what they were doing. They would have no problem following his trail in the light of day, for he had made no effort to hide it.

He sat staring down the mountainside for the next hour, but nothing was stirring. Finally he lay down on his back with his arms behind his head and, within minutes, drifted off into a sound sleep. He later awoke with a start, for he could tell by the position of the sun that his nap had been a long one. A glance at his watch told him that he had slept for more than two hours.

He took up his vigil of the switchbacks again, eating some of the Bologna sausage as he watched. He had just shoved the remainder of the sausage into his saddlebag when he saw movement on his back trail. Seven riders had suddenly appeared, and though they were probably no more than half a mile away as the crow flies, the circuitous route they would have to travel would probably be ten times that far.

Having no doubt that he was looking at Bill Fink and his posse, Free lay watching them for the next hour. Though they were halfway up the mountainside now, he knew that they would have to slow down very shortly, for the closer they got to the top, the more treacherous the footing. And although he would not interfere with their progress for another hour or more, he knew that he could stop them any time he took a notion. After all, the Winchester did its traveling as the crow flies.

He brought the filly up and cinched down the saddle, then tied his bedroll and his heavy coat behind the cantle. He laid the sack containing the remainder of his food across the saddle, then tied the animal to a bush a few yards away. Then, with his rifle in his hand, he returned to the drop-off, this time taking up a position behind the boulder. He remembered that, being the narrowest of the lot, with tons of loose shale underfoot, the second switchback from the top was the most difficult to negotiate. The riders were nearing it now.

He eased a shell into the chamber of the Winchester and sat waiting. He had no way of knowing whether the rider in front was Bill Fink, but he seriously doubted it. Although it required no more than a little common sense to realize that the first position in any line of men could very easily turn out to be the most hazardous, Fink probably had at least one man in the bunch who would eagerly volunteer to lead the way up the mountainside.

On they came. Billy held his fire till three of the riders were visible on the narrow ledge, then he squeezed off a shot between the first and second horses. The second horse squealed at the top of its lungs, then reared on its hind legs and attempted to wheel around in the direction from which it had come. The rider slid off the animal's rump and landed safely in the middle of the ledge, but the horse, whirling around blindly, failed to find solid ground with its front legs. After scrambling in vain for a foothold, the big bay was still squealing as it disappeared over the edge.

Though Billy felt a quick pang of sorrow at watching the terrified animal plummet to its death, he had a different problem at the moment. The horse that had been carrying the first rider, hearing the shot hit the rocks and the squealing of the animal directly behind it, had begun to scramble toward the top of the mountain at a breakneck pace.

Although the rider was attempting to bring it to a halt by seesawing on the reins, the frightened animal had become uncontrollable. Even the two shots that Free put in front of its nose failed to slow it down. Finally, not having any other choice, Billy shot the animal between the eyes just before it reached the summit. The trail was much wider at this point, and the rider had no problem stepping from the saddle as the horse went down. Less than a hundred feet away, close enough that he could see the muzzle of Free's Winchester, the man threw up his hands the second his feet touched the ground. "Please don't shoot, Mr. Free," he said in a high-pitched voice. "I've got a family."

Billy chuckled. "Mr. Free?" he asked. "How come I've suddenly become mister? Would it have anything to do with the fact that I've got a Winchester repeater trained on your nose?"

The man continued to hold his arms high above his head. Appearing to be about forty years old, he was of medium height and build and had a leathery face with gray hair around the edges of his hat. "I . . . guess so," he admitted.

Looking down, Billy could see that all of the other riders had dismounted. The ones who had enough room had scampered out of sight, and the others stood hiding behind their horses. Turning his attention back to the man in front of him, Free asked, "What's your name, fellow?"

"Clete Granger."

"You say you have a family?"

"Yes, sir."

"Then why in the hell ain't you at home with them?"

The answer was a long time in coming—so long that Billy was about to ask another question. "Just . . . just listened to all that stuff the marshal was saying, I reckon," the man said finally.

"I'm sure you did!" Billy said loudly. "But now you're gonna listen to me." He told Clete Granger the whole story, including the fact that Fink was married to the Poe brothers' sister, and that she was the driving force behind the two murder warrants. Everybody in Tom Green County knew that the Poe brothers themselves had started the fight that brought on their deaths, he said, and the only two people in the world who demanded his scalp for killing them were their sister and brother-in-law. Free also told him that Bill Fink was known far and wide as one of the crookedest sheriffs in Texas long before he discovered a way to finagle a U.S. marshal's badge. "He's a no-good bastard who don't give a damn about anybody but himself," Billy said in conclusion. "Why do you think he had you riding up front? If somebody got killed, he wanted it to be you, not him."

Clete Granger stood staring at Free with his hands over his head. "I'm inclined to believe what you've been saying," he said, "and it ain't just 'cause you're the man with the gun right now. I don't doubt for a minute that you could have killed me just as easy as you shot my horse. Fact is, you could have picked a bunch of us off on that last switchback down there.

"It would have been like shooting fish in a barrel, and it seems to me that if you'd been the wanton killer Bill Fink told us about, you wouldn't have passed up a clear shot like that." He glanced down the trail, then turned to face Free again. "I don't reckon Fink even told any of us that he used to be a sheriff, and he sure didn't tell us that the Poe brothers were relatives." He coughed several times and spat something large over the cliff, then continued: "Like I say, I'm inclined to believe what you say."

"You can believe me, Mr. Granger, 'cause every word I spoke was the truth. I wouldn't really have any reason to lie to you anyway, 'cause like you say, I'm the man with the gun and I could have eliminated you a long time ago."

Appearing to be convinced, Granger nodded several times. "I ain't got no gun on me, and my Henry's in the saddle scabbard under that dead horse. Can I put my hands down now?"

Billy nodded. "What are you gonna do if I let you walk back down that hill, Mr. Granger?"

"I'm gonna tell all of 'em what you said, and I'll tell 'em that I believe you. Everybody down there except Fink is a relative of mine, and they're pretty likely to go back to San Marcos with me when I tell 'em you ain't no killer."

"You do that, sir. I'll be on this mountaintop for two more days, so don't show yourself around here again during my stay. Any time after the second day you can come back and get your saddle and your rifle off that horse. Tell the man who was riding behind you that I'm sorry about his mount going over the edge."

"I'll tell him." Granger said. "He's my first cousin, and the horse belonged to me." He began to shake his head. "I ain't gonna let losing a coupla horses worry me none, though. Hell, it could just as easily have been some of us that went over that cliff." He stood quietly for a few moments, then asked, "Can I go now?"

Billy nodded. "Go on home to your family, Mr. Granger, and tell the others to do the same. Tell them that I'll start playing for keeps if they get on my trail again."

"They won't," Granger said, then began to walk down the hill. "I'll come back after my saddle and rifle three days from now," he added over his shoulder.

Billy maintained his position behind the boulder as he watched Granger's retreat. The man never looked back until he had reached the posse members who were standing behind their horses. Then he began to speak to the men animatedly, pointing to the top of the mountain. Billy could easily see that Granger had their attention. Even those who had been hiding beside the trail stepped out to listen.

Free could read the conversation fairly well just by watching the men's hand gestures. One man in particular continued to shake his head and wave his arms to emphasize whatever point he was trying to make. That man would be Bill Fink, Free supposed, probably arguing loudly that the only right thing to do was to keep hounding Billy Free. When Granger passed up all of the riders and began to walk down the trail alone, several men, all leading their animals, fell in behind him.

After a while, only one man was left behind, waving his arms and shouting after the others. No doubt about it, Free said to himself, that man simply had to be Bill Fink. Billy took careful aim and squeezed off a shot, then chuckled softly and smiled broadly as he saw the slug kick up dirt no more than two feet from Fink's boots. The man made one quick jump, then he was out of sight beside the trail again.

Billy held his position and kept his eye on Fink's horse, which was still standing in the middle of the trail and facing the top of the mountain. After a few minutes, Fink had obviously decided that if Billy had wanted to kill him he could have easily done it already, for the man walked out of hiding and turned his horse around. Then, no doubt realizing that he no longer had a posse, he began to lead the animal down the trail behind the others.

Free watched the disbanded group for more than an hour. When they reached the last of the switchbacks, three of the men took off their hats and stood waving them toward the top of the mountain. As Billy waved his own hat in return, he doubted that he had seen the last of Bill Fink, but he did not expect to see Clete Granger or any of his relatives again.

He led the filly to the seep and watched her drink it dry again, then mounted and headed down the north side of the mountain. He had lied to Granger when he said that he would be around for two more days. Two more hours would have been closer to the truth.

Although going down the mountain was anything but a pleasant experience, it was by no means as difficult as had been coming up the other side. The north side had the same hairpin turns as the south side, but they were not as steep, and the trail was wider in most places. After a while, as he had done coming up the south side, he dismounted and led the filly.

When he reached the foot of the mountain almost two hours later, he halted before leaving the woods, for far off in the distance, he could see several riders traveling in a south-easterly direction, toward San Marcos. He could not be sure, but it appeared that two of the horses were carrying double. If so, he had little doubt as to who those riders were.

He sat waiting till the riders disappeared, then rode out on the open plain behind them. The girl that he intended to marry lived in this direction, and besides, he preferred being behind Bill Fink to being in front of him.

He reached the Blanco River an hour before sunset, but continued along the north bank till dusk. He had seen no reason to make camp earlier, for having no coffeepot and no food that needed cooking, he would need no time to hunt up fuel for a fire. All the daylight he needed was enough time to select the best grass on which to picket the filly. Then the dark of night would not only be welcome, but would be appreciated.

He watered and staked the animal out, then spread his bedroll no more than thirty yards away. He walked around till he understood the lay of the land, then took a seat on a folded blanket and began to eat his supper in the dark. When he had finished, he had only to lean back in order to stretch out on his bed. He went to sleep a few minutes later with his arms lying across his stomach, the right hand clutching the deadly Peacemaker.

He awoke shortly after daybreak with a strong feeling that something was out of kilter. He had long ago fallen into the habit of giving credence to such intuitive warnings, and this morning would be no exception. He stood up on his bed and looked the area over quickly, but saw nothing. Even his filly was grazing peacefully a short distance away. Nonetheless, he sat back down and pulled on his socks and his boots hurriedly.

When he got to his feet again, he saw a different picture. Miss Muffet was no longer busy grazing, but was standing with both ears funneled toward the wooded hillside half a mile away. Billy needed no other signal. He ran to the filly and trotted her back to camp, then threw on the saddle. He rolled up his bed and tied it behind the cantle, then laid his saddlebags across the animal's withers and shoved the Winchester into the boot. Then, with the sack containing his food draped across his left shoulder, he stepped into the saddle.

He had not yet chosen which way he was going to point his mount, but made up his mind very quickly when he saw five horsemen leave the woods at a hard run. He turned the filly north and headed back toward the same mountaintop he had been on the day before. He would not climb the mountain this time, however. He had chosen to ride north only because it better served his purpose. He already knew the area in this direction, and there would be no surprises.

He rode along without haste. The country ahead was relatively flat for at least five miles, plenty of distance for him to find out what kind of horseflesh the men had under them. Bill Fink had obviously managed to put another posse together, and if their horses had traveled all the way from San Marcos during the night, Free did not expect them to last long if it came down to a horse race.

And the posse seemed eager for it to begin. Even now they had spurred their animals to a gallop and were slowly gaining on the filly. Billy was in no hurry at the moment, however; he himself would decide how the race was to be run. He headed across the wide plain at an easy, horse-saving canter. By the time the riders had cut the distance in half, he had grown even more confident.

Looking over his shoulder, he could see that at least two of the men had already gone to the whip. He smiled and kneed Miss Muffet to the slowest of her galloping gaits, for he wanted the men behind him to think that she was running as fast as she could. He seriously doubted that there was an animal in the pack that, even when fresh, could hold a candle to the filly.

Besides, she had been grazing and resting all night while they had been hauling their riders over one hill after another. Therefore Billy thought it highly unlikely that, once he had called on the filly for more speed, a single one of the animals behind him could keep its master within seeing distance.

He held his mount to the same gait and, after another mile, could see that the distance between himself and his pursuers was increasing; that their horses were about spent. Although his own animal had not even worked up a sweat, he had no intention of pushing her any harder than was necessary. He suddenly pulled her to a halt, then turned to face the oncoming posse.

To his surprise, the riders behind him also stopped, and Billy saw one of the horses stumble. He sat watching them for a few moments. One man in particular seemed to be doing all of the talking, holding one rider's ear for a moment, then turning about and leaning over to gain the attention of another. Free was satisfied that, even at such a long distance, he had identified Bill Fink.

Billy decided that it was time for the chase to begin, for he had no intention of giving the posse any more time to rest their horses. He kneed the filly and sent her across the plain at a fast clip, caring little about whether or not the posse had taken up the chase again. He rode all the way to the foot of the mountain before he looked back, then only after he had brought his mount to a halt.

The posse was now about half a mile away, and Billy could see that one member of the group was lagging badly. He was probably fifty yards behind the others, and his animal was moving at a faltering gait. Free sat patting the filly's neck and talking to her softly, waiting for them to get closer. Then, just before they came into effective rifle range, he was off again.

He led them on a quarter-mile run in an easterly direction, then just as he neared the trees, turned back south and headed across the grassy plain at a gallop. After a few minutes he would be back at the river, and would have led the posse on an eight-mile chase that put them right back where they started.

But their animals were not going to make it to the river. When Billy slowed the filly halfway across the plain and looked over his shoulder, he saw that two of the horses were already down, and that all of the other riders had stopped and dismounted. He doubted that Fink had halted his own animal out of compassion. He had more likely done it only because he was afraid that he might be left afoot. Looking back at the panting animals, Billy began to shake his head. He knew that Fink was already afoot, for none of those horses was going to live out the day.

When he reached the river, Billy sat his saddle for a few minutes watching the stranded posse. Then he guided the filly across the shallow ford and struck a ground-eating trot in a southeasterly direction, intending to give the town of San Marcos a wide berth. He would pass to the south of New Braunfels and skirt San Antonio on the north. Then he would be on a straightaway course to the town of Edna and the welcoming arms of Bess Noble.

35

★

He avoided the beaten paths all day long, but just before sunset, turned onto what a roadside sign identified as Wolf Creek Road. An hour after dark, he came to what he supposed was Wolf Creek. Then, just as he had done on Brady Creek, he put the filly in the water and waded downstream for a while.

An hour later, he spread his bedroll in a cluster of cedars and picketed Miss Muffet on a grassy knoll nearby. Then, sitting on his bed in the dark, he ate the last of his food. He would have to shoot something tomorrow, he was thinking, for he had learned from the San Marcos incident that stopping in a populated area to buy groceries could have consequences.

He shot a rabbit the following morning without having to hunt. The animal hopped within thirty yards of his bedroll, then sat twitching its nose and staring, evidently trying to figure out exactly what kind of creature Billy was. And it was not afraid, for even though it required a great deal of movement for Free to reach for his rifle, press it to his shoulder, and take aim, the rabbit watched it all with no sign of apprehension.

An hour later, when Billy had eaten the last of the little animal, he kicked dirt over the fire and caught up his mount. He rode out of the cedars shortly thereafter and headed back down to the creek. He watered the filly, then began to ride along the south bank. At the moment, the stream ran in the exact direction that he needed to travel, and besides, he stood a better chance of picking up a hind quarter off something bigger than a rabbit if he stayed close to the water. A fat fawn's hind quarter would provide enough meat to hold him all the way to Edna now, he was thinking, for he believed that he was no more than a hundred miles away. Only three more days—even at a horse-saving gait.

He followed the creek till midmorning but saw no game. He said good-bye to the stream at that time, for it had begun to meander back toward the north. He continued on a southeasterly course and, just before noon, climbed the bank at the end of a deep gully and came face-to-face with an old man seated beside a smoldering campfire. A donkey grazed a short distance away, and there was a small spring nearby.

Free had been making it a point to avoid people, as well as places where people might be found. There had been no avoiding this meeting, however, for Billy had been almost on top of the man before he saw him. In fact Free had seen and been seen at exactly the same time. "Come on up and set, young man," the bearded old-timer said. "I can heat this coffee up again right quick."

Looking the man over, the only gun Billy saw was a Henry rifle. The barrel of the weapon was leaning against the lowest limb of a stunted mesquite, well out of reach of its owner. Free kneed the filly toward the spring and continued to sit his saddle as she drank. All the while, he had never taken his eyes off the old man.

Moments later, he dismounted and led the animal back to

the fire, where he loosened the cinch and tied her to the mesquite. "I'd take you up on a sip of that coffee if I had something to drink it out of," he said. He pointed to the canteen hanging on his saddle. "I've done all of my drinking out of that thing since my cup came up missing about a week ago."

"Well, now," the old-timer said, "that ain't gonna be no problem." He fished around in his sack for a moment, then handed Billy a tin cup. "Walk over there and wash it out if you want to. I'll be trying to fan some life back into this fire."

Billy washed the cup, then the two men sat watching the fire in silence till the coffee was hot. The old man poured Billy's cup full, then motioned behind himself with his head. "I decided to camp a few days right where I shot the deer," he said. "Save lugging all that meat around."

Looking in the direction that the man had indicated, Billy was more than a little surprised that he had failed to spot it on his own. There, in plain view and less than fifty feet away, lay the carcass of a half-grown doe. "Ain't no way in the world that I can use more'n a few pounds of that before it spoils," the old-timer said. Then he handed Billy a hunting knife. "Cut yourself a few pounds of meat off of one of them hind quarters, then broil it over this fire.

"You don't have to cook it all the way now, just heat it up enough to keep it from bleeding as you carry it along. Then all you gotta do is stop and finish broiling it any old time you get hungry. You got salt and pepper?"

"Yes, sir," Billy said. "I've got as much of both as I need." He tested the edge on the blade of the hunting knife with his thumb, then added, "I shouldn't have any problem cutting meat with this thing. It's about as sharp as a razor."

"A dull knife ain't worth a shit for nothing," the man said, beginning to stoke up the fire for the broiling. "I've got a good rock in my sack, and I keep both of my knives sharp like that on purpose."

Billy nodded, then got to his feet and took his own gunnysack out of his saddlebag. Then, without another word, he headed for the doe.

Twenty minutes later, using sticks broken off a green mesquite limb, both men sat holding thick slabs of venison over the fire. "Don't take but about five minutes in an open flame like this," the old-timer was saying, "then the meat'll keep for nigh onto a week."

Within the hour, Billy rolled up several pounds of partially cooked venison and stored it in his saddlebag. Then, spearing the last chunk with another green stick, he sat down and began to broil his dinner. When the meat was done, Free used his benefactor's salt and pepper, for the old man had shakers.

When he had eaten the last of the sweet-tasting venison and drunk his final cup of coffee, he washed the cup and returned it to the old man. "Thank you for the coffee and the venison, mister," he said. "It's been a good thing for me that I ran across you, and I appreciate everything you've done, but I've got to be on my way."

The old-timer sat shaking his head. "You ain't caused me no trouble, boy. And that venison you're taking ain't gonna hurt me none either. Hell, I'll have to fight over the rest of that deer anyway once the predators get a good whiff of it. You just be careful where you ride, and I hope the wind always blows on your back."

36

Billy traveled steadily for the next three days and at midafternoon arrived at his old campsite on the Lavaca River. He was happier right now than he could remember ever being before, for the girl that he was going to marry was at this very moment no more than ten miles away.

After looking the site over closely, he decided that he himself had been the last party to use it. He staked out the filly, then went about gathering deadwood for a fire over which to finish cooking the last of his venison. He was very hungry, for he had eaten nothing at all this day.

He had soon kindled a small blaze, and while he was waiting for it to become a cooking fire, he walked into the small thicket and spread his bedroll in the exact same spot as before. He knew that he would be riding into Edna some time after dark, and the presence of his bedroll would be a signal to any other camper who happened by that this particular campsite was already in use.

Once the fire was burning to his satisfaction, he dug his

salt and pepper out of his saddlebag, then sat down to broil the venison. Holding it over the gray coals instead of the flames so as not to burn his wooden skewer in two, he cooked it to a golden brown in less than an hour. Then, after laying the full-pound chunk on a piece of bark and allowing it to cool for a while, he ate it all.

Then he lay down on his bedroll with the intention of taking an afternoon nap, but sleep would not come. His mind was on Bess Noble, and the thought that he would soon have her in his arms gave him a warm feeling. She was on his mind for most of his waking moments nowadays, and sometimes it seemed that he spent the entire night dreaming of the life that they were going to have together in California.

He alternated between lying and sitting on the bedroll till sunset, then led the filly into camp and cinched down his saddle. He watered the animal from the river, then stood beside the big willow for a while. Anxious as he was to see Bess Noble, he had decided that there was still too much daylight left for him to start moving around. As long as he had been traveling it had been necessary, but now it was not. He wanted to be seen by as few people as was possible, and he could very easily make his way to Edna after dark.

When darkness finally closed in, he mounted and headed south along the river. He held the filly to a walk for the next two hours, and turned east when he reached the main road. Then, after riding for two miles at a fast trot, he stopped where a private driveway led off to his left, for he knew that Bess Noble lived at the end of it. Though he could not actually see the dwelling in the dark, he could see the light shining through the windows, which suggested that Bess had not yet gone to bed. He kneed the filly down the narrow driveway.

A dog began to announce his arrival as soon as Billy left the main road, and continued its yelping even as he rode into the yard. A moment later the front door opened and Bess Noble stood in the doorway, the lamplight behind her outlining her shapely form very well through the thin night garment that she wore. She silenced the dog with a single word, then spoke into the darkness. "Is somebody out there?"

Free continued to sit his saddle just beyond the glow of light shining through the doorway. "Just a fellow named Billy Jones," he said softly, "stopped by to have a word with his betrothed."

"Billy!" She bounded into the yard and almost pulled him from the saddle. "I can't believe that you're back already."

He stepped to the ground and held her tightly, kissing her lips and her eyes over and over. Then, holding her at arm's length, he said, "It's so good to hold you again, little one. I've thought of you constantly since the last time I saw you."

She kissed his hand several times, then placed it against her cheek. "I don't ever stop thinking of you, Billy," she said. "Oh, I love you so much that I just don't know how to tell you." She dropped the hand and grabbed him around the waist, burying her face against his chest. "You can put your horse out back and spend the night right here. We've got a spare bedroom, and Aunt Esther wouldn't mind at all."

He touched her nose with his tongue. "I'd like to, sweetheart, but I simply can't. I've got a problem that I need to discuss with you. In fact, we need to talk about it a whole lot." He kissed her long and hard, then continued, "I want you to meet me sometime tomorrow at our old camping place on the Lavaca River. Don't tell a soul where you're going, not even your aunt. And most important of all, don't tell anybody that you've seen me." He squeezed her again. "Can I count on you, honey?"

"Oh, yes, Billy, you know you can. I'll do exactly like you said."

"I'll see you on the river tomorrow, then," he said. He kissed her good-bye, then remounted. "Bring something to eat if you can," he added over his shoulder. "I'm completely out of food." He guided the filly back toward the road at a trot. Once he left the driveway he pushed the animal to a canter, for he did not want to spend any more time on the main road than was absolutely necessary.

He turned north again when he reached the river, and very quickly got the impression that the filly knew exactly where he was headed. Now at a walking gait, he simply gave the animal her head and went along for the ride. Two hours later, she carried him into his camp and, of her own accord, came to a halt beneath the big willow. Billy dismounted and led her to water, then stripped the saddle and staked her out in the small meadow that she was by now very familiar with.

A few minutes later he stretched out on his bedroll, unable to remember any time of late when he had felt so at ease with the world. The remembrance of seeing his love again and the anticipation of what was to come with a new day gave him a good feeling. He lay awake thinking about it for a long time. He had just held the soft and shapely Bess Noble in his arms and kissed her repeatedly, and tomorrow she would be lying beside him with her head on his chest. The thought made him warm all over.

37

★

The sun was three hours high when Bess came into view next morning. Billy had been sitting at the edge of the thicket looking downriver for more than an hour when he saw her come around the bend. He was on his feet instantly, waiting for her to close the distance. He noticed right away that she had either traded horses or borrowed one, for she now rode a small black gelding.

Pulling alongside, she handed him a pillowcase filled with food, then jumped to the ground. He laid the bundle on the ground, then took her in his arms. He kissed her face all over, then held her tightly for a long time. "I've missed you so much, honey," he said finally. "I think I'm happier right now than I've ever been before."

"I know I am," she said, locking her arms around his neck and lifting herself off the ground. "I want to be with you forever, Billy. Please don't go off and leave me alone again."

He handed her the pillowcase, then scooped her up in one arm and led her horse with the other. Moments later, he tied he animal to a bush beside the willow. "What did you do, rade horses?" he asked.

"Yes," she answered, "and I got the best end of it. At east, I think I did. I got what I believe is a better horse, and nade the man give me ten dollars to boot."

Billy chuckled and pinched her on the cheek. "Remind me o let you do all of my trading in the future," he said. He laid he pillowcase beside the ashes of his last campfire, then cooped Bess Noble up in his arms and headed for his bedroll. 'or the next two hours, they made love like neither of them ad ever even dreamed about before.

Finally Billy sat up on the bedroll. "I hate to mention food t a time like this, little one, but what did you bring in the pil-owcase?"

"Everything I could think of," she answered sweetly, "or t least everything that we had on hand. I cooked a beef roast fter you left last night, and about half of it's in there. I baked pan of biscuits right after daybreak and put them in there, oo. I brought a pot and one big spoon, and most of that other tuff is dried beans, potatoes, and turnips. I wrapped up about dozen raw eggs, too, 'cause I remembered that you like to oil them and eat them with salt and pepper."

Billy kissed her, then squeezed one of her firm, round reasts. "You're the best thing that ever happened to me, lit-le one. Now that I've had you around for a while, I doubt ery seriously that I could even make it by myself."

She blew him a kiss. "Of course you're joking," she said. You'd make it just like you always have, but I certainly vouldn't like it." Neither of them spoke again until both were ully dressed. "By the way," she said as she fastened the top utton of her blouse. "What is it that you wanted to talk bout, and why did you quit the trail drive?"

He pointed toward the pillowcase. "Let's eat first, then 've got a lot of things to tell you."

Half an hour later, after he had eaten as much beef and iscuits as he could, he took a long drink from his canteen and

wiped his mouth on his sleeve. "I'm gonna start at the begin
ning," he said, reaching for her hand. "You just sit here and
listen. First of all, my name is not Jones. My name is Billy Free
and I came from Leakesville, Mississippi."

He told her the whole story: the false accusation that had
first put him on the run, the killing of the Kipling brothers to
protect his mother and his siblings, and the shooting of the
Poe brothers in defense of his own life. He told her about
Willy Bouton, who had betrayed their friendship and tried to
shoot him in the back for the reward. And about a former
sheriff and now United States marshal who hounded him con
stantly, knowing full well that he had committed no crime.
"I've never picked a fight in my life, Bess," he said in conclu
sion, "but I've killed five men in the past sixteen months. In
every single instance I've had no other choice."

She wiped her wet cheeks, then laid her head on his shoul
der. "Why does the marshal keep chasing you if he knows
that you're innocent?"

"Because his wife keeps pushing him into it. Frank and
Foster Poe were her brothers, and she's determined to have her
revenge."

"Is the marshal the reason you quit the cattle drive?"

"Yes. When we reached the town of Brady, he decided to
ride out to the herd and look the drovers over. I would not
have survived his inspection."

"Are your mule and your packsaddle still with the herd?"

"No. They're at the Circle K, and that's where I intend to
leave them."

She sat quietly for a while then wiped another tear off her
cheek. "Why do you think all these bad things keep happen
ing to you, Billy?"

"I sure wish I knew, little one. A fellow who is supposed
to be a whole lot smarter than I am told me that a man's des
tiny is preordained; that the cards he draws in the game of life
were carved in granite long before he was born, and the best

hat he can even hope for is the chance to play out the hand
with dignity."

"Do you think that man was right?"

"I don't know what to think, Bess, but I sure haven't run
into anything yet that proves him wrong."

He pulled her closer, then broached the subject of California. He had been thinking about going out there by himself, he explained, then sending for her when he had a good
job and a place to live. Traveling with a wanted man was entirely too dangerous for a woman, he added.

Bess began to shake her head emphatically. "No, Billy,"
she said. "No, no, no. I don't want to stay in Edna for another
day while you're off somewhere else. I don't care if it is dangerous, we'll go to California together. Anyway, I wouldn't
trade a short time with you for a lifetime without you."

He sat thinking for a long time, then kissed her hard on
the lips. "We'd need another pack animal and a packsaddle,"
he said finally. "If we carry enough food with us we can stay
off the beaten paths, and the fewer people we run into, the
better our chances of making it to California without a fight."
He sat quietly for a few moments, then asked, "By the way,
how'd you get away from home without telling your aunt
where you were going?"

"I didn't. I told her that I was going to meet you this
morning, but I didn't tell her where. I waited till she went to
open up the store before I started gathering up things. The pillowcase was the only sack I could find that was big enough.

"As for the pack animal and the packsaddle, I can get
both of them at the livery stable." She smiled sheepishly, then
continued, "One of the liverymen is not much older than me,
and he's been asking me for a date for several years now.
I've always said no, but I didn't say never. Anyway, he'll do
whatever I ask within reason, and he'll keep his mouth shut
about it."

Billy chuckled. "Sounds like he's the man we need to do

business with, then. I'll just give you the money and let you take care of it." He kissed her wetly, then slid his hand inside her blouse. "Right now I've got a strong urge to go back to bed." Getting to his feet, he took her hand and led her back into the thicket.

Bess stayed in his camp for four days, then headed back to Edna early on the fifth morning. She intended to do the things that she must, then be back at the camp long before sunset. Billy had given her money for a pack animal, telling her to choose a horse because a mule was "too slow and too damn stubborn." She would also buy a packsaddle, along with the rest of the equipment that he said they would need. When she reached the bank she would withdraw her hundred and ten dollars, then ride back to the livery stable and buy the pack animal. Then she would circle the entire town before going home, for the last thing she wanted right now was for somebody to see her leading an extra horse.

She would load her clothing on the pack animal while her aunt was at work, then leave a note for her on the kitchen table. As Billy had suggested, she would not tell Aunt Esther where she was going. She would also help herself to her brother's extra bedroll, for she knew that he would not mind. She and Billy had talked about Lenny several days ago, and Billy had said that he liked the young man very much. He told her about taking up her brother's end of an argument on the trail drive and about offering Lenny a home with them when they got settled in California. She had been pleased to hear that.

She would take nothing from home except the bedroll, two blankets, and some of her shoes and clothing. Billy had told her not to concern herself with food, a coffeepot, or cooking and eating utensils. They would buy all of those things when they got someplace where it seemed safe to do so.

She rode the entire distance from Billy's camp to Edna at a fast trot. Once there, she spoke to no one unless it was absolutely necessary, and was out of town in less than two hours.

When she had finished taking care of business, she circled the settlement and rode to her aunt Esther's house. She spent less than an hour inside the building, then headed for the camp with the newly bought pack animal trotting along behind.

Billy had been sitting at the edge of the thicket watching for more than two hours when he saw Bess come around the bend leading a big sorrel. He was on his feet quickly and stood waiting. Moments later, she stepped to the ground and handed him her saddle horse's reins and the pack horse's lead rope. "I made the trip as quick as I could," she said. "I hope I didn't forget anything."

He kissed her and hugged her around the shoulders with one arm. "You did good, honey," he said. "The pack horse looks good, and he's big enough to carry a load."

"That's the same thing Jubal told me at the livery stable. He sold me the horse, the packsaddle, and the ropes and pins for twenty-four dollars; said that was exactly what he had paid for it all."

Billy looked the horse and the packsaddle over a little closer, then nodded. "That sounds about right to me," he said. He goosed her in the ribs, adding, "I guess he was willing to give up his profit because he hoped that you'd give him something better one of these days."

She ignored his remark and walked to the dying campfire, where Billy had just finished cooking a pot of beans. Using the oversized spoon, she began to eat right from the pot, as she and Billy had both been doing for almost a week now.

Free stripped the saddle from Bess's mount, then unburdened the sorrel. He led both animals to water, then picketed them in the meadow beside his filly. He dragged the saddle and the packsaddle into the thicket, then seated himself on the ground beside the fire. After watching Bess eat with the big spoon for a few moments, he said, "We'll buy some spoons that are closer to your size, the first chance we get."

She nodded and continued to eat.

As he had done several times during the past few days,

Billy spent the next few minutes quietly poring over his map. "I want us to go through the Hill Country and get into New Mexico Territory as soon as possible," he said finally. "Tom Green County is also in that direction, but we'll cross the Middle Concho River in Reagan County, far to the west of San Angelo."

"I don't know anything about stuff like that, Billy," Bess said around a mouthful of beans. "I can't even read a map."

"That's all right, little one, you're not alone in that regard." He folded the map and shoved it into his vest pocket. "We'll get a good night's sleep and head northwest at sunup." He tickled her under the chin. "You will let me get a good night's sleep, won't you?"

38

They ate cold beans for breakfast next morning, and one hour later, forded the river and headed northwest. Within the first few hundred yards of travel, Billy decided that Bess's friend at the livery stable had treated her well. The sorrel had definitely packed before. The horse obediently followed Miss Muffet at a distance of about fifteen feet and always kept a little slack in the lead rope so that Free never actually felt the heavy animal at the other end. In fact, Billy had not had to pull on the rope even at the start. The big gelding had started moving at the same time the filly did, seeming to instinctively know ahead of time which direction it was expected to go. After a while Billy spoke to Bess, who was riding close beside him. "I like that sorrel back there," he said. "He's strong and easy to lead. I think he's worth a good deal more than the fifteen dollars you paid for him."

"I didn't get him for fifteen dollars, Billy. I paid eighteen."

"Oh."

They traveled steadily hour after hour, and at midafternoon pulled up at a boxed-in spring. They could see a small
town from where they sat, and Billy mentioned it. "That little settlement up ahead might be a good place for us to buy the
things we need," he said. "Don't look to be more than a mile
away."

Bess waited till both had dismounted, then said. "That's
Cuero, Billy. I've heard that it's such a wild town that women
and children are forbidden to even be out after dark. My
brother's first job was right there. Lenny spent all of the summer he was fourteen working at the Cuero General Store. It's
on this side of town, even before you get to the livery stable,
so you might be able to go there without being seen by very
many people."

A tin cup hung from a nail that had been driven into one
of the boards that boxed up the spring. Billy filled it with
water and handed it to Bess. "I'd like to prevent even one person from seeing me up close till I get out of Texas," he said.
"I think you should be the one to do the buying, while I find
someplace outside the store to stay out of sight."

They watered their horses, then Bess stepped into her saddle. "I'm ready," she said.

"Here," he said, fishing around in his pocket. "Let me
give you some money."

"Thank you, sir," she said, shaking her head, "but I'll
make out fine. I've got some money of my own, and I'll spend
it. I have to eat too, you know."

No horses stood at the hitching rail when Billy and Bess
arrived at the store, which pleased them both. Billy tied their
animals, and while Bess disappeared into the building, he
crossed the street to a vacant lot and took a seat on a short
stack of lumber. He would come face-to-face with nobody sitting here, for he could see for a long distance in every direction. If anybody should head toward him, he would simply get
up and walk away.

It was the longest half hour he could remember ever

spending, but when he saw how many sacks Bess had set on the porch beside the hitching rail, he began to wonder how she had done it all so quickly. He walked across the street and began to load the goods on the pack animal in a haphazard fashion, any old way to get them and himself out of town in a hurry. "Be careful with this," Bess said as she handed him the last of the packages. "It's got two dozen eggs in it."

One minute later, they were headed back in the direction from which they had come. "We'll turn south when we get to the spring," he said. "We'll circle this town and make camp a few miles west of it, at the Guadalupe River." When they had passed the spring and made their turn, he asked, "How many people were in the store, Bess?"

"Just one," she answered. "He seemed alert enough, and I think he added up the charges right, but he sure did look old, Billy; I mean real old." She paused for a few seconds, then added, "He started flirting with me the instant I walked through the front door, and he never stopped." She was thoughtful for a moment, then asked, "How old does a man have to be before he gets to the point that he can't do anything with a woman?"

"I suppose it varies," he answered. "At least that's what I've been told."

"In other words, I'd have to ask somebody older than you, huh?"

"Yep."

They forded the Guadalupe an hour before sunset and camped on the west bank. Deadwood was plentiful, and anxious to sample whatever Bess would fix for supper, Billy tied the horses to a bush and kindled a fire. Then, as he listened to the familiar sound created by the rattling of pots and pans, he unburdened all of the animals, then led them to good grass. He stomped their picket pins into the ground, then walked back to the river, where he stretched out on his stomach to wash his face, neck, and hands.

When he walked back to the fire, Bess handed him a

brand-new coffeepot and pointed toward the river. "Yes, ma'am," he said, smiling, already anticipating the biting taste of his first cup of strong coffee since meeting the old-timer on the trail. He delivered the pot of water, then went about selecting a place for their bedrolls. As far as he was concerned they needed only one bed, but he spread both of them out anyway.

That done, he sat on his own bedroll watching Bess as she moved back and forth around the fire. In less than an hour, she called him to come and eat. The sun had disappeared and the night was dark as pitch when they sat down to a meal of smoked ham, scrambled eggs, and johnnycake. Bess loaded up his plate, saying, "Since you didn't have anything but cold beans this morning, I thought you might want some breakfast now."

"You thought exactly right, honey." He took a sip from his steaming cup, then smacked his lips. "I believe this is the best coffee I ever tasted," he said.

They ate the meal in silence for the most part, then Billy smiled at Bess, who sat beside the fire with one of her brother's old hats pulled low over her eyes like a man. He washed the last mouthful of his food down with coffee. "That was wonderful," he said. "Like I told you once before, I'm not sure that I could make it without you now."

She chuckled, then flashed two rows of perfect teeth. "I hope you still feel that way forty years from now," she said.

He carried the skillet and the eating utensils to the river and washed them, then dragged the packsaddle up to the head of their bedrolls. "Lots of wild animals prowl at night," he said, "and some of them like the same kind of food that we do. They're not likely to bother our pack when it's this close to us, though. The human smell should be all it takes to send them in the opposite direction."

"Ooh," she said, faking a shiver. "Just thinking about them scares me."

"Good," he said. "Maybe that'll keep you in my bed all night."

She did stay in his bed all night. After making love for the better part of two hours, they slept the remainder of the night away. The very second that their eyes opened at daybreak, they reached for each other again.

Life was great at the moment, Billy was thinking later as he began to dress himself. And if he could just put a couple thousand miles between himself and Bill Fink, things might get even better. He pulled on his boots and kindled a fire, then walked down to the river to fill the coffeepot. Moments later, after Bess had insisted on taking over the breakfast preparations, he headed for the meadow with three bridles hanging on his shoulder.

He watered the horses, then led them into camp. He saddled Miss Muffet and Bess's gelding, and by the time he was done balancing out the packs and buckling the packsaddle harness on the sorrel, Bess called him to breakfast. "Just more of the same this morning," she said as he sat down beside the fire. She handed him a plate, adding, "I thought we should go ahead and use up the eggs. I've heard that the constant jostling motion of a pack animal will make them go bad after a few days."

"I don't know about all of that," he said, accepting the plate. "But if you'll just keep cooking 'em for me they won't be around long enough to go bad." He took a sip of his coffee, then began to concentrate on emptying the plate.

When breakfast was over, Billy kicked dirt over the campfire. He washed the utensils and returned them to the bag that had been supplied by the storekeeper, then tied the bag to the packsaddle. He lifted Bess to her saddle, then mounted the filly and tightened up the slack in the pack horse's lead rope. Then, with the sun at least two hours above the treetops, they rode out of camp. They would ride due west for the next three or four days, for Billy intended to pass far to the south of San

Antonio. Once past the big town, they would head for New Mexico Territory.

They traveled west and then northwest uneventfully, and nine days later set up camp on the north bank of the Middle Concho River, halfway across Reagan County. One whole county and half of two others lay between his campsite and the town of San Angelo, so Billy felt about as safe here as he did anywhere else. He built a small fire and allowed it to burn long enough to heat some ham and boil a pot of coffee, then extinguished it immediately. For the next half hour, he and Bess sat sipping from tin cups as they ate the last of their smoked ham. As darkness closed in, they pulled a blanket over them in hopes of discouraging the blood-sucking mosquitoes, then cuddled up on Billy's bedroll.

As had become the rule rather than the exception, they got another late start next morning. Still traveling northwest, they had ridden for only about an hour when Billy suddenly kicked the filly with his heels and guided her off the road, motioning for Bess to follow. He moved behind a thick stand of trees, then turned back to face the road. "Somebody's coming," he whispered.

Straddling a tall roan and leading a black pack horse, a lone rider topped the hill a few minutes later. Even from a distance, Billy decided that the traveler sat his saddle exactly like someone he had known in the past. As the man continued on down the hill, Free became more convinced. By the time he drew abreast of the trees there was no longer any doubt. Billy smiled and handed Bess the pack animal's lead rope. "Stay here and be real quiet, baby," he said. "That man may be the best friend I've ever had."

Billy had recognized the rider as Casey Springer, foreman of the Flying W Ranch. He was leading the very same animal that Billy had traded him for Miss Muffet, and the horse was carrying a heavily loaded packsaddle at the moment. Billy rode out of the trees to meet his friend.

Springer recognized him immediately and brought his animals to a sudden halt. "Damn, it's good to see you, Billy," he said, turning his horse sideways and extending his right hand. "I've been thinking about you a lot lately and wondering what the hell became of you. I don't ever run across anybody who knows any more about you than I do, though."

Free accepted the hand and returned its firm grip. "I'm doing as well as I could hope to, I guess. So far I've managed to stay out of Bill Fink's clutches."

Springer began to shake his head emphatically. "If you're riding west or northwest you ain't gonna stay out of his clutches much longer. I've been over in Upton County taking care of some business for Mr. Winter, and I've been stopped three times in the past two days by groups of men looking for you.

"I tell you, Billy, these hills and gullies are full of men trying to collect that reward. It's up to three thousand now, and that's enough to turn ordinary men into bounty hunters." He paused for a moment, then added, "Unless I miss my guess, that's exactly why you or one of your friends killed Willy Bouton."

Billy sat his saddle quietly. He was not about to admit anything concerning Willy Bouton. "You said there are several groups out looking for me, Casey. Is Bill Fink with them?"

"He was in the first bunch that stopped me. Seven in the group counting him." He waved his arm toward the west, then the northwest. "There really ain't no telling how many of them bastards are out hunting you." He waved the arm again. "They're just making a big sweep, Billy, seining these hills and hollows with a net so fine that a damn rabbit would have to be lucky not to get snared.

"I don't know which way you're headed, and I don't want to know, but I'm begging you not to ride into that trap. Just hole up somewhere for a while. All these hunters'll get tired in a month or two and go home." He glanced toward the northwest, then began to talk even more hurriedly. "I've got to be going, and you certainly don't need to be sitting out here in the road like this. Hell, I've run into two different groups of them bastards within the past two hours." He kneed the roan and pointed its head east. He turned in the saddle as he rode away. "I can see that you're treating Miss Muffet good, Billy," he said.

Free rode back behind the trees at a gallop. He accepted the lead rope Bess handed him, then sat staring between the filly's ears with a heavy heart. "We've got to turn back, Bess," he said finally. "Casey says that bounty hunters and lawmen have got us cut off on the west and the northwest both. He's run into two different groups this morning already, and they're all hunting me."

"Oh, Billy," Bess said softly, putting her hand on his arm. "What in the world can we do?"

"Casey says that if I hole up somewhere for a month or so, they'll all get tired and go home." He sat looking toward the northwest for a moment, then added, "I know a place where we can hide if we can just get there."

"Then let's go there, Billy. Let's go now."

He leaned over and kissed her lips. "It's northeast of here," he said. "Let's try to find a good place to hide for the rest of the day, then we'll ride all night. If we spend the night in the saddle, I believe we'll be there by daylight." He pointed the filly's head northeast and took the slack out of the pack animal's lead rope, then led off toward the old Conner cabin.

Riding at a trot, he left the road immediately to seek out rougher terrain. Within the hour, he found what he was looking for. A narrow ravine that was at least six feet deep in most places ran east and west. As crooked as a snake's path, it almost curved back into itself every hundred yards or so.

He sat looking the gully over for only a few moments before deciding that it was their best bet. It was too narrow for several men to ride abreast of each other, and with the summer sun bearing down and no air circulating, it would be hot enough down in that ditch to discourage man or beast.

The biggest thing in their favor was the fact that the gully curved around in a new direction every forty or fifty feet, making it a certainty that if anyone found them here it would be purely accidental. A man would have to ride directly up on their particular short section of the ditch and look down, all of which was highly unlikely. "It's gonna be mighty hot, Bess," Billy said, pointing to the gully. "It very well might get so hot that we can't stay down there, but if we can, I believe it's our best chance."

Bess nodded. "Let's do it, Billy. We've got four canteens full of water."

"I know," he said. "But the horses don't have any canteens." He continued to ride along the bank and after a hundred yards or so found an easy way down. He guided the filly into the ravine and turned east. Just before he rode into the gully he had been pleased to see a place up ahead where a lot of brush and several saplings grew along the bank. When he arrived there and saw that the tree limbs actually hung over the ditch and created a thirty-foot section of shade, he was doubly pleased.

He dismounted quickly. "Might not be as hot as I thought," he said, leading Bess's gelding and the pack horse into the shaded area beside the filly. "With all of these bushes growing along the banks, we can raise our heads up into the cooler air occasionally." He swatted a horsefly that had taken up residence on the filly's rump, then added, "I believe these animals'll be all right as long as we can keep 'em out of the sun."

They stayed in the ravine until after sunset, and it was the most miserable day either of them had ever spent. The only relief they found from the oppressive heat was to occasionally crawl up the bank and let the faint breeze blow against their sweat-soaked clothing. And though the horses became lathered and stood with their heads hanging low, Billy thought they would recover quickly once the sun went down. At midafternoon, he had emptied two of the canteens into his hat and gave each of them a small drink, which they sucked up eagerly.

39

When they headed northeast at dark, the thing uppermost on their minds was water. They had ridden no more than a mile, however, when they came upon one of the Middle Concho's tributaries. Billy filled the four canteens, then allowed the horses to stand in the knee-deep water for a while. While he and Bess sat passing a canteen back and forth every few minutes, the animals were doing their version of the same thing: drinking a while, waiting a while, then drinking again. They, like their passengers, had become dehydrated in the gully.

They stopped only once more during the night, which was at another stream. Billy believed that it was at least an hour past midnight, and so informed Bess. "I don't have any conception of time," she said. "It seems to me like two or three days since you talked with that man on the road." Billy leaned over quietly and kissed her, then tightened the lead rope and led off again.

They pushed their tired animals throughout the remainder

of the night, and just as the eastern sky began to take on a pinkish hue, broke out of the woods and onto a grassy plain. Billy knew exactly where he was now, for it was the same flat meadow he used the day he had decided to find out whether or not Miss Muffet could run. The old Conner cabin was only one mile ahead.

"We're almost there, sweetheart," he whispered. He had spoken quietly because he did not know for sure that the cabin would be unoccupied, and he had deliberately slowed their pace for the same reason. He intended to stay near the woods and stall for daylight before approaching the building.

When they reached the east end of the plain, they pulled up and waited quietly. Then, after twenty minutes or so, Billy kneed Miss Muffet up the hill. It was almost full daylight now, and he could see well enough as he rode into the yard to look things over. The tall weeds growing all the way up to the door told the story, but he helloed the house anyway.

When he got no answer, he dismounted and knocked. A moment later, he pushed the door open and stood looking into the empty cabin. Even from where he stood he could see the large pile of things in the corner. He walked to the back of the building for an inspection. Nobody had been in the building since the last time he had seen it, he decided quickly. The buffalo robes, the blankets, the cooking and eating utensils— everything was just the way he had left it, right down to the big stack of wood beside the fireplace. He walked back into the yard and motioned Bess up the hill.

She rode into the yard leading the pack animal, then sat looking at the cabin thoughtfully for a few moments. "It won't fall down, Billy?" she asked.

He chuckled, and shook his head. "Nope," he answered. "The top's a little farther south nowadays than the bottom is, but it'll stand." He unburdened the horses, then took the saddles and the packsaddle into the cabin. He dropped them in a corner, then pecked Bess on the cheek. "You can get something started to eat while I take care of the horses," he said, handing her a few sulfur matches. "The spring's right across the yard, and there's plenty of wood by the fireplace."

He watered the animals from the spring's runoff, then led the sorrel and Bess's gelding to the little knoll above the cabin, where he picketed each of them on a forty-foot rope. Then he staked the filly out halfway up the little rise on the east side of the building. The grass looked especially good there, and she would be closer to hand if she was needed in a hurry.

After a late breakfast of potatoes, turnips, and johnny-cake, Billy began to nod back and forth sleepily. Bess took the coffee cup from his hand. "Go back there and lie down on one of the buffalo robes," she said. "I'll join you as soon as I get done here."

With his eyes half closed, Billy walked lumberingly to the back of the room. Two minutes later, he was snoring lightly.

40

★

They had been here for a full week now, and Bess said that she was beginning to like living in the cabin. The only drawback, she said, was not having a cookstove. She had turned out some excellent meals over the open fireplace, however, and this morning she was busy frying a rabbit that Billy had shot just before dark. Billy himself was at the moment lying on the buffalo robe, waiting for his call to breakfast.

He had already been up once this morning, but then had lain back down and slept for two more hours. He had watered the horses at daybreak, then picketed them down in the meadow, for they had eaten everything closer to the cabin. Then, with nothing else to do and the sky looking like it might start raining any minute, he had gone back to bed.

On his feet instantly when Bess issued the breakfast call, he was standing beside the fireplace reaching for the coffeepot when he heard somebody call his name. "Billy Free!" the voice called loudly. "This is United States Marshal Bill Fink!" Billy's hand froze in midair, and Bess looked as if she had just seen a

,host. "Come on out with your hands up, Billy Free," Fink ontinued. "We've done got all three of your horses, and ou're not going anywhere. Tell that fellow in there with you o come out, too!"

A thousand thoughts raced through Billy's mind during he next few seconds. Had Casey Springer sold him out? The nswer was apparently yes, for Fink could not possibly have racked them after all the evasive measures they had taken.

A heavy-caliber rifle roared outside and a small piece of vood splintered off the inside of the plank door. With all of is attention focused on the noise outside, Billy had no idea hat Bess had been hit until he heard her body hit the floor. He urned to see her lying facedown, a splotch of red between her houlder blades that was spreading fast. Feeling as if his in-ides were all in his throat, he turned her lifeless body over. Ier eyes stared at the ceiling. Her mouth was open wide and few drops of blood trickled onto her chin. Bess Noble was lead.

"That shot was just a warning, Billy Free!" The voice ounded as if it was a mile away now, even though he knew hat Fink was no more than fifty yards from the cabin. "I'm ;iving you two more minutes to come out of there with your ands up, Billy Free. Otherwise, we're gonna riddle that cabin ill it looks like a sieve!"

As Billy sat staring into Bess's sightless eyes, he recalled the vords of his cousin Walt Endfinger. "The cards a man draws n the game of life were carved in granite long before he was oorn," the old man had told young Billy on more than one oc-:asion, "and the best that he can even hope for is the chance o play out the hand with dignity." Still staring into the face of his dead lover, Billy wiped a tear from his cheek. He un-lerstood Cousin Walt a little better now. What the old man had really been saying was that even though life might deal a nan some lousy cards, he had no choice but to play out the and. Free hesitated no longer. "Marshal Fink!" he yelled at he top of his lungs. "I want to talk, Marshal Fink!"

"What do you want to talk about?"

"I want to make a deal before I surrender. You just keep me from hanging, and I'll tell you some things that'll help you wrap up a lot of cases. Information that nobody but me knows. Do you hear that, Marshal Fink?"

"I hear you and I'd like to hear the rest of what you've got to say, but I won't meet you alone. I'd need another man there for a witness."

Billy opened the door and peeked outside. "That's all right," he said. "That same man will be my witness, too. Just start walking on up the hill, and I'll walk down to meet you."

"All right, we're on our way. You'd better come out of there empty-handed, though."

Billy stood watching while Fink and another man climbed out of the ditch and headed up the hill at a slow walk. Fink wore a holstered weapon, and his friend carried a rifle at arm's length.

When they had covered several yards, Billy stepped through the doorway and began to walk in their direction. Apparently unarmed, he held his empty hands up even with his shoulders. Looking down the hill past Fink and his man, Free could see several more heads peeking from the ditch. He disregarded them for the moment, however, and concentrated on the two men in front of him.

The three men walked slowly, as if counting the steps. When they were about forty feet apart, in a maneuver that Free had practiced many times, he suddenly reached behind his back and jerked his two Peacemakers from inside his waistband. His first shot dropped Bill Fink in his tracks, and the second and third shots went into the man with the rifle. Heavy fire was coming from the ditch now, and Billy had already been hit low in the abdomen.

Nonetheless, he began to move down the hill at a staggering trot. Even as he took more lead himself, he put another bullet between Bill Fink's eyes as he passed the man's body. That done, he headed for the ditch with both of his Colts spitng fire. He had been hit several times by now, but continued to stagger on crazily. Then, twenty feet before he reached the itch, the hammers of both of his weapons clicked on empty chambers. He stood reeling while several more slugs tore into im, then fell forward on his face. With the last bit of strength ft in his body, he turned himself onto his back, kicked his ght leg convulsively, then lay still.

The guns of Billy Free had been silenced forever. The date as August 6, 1878. A Monday.

EPILOGUE

★

Around a campfire in Arizona Territory in 1885: "Bill Free was the fastest gun ever to come out of Texas," an ol man was telling his companions. "Killed twenty-five me durin' a span o' less than two years. He enjoyed it, too. He' blow a man's brains out jist fer lookin' at 'im crossways."

And on a Montana cattle roundup in 1890: "I know fer fact that Billy Free killed thirty-three men. Th' girl that die in that shack with 'im killed more'n half that many her ow self."

And the legend continued.